"Melee mode engaged."

The ever-present feeling of buzzing electricity grew to an uncomfortable pitch that ran from the fingertips of both hands in to his spine, causing Mal to almost lose his footing as he leaned his head down to rush the men. From the corner of his eyes, Mal watched as one arm molded itself into a nearly three foot long blade of glimmering steel, thrusting out from where his forearm had been. The other arm seemed to bulk up, metal plates flanging and flaring out, and his fingers elongated into five claws that would have made Wolverine shit himself with

envy.

The GMRs were fast and raised their electrified clubs into position to strike him as the distance closed, but Mal was infinitely faster. The man on Mal's left was split in half, from groin to collarbone, dead before he realized it, and flopped to the nylon gray carpet. Seemingly of its own accord, Mal's bladed right hand shattered the second man's club in its grip, completely unaffected by the charge it held, and ripped through his chest, the Kevlar vest offering no more protection than a cloth t-shirt.

The fight was over in less than a second and two of Mal's unknown opponents lay at his feet, dead and nearly unrecognizable as having once been men. Barely breathing heavy, Mal stared at the implements of death his hands had become and shook with quiet emotion, ignoring the silent voice that spoke once more from somewhere deep inside his mind.

"Four hostile units approaching at six o'clock. Unit Designate Gauss considered preliminary threat," it droned.

"What am I?" muttered Mal on the verge of collapse.

"You're dead is what you are, Cestus."

THE CESTUS CONCERN

BOOK 1 OF THE WEIR CODEX

BY MAT NASTOS

DEDICATION

To Alden, one of my oldest and dearest friends, for going to see way too many questionable movies with me in high school.

CHAPTER 1

It has been said being born is one of the most painful and traumatic events in a person's life. For Malcolm Weir, being reborn was far worse.

The first thing Mal noticed as the warm, floating feeling only an especially heavy dose of morphine can give started to fade was the telltale itch in all ten of his toes and the balls of his feet.

Strangely enough, the itch didn't reach his hands. From the middle of his pecs, into his shoulders and down through both arms, there was an odd buzzing feeling, almost as if the Army Ranger was holding a faulty power cord in his hand—not quite the pain of electrocution, but an uneasy feeling that lay just below the surface and culminated in a pinprick discomfort in each of his fingers.

As consciousness returned, a number of other tidbits of information began registering in Mal's brain, the most troublesome being that his head felt as if a thick railroad spike had been inserted into it just below the base of his skull, and whatever caused the ache seemed to steal away his ability to move his head freely.

His mouth was dry; so dry, it felt as if Mal had been sucking on cotton balls and Brillo pads for days, his tongue cracked and devoid of even the slightest hint of moisture. Mal couldn't remember the last time he'd had anything to drink.

Panic and worry struck with the force of a hammer between his eyes as the man realized he couldn't remember anything at all. Mal had no idea where he was or how he got there. The worry quickly turned to fear as the soldier found himself unable to open his eyes.

Where am I, thought Mal, as his darkness seemed to suddenly swirl with chaos and terror. What happened? Why can't I see?

Frantically, Mal reached up with his left hand to touch his eyes, barely noticing the feel of metallic and leather arm restraints tearing apart from his movement. His outstretched finger struck his face with more force than he intended. The tip felt numb, almost as if his hands were wrapped in a wet sock. A shaking hand traced the outline of the tape cover his eyelids as the surrounding sounds returned all at once as if someone had switched them on like a radio.

A woman's voice near his right shoulder caused him to jump and to rip out half of his eyelashes along with the sticky substance that robbed him of sight.

"Oh, my God! He's awake!" came the startled throaty voice of the woman. Mal guessed she was middle-aged. He could also tell from the way her words echoed out across the room that he was in a fairly large area with tall ceilings.

"He should have been out for at least another four hours while the upgrade was being processed." The voice sounded annoyed more than concerned. Directly into his ear, and louder than Mal would have liked, he heard, "Designate Cestus, please return to diagnostic mode. Medical override five-two-six-alpha-nine."

For a split-second, the strange words took control of Mal's befuddled mind and he dropped back down to the position he awoke in, flat on his back, with arms calmly to his side. The urge to obey was quickly dispelled by an increased electric-shock sensation flowing from the back of his head into his chest and down into Mal's hands.

He had no clue why her command affected him so and didn't want her to try it again. Mal flapped his arm in an effort to shoo the woman away from him.

"Let me up," he whispered.

"Shit...he's ignoring the override." The annoyance transitioned into audible and obvious worry. "Monitors show the AI has been corrupted. We're going to need to restrain him!"

"I'm on it!" snapped another, much deeper male voice, this time from somewhere down near Mal's left foot.

Mal's eye finally came unstuck, but the lights in the room were too harsh, too bright for him to be able to see properly. Everything was a painful white blur. A shadow fell across his face, blocking some of the light, for which Mal was most thankful. Two large hands pressed down on his eerily numb shoulders, trying to stop him from rising. In spite of the reduced sensation his back and arms were experiencing, Mal could tell he was lying on a hard bed or table of some sort. The cold touch of metal along his spine suggested it was probably the latter.

"Hold him down!" screeched the woman. Mal decided she sounded like his Aunt Nancy, an even more disquieting fact than waking up on an operating table, blind and numb. God, he hated his Aunt Nancy.

"Damn it, I'm trying!" yelled the Southerner with increasing agitation. The man pushed harder, trying to keep Mal on the table. "Hit him with a shot of Midazolam, quick!"

Mal fought against the power of the man attempting to hold him down. With a quick twitch, his right arm came free and started to push his body into an upright position. As the motion caused his head to tilt out of its supine position, a new pain exploded in the back of Mal's skull, threatening to split it in half.

"Got it," the woman shouted from across the room!

Not wanting to wait around and find out what exactly "Midazolam" was, Mal shot his left hand out in an effort to get his male captor away from his body. From Mal's perspective, it was only a half-hearted backhanded slap. However, a grunt from the man and a loud crash a long distance away revealed it to be something more.

The woman screamed as she observed whatever Mal was unable to see, "Bradley!"

Mal ignored the sounds of the woman's footfalls heading for the body of "Bradley," and reached up with now-freed right hand to figure out what was holding the back of his head down to the table. Groping blindly, the confused man felt wires leading into a solid casing of some kind. It was hard and warm to the touch, and pulsed with the same shock of electricity Mal felt in his arms.

Most disturbing of all, however, was that the whole thing

seemed to be attached to a metallic plate mounted on the back of his head. Mal screamed in horror and pain as his hand gripped the slightly vibrating rod and yanked it from his head. He could feel the tip of it sliding out through the rear of his skull and his entire body jerked upright as he nearly retched from the experience.

"What have you done?" Mal howled.

The sounds of electronic equipment overloading and shorting out filled the room, along with the acrid smell of burning plastic and wiring.

Cupping the back of his head and its newly exposed hole with one hand, Mal reached up with the other to remove the remaining tape from his right eye. In the background his ears picked up the woman—a nurse?—as her shoes slapped against the hard floor of the room. Mal was finally blinking his way back to the land of the sighted when the sound of cracking glass and a shrill alarm filled the room.

The woman's voice, filled with worry and anger, fired off, presumably into an intercom somewhere behind the table Mal sat on. "Emergency! Send Gee-Em-Ars to surgical suite eight! We have a rogue unit! I repeat: we have a rogue unit!"

Mal's bare feet were dropping down to the cold floor of the operating room as a reply came over the speakers hidden somewhere in the ceiling, "GMRs in route. Stand by for assistance."

Spinning to face the nurse, as well as locate an exit, Mal's still squinting eyes were finally able to take in the room itself.

The pale cream room was just as Mal had feared: an operating suite about forty feet long by twenty-five or so wide. While the room itself was well lit, the area where he had been lying on a slightly inclined hydraulic surgical table was flooded by a series of four high-powered operating lights, mounted on a frame directly overhead.

A giant robotic arm, decorated in the same off-white color of the walls, reached out and engulfed the bottom quarter of the table, looking as much like a giant mechanical crab claw as the scanning device it probably was, with twin sensors above and below. A bank of blue glowing flat-screen monitors extended down from the ceiling and was linked to Mal by a mismatched multicolored series of cables and tubes which pierced his body at a number of locations.

Dominating the immediate area, though, was an evil looking rack of computers that was now smoking, sparking and seemingly on the verge of exploding. Mal's eyes lingered for a moment on the large bundle of cables that terminated with the large, glistening spike he had just removed from his skull. His hand started up to touch the hole left behind from the extraction when movement over the confused man's left shoulder caught his attention.

One wall seemed to be fashioned entirely of glass and, although he knew it was impossible, Mal could sense a number of people were watching him from the other side. Somehow he knew there were four human heartbeats in his immediate vicinity, all but one beating well-above normal rates.

Aside from the large, crumpled form of Bradley near one of the exit doors, the only other person Mal saw in the room was the woman who stood near an emergency call box. She was a harsh looking woman in her mid to late thirties, with light brown hair pulled tightly back into a bun. So tight, in fact, was her hair tied back that it caused the skin of her face to be stretched tight over her skull, which only increased the sharp appearance.

Even at nearly thirty feet away, Mal could read the small white name-tag pinned onto the blue hospital scrubs the woman was wearing. It read "Rebecca Clark, MD." When Doctor Clark's eyes finally locked onto Mal's, he could tell she was as confused as he was. Well, almost. At least she knew why he was standing, stark naked, in a cold operating room instead of being fully clothed and sweating like a pig with his battalion on maneuvers in Afghanistan.

"Wh—where am I?" stammered Mal.

"You are in surgical suite eight, Designate Cestus," replied Doctor Clark nervously as she took a step forward to the patient she had been working on. "Everything is all right. Please stand down and return to the table."

"Why do you keep calling me that?" Mal snapped back,

anger building in his chest. "My name is Captain Malcolm Weir, Third Battalion, Seventy-Fifth Ranger Regiment."

Holding her hands out in front of her body, the female doctor responded calmly, "No. You are Designate Cestus; we're at Project: Hardwired. Everything is fine…your programming has just gone a bit haywire and we need to get you back onto the table to get it fixed."

"There's been a mistake," the words tore themselves out from between Mal's clenched teeth. "I'm a Man. Look at me!"

Malcolm Weir gestured wide in an attempt to show the doctor how wrong she was and was surprised at her reaction. "You look, Designate Cestus. See what you are."

Confused and shaking, Mal stared down at his body to see what she was talking about. What he saw caused his world to shatter.

A spider's web of scars, long healed over, crisscrossed his chest and ran down his sides. The scars' state and pale white appearance spoke volumes as to just how long Mal had been blacked out. It would take a very long time, many, many months for wounds such as the ones he was looking at to close up and heal like that.

He had been out for a very long time.

What happened to me, he thought, eyes going fuzzy around the edges as they glazed over with tears.

Moving his hand to trace a finger over the network of off-white tissue is when Mal finally noticed his arms. What he saw stole the breath from his chest.

His arms, hands and upper chest were covered in metal. At first, Mal thought he was wearing some sort of armor made up of uneven, interlocking chromed plates, but where the armor met his flesh there were strange puckered scars and the metal itself seemed to merge with his skin. Whatever had happened to him, whatever it was, the armor was part of his body.

Clark's calm, self-assured voice rolled over Mal's shaking form, "You are Designate Cestus. You are property of Project: Hardwired and were brought in for a system upgrade when you were damaged," she moved closer to the man, oblivious to what was building inside of him with every word she spoke.

"Something compromised your AI and shorted out our system. Now I need you to return to the table."

With the truth slamming into him with the force of a freight train, Mal let loose with a primal scream—a scream of rage and despair and terror all rolled into one; a scream that, for a moment, drowned out even the noise of the still-sounding alarms.

The desperate man tore at his own flesh with fingers of metal, trying to rid himself of whatever had been done.

"Stop! You'll destroy your implants!"

Mal's eyes became the hate-filled eyes of a predator as they focused on the tall woman. A second scream seemed to propel the man in a leap that covered the nearly twenty foot distance between he and the doctor, the sudden burst of movement tore the tubes and wires from what remained of his human flesh, and left a fine mist of blood and IV fluids in his wake.

Fueled by anguish and fury and wildly pumping adrenalin, Weir reared back with a fist of unyielding metal and struck out against the only thing he could: Doctor Rebecca Clark. For ten long seconds, hands that were now cruel weapons of unbreakable titanium and unknowable technology rose and fell, each blow met with increasingly wet sounds, and less and less resistance.

With a final blow that cracked the floor beneath his feet, Mal stopped his assault, breathing heavily from the exertion, rivulets of sweat stinging each of the multitude of tiny wounds left behind by the IVs and monitor wires being wrenched from his skin. For a long moment he stared down at the crimson and black mess before him, unable to comprehend what was once the head and torso of the middle-aged doctor, but was now an unrecognizable mess of shredded flesh, broken bone and spent life.

Realization dawned on Mal as his senses now told him there were only three heartbeats registering in immediate proximity to him. Holding up his hands, Mal stared at them, dumbstruck. His fingers, now covered in dripping red gore, had elongated into terrifying looking claws, and the armor along his arms was now covered in one and two inch spikes.

All the better to kill you with, he thought grimly, rising to his feet unsteadily. Mal couldn't believe what had just happened. He'd never killed anyone before. Not once during his time as a ranger and never ever in cold blood.

"What have I done?" he whispered to the bloodstained weapons that had taken the place of his own hands.

Mal was a killer now. A murderer. He needed to find someone in charge to get things sorted out and turned over to the authorities, decided the soldier.

Before he could move toward the door, Mal's new senses screamed at him. Six heavily armed hostiles were swiftly approaching his location. Something from the base of his skull commanded him to flee the area or prepare for aggression, but Mal ignored the voice and stood still, his nude, muscular frame still half-coated in blood that was rapidly drying under the room's ever-present air-conditioning.

Mal turned to face the only entrance to the room as he waited to turn himself in, his head tilting up as he heard a group of people stop just outside.

"Rogue unit, Designate Cestus, located," said the muffled voice of either a military or law-enforcement officer.

That's really starting to get on my nerves, thought Mal at the newcomer's words.

The electric buzzing in Mal's metallic arms spiked in intensity, warning him once more of his imminent danger. "Target locked."

"Fire!"

Even as his mind was still registering what was happening, Malcolm Weir's body took over on instinct and reflex alone, diving wildly to his right as the door and wall in front of him disappeared in a torrent of gunfire. Whatever they had done to him, whoever "they" were, they had given the ranger a speed that defied imagination.

Faster than a speeding bullet, was what crossed Mal's mind. Unfortunately, that illusion was quickly dispelled as a second hail of gunfire tore into him, his new body armor absorbing all but a single shot, which lodged itself in the thick muscles of his upper thigh, and spun him across the now debris-laden floor.

Mal grunted with the impact as his mind analyzed his situation. Wounded, nude and trapped in a room with only two available exits, Mal was already leaping over the surgical table he had been strapped to even as his newfound senses worked through the problem.

Mal ducked down low behind the hydraulic and metal table in hopes it would shield him from more gunfire, grabbing the starched white sheet still draped across it to cover himself. Hazarding a look back towards the door, Mal tried to figure a way out while tearing a strip of cloth off to use as a tourniquet for the bullet wound in his leg.

Reaching down to try and remove the bullet with his fingers, Mal was surprised to see the projectile push itself free when his hand approached, as if by magic. The words "initiating repairs" sounded silently in his head. Mouth open in stunned amazement, Mal watched as the hole in his leg stopped bleeding and began to slowly knit itself closed. Further inspection revealed the array of nicks from the numerous intravenous needles had nearly vanished fully from sight, leaving behind only the smallest of red welts.

Another chorus of semiautomatic gunshots interrupted any astonishment the man was feeling over his rapidly healing wound. Mal was stunned that he could identify the weapons and number of said devices that were shooting at him: five Heckler & Koch MP5/40 submachine guns, fired in overlapping bursts of three rounds each.

Being able to identify the guns shooting at you was a neat carnival trick, but it wasn't going to help get him out of danger, Mal told himself harshly. Any second his attackers were going to resolve it was time to charge into the room and, when that happened, no amount of gun identification was going to save his sorry butt.

If these people had done whatever it was they did to him, Mal was sure they would know how to neutralize him as well.

The sight of a tall, muscular, dark-haired man half-wrapped in a sheet drew Malcolm's attention. At first, he didn't realize he was gazing at himself in the wall of glass separating him from eight heartbeats—his hair was cut down almost to the scalp and his icy blue eyes were sunken. His entire face was almost unrecognizable, even to himself.

That's when it hit him: "two available exits."

Mal was charging head first for the mirrored wall at the back of the room when hell came through the door behind him.

CHAPTER 2

The operating room's only door was blown inward from the force of a thunderous impact as Malcolm Weir raced across the cold tiled floor at breakneck speed, heading for what he hoped to be an escape.

Senses obviously operating on overdrive told the man the half-dozen hostiles had entered the room and were taking up position behind him. The rapidly increasing heart rates of the two people in front of him on the opposite side of the mirrored wall further informed him those hostiles were about to fire.

Well, to be fair, the sight of a six foot two US Army Ranger with wicked-looking blood soaked metal arms, hauling naked ass towards them at a pace that would make most Olympic sprinters envious, was probably enough to get anyone's heart racing.

The military-esque unit, which Mal could now see reflected in the ten by ten foot mirror in front of him, emerged from the dust cloud caused by their sudden entrance and had formed into two lines, with three black-clad, helmeted members dropping to one knee in front of the remaining three. All were dressed in a variation of law enforcement style tactical gear: visored helmets bearing the letters "GMR" emblazoned on the sides, each followed by a number, long-sleeved shirts with some sort of government insignia on their shoulders, covered by Kevlar vests loaded to bear with nylon gun harnesses. Every man wore a pair of pistols on their shoulders, Beretta M9s by the look of them, and some sort of large machine pistols Mal couldn't identify strapped to their right hips.

In addition to the HK-MP5/40s that five of them carried and

were currently pointing at Mal in a threatening manner, they were a formidable group for sure. The sixth man, whom Mal assumed was their leader, and only one without a helmet, held an AA-12 automatic shotgun that, in the tight confines of the surgical theater, worried him more than the other weapons, and the grenade launcher mounted to it didn't help matters.

If Mal hadn't been running for his life, he might have noticed the inhuman way five of the members of the GMR-team moved in conjunction with one another, the metallic cables which replaced the thick neck muscles of their fair-haired leader or his chrome right eye. Of course, with escape and self-preservation at the forefront of his mind, it was excusable for him to miss such details.

Mal felt the dull impact of at least six shots against the thick armor that now made up most of his wide back as a stream of bullets, laced with tracer fire, punched holes in the ultra-polished surface of the one-way observation wall a split second before his powerful legs catapulted his body through it. The eerily heightened senses he now possessed notified the soldier that one set of heartbeats in the darkened room he landed in had been silenced by the gunfire.

Shit, thought Mal as he planted one titanium-steel hand onto a desk and vaulted behind a bank of electronic equipment, they're killing their own people!

Only half acknowledging the body of a poor lab technician slumped over a computer terminal and missing the rear half of his skull, Mal headed for the door on the opposite side of the room, drawn by the bright light pouring in from the outer hallway. Bullets continued to pepper the room in increasingly uncontrolled bursts of fire.

Somehow, through the staccato drumbeat of the semi-automatic weapons' fire, Mal's ears picked up the sound of a woman whimpering just to the right of the door, hidden under a desk. His eyes found the young blond woman without much effort, curled up into a fetal position. She was dressed in a dark blue blouse, borderline inappropriately short black skirt and a standard-issue white lab coat. Most of her face and chest were covered in the steaming gore from her co-worker's death, and she was missing a black high-heeled Oxford that, amusingly enough, the silent voice in Mal's head had already located under an over-turned faux-leather office chair four feet to his left.

Normally Mal would have left the attractive woman behind— she had, after all, been part of whatever group had brought him here and did whatever it was they had done to him—but the soft pop and whoosh of a grenade being fired from the other side of the fractured and fragmented wall caused his Ranger training to kick in and the world seemed to slam into slow motion.

Perception kicking into high gear, Mal could see the motion trails and air disruption of hot projectiles flying through the surrounding air, easily dodgeable. A quick look over his left shoulder showed the fast approaching grenade round, spinning fiercely even in the hour it seemed to take for a second to tick off the clock.

A clawed hand grasped the cowering woman's shoulder and yanked her to her feet, forcibly dragging her along behind the soldier who was now moving at nearly an imperceptible speed. The living metal of Mal's shoulder caused the wooden and glass door to vaporize under its weight, slowing his momentum not one iota and allowing him to bounce out of the workroom's doorway even as the grenade exploded.

Flames licked out into the hall, followed by oily gray smoke and the smell of scorched plastic, quickly filling the corridor from floor to ceiling.

His powerful body shielding the woman from explosion and raining debris, Mal used one hand to turn her face toward his, leaving a grisly, clawlike handprint across her cheek, and demanded, "Who are you people? Where the hell am I?"

"Don't kill me!" was all she responded; mascara and tears ran down her now soot covered face. All that followed was incoherent blubbering.

The grating sound of stone being ground to dust spat from Mal's mouth as teeth ground themselves against each other in anger and frustration. He didn't have time for this. Those "GMR" guys were going to realize he survived the room's obliteration and come for him, guns blazing any second. Mal hauled the woman to her feet with an ease that surprised him: the arms, whatever they were, increased his strength dramatically. As long as his feet were planted, the super-soldier guessed he could probably lift a few thousand pounds without much trouble.

A quick once-over of the woman, whose nametag Mal saw was "Grace Talborg," helped him decide "good cop" was probably the best interrogation technique to use. She was fragile and looked like she'd shatter if he breathed too hard on her.

"Look, Ms. Talborg," voice shifting into comfort-mode as years of polite Southern upbringing took over, Mal held his hands up, palms out, to show he meant her no harm, "I don't know what's going on here, or where I am or why I'm here… please. Help me."

Her response left much to be desired, at least from Mal's point of view.

A gun pulled with amazing speed out from under her coat and a trio of bullets fired with amazing rapidity into his chest caused Mal to rethink his manners. The pistol was a tiny .22 caliber job and Grace wasn't the most skilled of marksmen, but only his hyper-enhanced reflexes and speed allowed Mal to avoid taking a slug to his vital organs: two bullets flattened themselves against his chest armor, harmlessly, while the third pinged off the forearm he threw up to shield his face and ricocheted up to leave a nasty gash across his right cheek, burrowing a burned and bloody line into his face.

Grace moved to fire her weapon again but Mal was quicker and caught her hand in his increasingly savage looking one. All she could manage was a sharp intake of breath as a quick flex of the soldier's gleaming chrome muscles crushed the gun in her hand, and the fingers around it.

"My, God," croaked Grace as the pain from her pulverized hand slowly registered in her brain. Mal didn't give her time to scream as he did the chivalrous thing and head butted the woman into unconsciousness.

Smoke from the fire continued to billow into the passageway and gave everything a red hue. Mal's sensitive hearing picked up the sound of sprinklers going off in the room next to where he stood. The sound of heavy booted feet stomping through water allowed him to identify where the armed group of men were—they hadn't charged in right after the grenade went off, which was the only thing that had saved him from taking a barrage of bullets from behind as he dealt with Grace.

Eyes narrowing in an effort to block stinging smoke, Mal squinted to try and find an escape route before he was discovered. Down the hall and away from the rooms he had just vacated were a series of doors and a T-junction at the end, perhaps a hundred feet or more away. Bright light, a clear blue sky and glimpses of buildings showed through a nearly floor-to-ceiling window in the opposite direction. One way led deeper into the unknown, the other to a freedom, but he'd have to make his way past two rooms filled with men who were armed to the teeth and ready to kill him.

Shouts from within the fire-engulfed room announcing his discovery spurred Mal's legs into action. He headed for the window and hoped there were no nasty surprises waiting for him from within the surgical suite's shattered doorway.

"Target locked!" shouted a voice from somewhere within the rooms and a nearly perfect horizontal line of armor piercing bullets tore through the wall right behind him.

Mal spit out a curse and sent his legs pumping.

Moving at full speed after only a few steps, Mal was able to outrun the rain of death from behind. Unfortunately, as he approached the well-lit doorway of the operating room, a pair of the GMRs emerged, wielding stun-batons loaded with enough electrical juice to take down an elephant.

Mal was about to stop and reverse direction when the inner voice chimed out, "Melee mode engaged."

The ever-present feeling of buzzing electricity grew to an uncomfortable pitch that ran from the fingertips of both hands in to his spine, causing Mal to almost lose his footing as he leaned his head down to rush the men. From the corner of his eyes, Mal watched as one arm molded itself into a nearly three foot long blade of glimmering steel, thrusting out from where his forearm had been. The other arm seemed to bulk up, metal plates flanging and flaring out, and his fingers elongated into five claws that would have made Wolverine shit himself with envy.

The GMRs were fast and raised their electrified clubs into position to strike him as the distance closed, but Mal was infinitely faster. The man on Mal's left was split in half, from groin to collarbone, dead before he realized it, and flopped to the nylon gray carpet. Seemingly of its own accord, Mal's bladed right hand shattered the second man's club in its grip, completely unaffected by the charge it held, and ripped through his chest, the Kevlar vest offering no more protection than a cloth t-shirt.

The fight was over in less than a second and two of Mal's unknown opponents lay at his feet, dead and nearly unrecognizable as having once been men. Barely breathing heavy, Mal stared at the implements of death his hands had become and shook with quiet emotion, ignoring the silent voice that spoke once more from somewhere deep inside his mind.

"Four hostile units approaching at six o'clock. Unit Designate Gauss considered preliminary threat," it droned.

"What am I?" muttered Mal on the verge of collapse.

"You're dead is what you are, Cestus," came the response from the doorway to Mal's left. A spinning hook kick from a steel-toed combat boot took Mal by surprise as it landed in the center of his back and drove him face-first through the opposite wall and into a darkened medical room.

All Mal could think as his head slammed into an examining table was that there was no way a normal man could have done that to him. It was impossible.

Whoever he was fighting, they were no more normal than he was.

"Gomer Units Theta-Nine, Theta-Ten and Theta-Fourteen, stand down, this asshole is mine."

Wiping blood from out of his eyes, Mal looked up to see the man his voice called "Gauss" stride out of the haze-filled hall, silhouetted by the flickering fluorescent lights in the ceiling behind him. Mal was shocked to see Gauss tear his shirt and Kevlar vest off with a quick motion, revealing a pair of slick, chrome metal arms underneath. Four two-finger thick bands of glowing material, spaced off every few inches, encased each arm.

Unseen, the three remaining Gomers sounded off in unison, "Standing down, sir."

The stereo effect creeped Mal out, although it was quickly forgotten as cold metal fingers grasped his neck from behind and jerked him to his feet.

"I've been waiting to take you down since they brought you in, Cestus."

A mouthful of spit and bile and blood accompanied a series of crushing blows to Mal's chest. He was sure he felt at least three ribs crack during the attack. Metal arms or no, Mal wasn't sure how much punishment he'd be able to take.

Gauss held Mal two inches off of the ground with an unyielding grip. "Let's see how much your 'badass Ranger training' helps you after I've ripped your spine out." The man's mouth literally frothed with his anger and spittle showered Mal's face.

Chrome fist clenched so tight his fingers seemed to disappear into a seamless ball, Gauss delivered an uppercut that rattled Mal's teeth and smashed him back through wood and drywall into the hall beyond. So furious was the blow that Mal found himself resting in a cratered floor on the verge of giving way to the level below.

In spite of his confusion and injuries, Mal decided he'd had enough. While he had no idea how exactly his new arms worked, he figured the best way to learn was to picture what he wanted and, as Gauss pushed his way through the half-collapsed office wall, Mal greeted him with two hands ending in five matching, six inch long blades each.

The two cyborgs rushed one another, each with death in his eyes. Mal was faster than the other man by far and left long gashes and bloody wounds on the man every time one of his claws connected. Unfortunately, Gauss was much fresher and far more powerful, with each fist strike or kick strong enough to pulverize concrete and shatter steel.

After one particularly intense exchange of attacks, Mal noticed Gauss's blows didn't have to connect to do damage. Whenever he threw a punch, the bands on his arms pulsed and seemed to amplify the man's strikes.

Mal was feeling bone-jarring impacts from open-palm strikes that stopped four or five inches from contact.

Panting and spitting gobs of thick, dark blood, Mal thought, what the hell is going on here? How do I fight someone who doesn't have to touch me to hurt me?

"Designate Gauss is equipped to affect, alter and manipulate magnetic fields in his immediate area," responded the calm voice that Mal thought sounded more and more like something you'd hear while on hold.

At least it's answering me now, Mal thought to himself as he blocked a leaping over-hand martial arts strike from Gauss that sent cracks throughout the floor beneath them and further threatened a collapse. If Mal didn't figure something out soon, he was a goner.

"Initiating dipolar counter charge in five seconds," the voice stated as a plan laid itself out for Mal.

"Four seconds."

The ferocity of the battle increased with the countdown. If Mal understood things, angling his back toward the window was going to be his best chance of getting away, and that whatever was going to happen was going to be rather impressive in nature.

"Three seconds."

Landing a particularly nasty cut down the face of Gauss that nearly took out his eye, the barest hints of a smile curled the edges of Mal's mouth. Gauss stumbled back a few feet in surprise. He was shocked Mal was able to hurt him.

"Two seconds."

Face flushing red Gauss put all of his power behind a strike he was sure would kill or incapacitate his opponent.

"You're dead!" screamed Gauss and his arm pistoned forward with the force of a canon.

"Dipolar counter charge initiated."

Hearing the words in his head and feeling the strange tingling in his arms, Mal lashed out with his own fist, directly into the path of the one Gauss had launched. The two hands, moving at rocket-like speeds, closed to within millimeters of one another before the reverse polarity field Mal's arms were generating took full effect, halting their power.

The resulting explosion caused the smoke-filled air to clear and, in a semi-circle of devastation, destroyed ceilings, knocked down walls and punched through concrete floors. The concussive force blew the three Gomer units spinning uncontrollable down the hall, quickly followed by an unconscious Gauss.

Mal blacked out from the powerful discharge.

He awoke less than three heartbeats later to find himself hanging over seventy stories up in the airspace just outside of the US Bank Tower in Los Angeles, surrounded by falling glass and debris. A cool wind massaged his body in some very intimate locations, reminding him of his lack of clothing. For a moment, just before mistress gravity reasserted herself on him, Mal felt just like Wile E. Coyote.

Mal wondered where he'd put his tiny 'HELP' sign.

"Y-Axis position: nine hundred sixty-three feet and falling. Time to ground impact: sixteen point three two seconds," Mal's inner voice told him in a flat, emotionless tone. "Chances of survival: zero point zero five nine one percent," it added.

"Oh, hell," was all Mal could manage before he dropped like a rock.

CHAPTER 3

When the security alarms began their shrill cackling, Gordon Kiesling cringed just a little—the sound reminded him very much of the way his mother-in-law cackled at the twice-yearly holidays of Christmas and Thanksgiving. During those times the only thanks Kiesling was giving came from the knowledge the old bat was old and would be dead soon.

As Kiesling reached for the intercom switch on his telephone, his tanned, manicured hand knocked over a pile of paperwork in transit, causing the handsome man to sigh. There were quite a few stacks of paperwork cluttering his desk, far more than he liked.

Although Kiesling absolutely relished the amount of power his position gave him—the power of money, the power of political influence and the power to defend his country from threats both foreign and domestic—the man loathed the tedium that it came with. He wished to himself, not for the first time, the reports were as easily dealt with as terrorist cells. At least those he could have shot.

"Yes, Executive Director Kiesling," Melissa's voice flowed out of the tiny black speaker box that sat next to an over-sized phone with more buttons than had right to exist on one device. Her tone was even and relaxed, as it always was. Melissa Roslan was the result of a million years of executive assistant evolution—smart enough to never question things she shouldn't, sexy enough to throw off the middle-aged politicians Kiesling was often forced to deal with and just perky enough to not be annoying. She was always dressed impeccably, with her blond hair pulled back into a sharp pony tail, her skirts perfectly wrinkle free no matter the time of day and the dull black Glock she kept in her top draw always well-oiled, loaded and ready to go.

The perfect accessory for a man like Executive Director Gordon Kiesling of Project: Hardwired. No slouch himself, Kiesling was a tall, handsome, fit man in his mid-forties with just enough gray in his jet black hair to rank well with voters on either side of the political divide. He was a man who had been groomed with a great destiny in mind and leading Project: Hardwired to success was but the first step.

"Melissa, what's going on with the alarms? Did Dr. Ryan's boys upstairs blow something up again?" Kiesling chuckled to himself at the comment. The last "mishap" caused by Doctor Jean Ryan's team had resulted in mass flooding on ten floors of the building from something they had done to the sprinklers. He'd instructed his assistant to have them removed from his office the very next day, fire marshals be damned. There was no way he was going to have another custom-tailored suit ruined.

The intercom popped and buzzed once more as Melissa's voice came over it once again, "No, sir. There's some sort of trouble in a surgical suite and one of the Cestus team has requested GMR assistance."

"The 'Cestus team?' Wasn't that unit just going through routine maintenance after Kabul?" It must be some sort of operator error, thought Kiesling to himself. After all, the program had been running like a well-oiled machine for more than eighteen months—once they had worked out the issues with the earlier 'Rebirth' units. Sure, those had been a mess, but it had been cleaned up.

"The unit Designate Cestus was undergoing reintegration with Abraxas-1. There had been...complications during its return from the assignment in Kabul."

"Complications?" That wasn't a word the head of a multi-trillion dollar top-secret government project liked to hear in relation to his department. Words like that tended to be followed by ones like 'reassignment' or 'termination,' neither of which Gordon Kiesling wished to experience. Eyes narrowed in concentration and jaw set solidly, the governmental overseer launched into the one kind of action his kind was best at: delegation. "Dispatch a GMR team to the location and lock it down...have one of the Prime units tag along just in case. Give me a full project report on Designate Cestus and his 'complications,' ay-sap."

The door to Kiesling's office slid open as his assistant strode in on five-inch black heels that matched the charcoal pants suit she had worn that day, arms loaded with files. He had to do a double take from her back to the intercom unit—he hadn't realized she was no longer at her desk.

Dropping the stack of stark white folders onto the only clean spot on her boss's desk, Melissa said curtly, "GMR team Theta is en route to surgical suite eight with Designate Gauss in command. They'll report back to you as soon as the location has been secured. Here are the files you requested. You'll find details of the operation in Kabul along with status reports for the Cestus unit from the past nine months."

Kiesling marveled for a moment at the woman's uncanny efficiency and damn near psychic ability to anticipate his every command. Without waiting for his response, the woman had spun on her heel and headed back to her own office.

Kiesling called out, "And, Ms. Roslan..."

"I'll send one of the interns in with your coffee, sir."

He was still smiling as the young woman disappeared into the bright fluorescent lights of her outer office and the connected reception area, the door closing silently behind her.

The late afternoon sun spread long bands of light across the heavy red cherry desk dominating the center of the office. The light added no extra warmth to the well air-conditioned room due to the heavy tinting on the windows—tinting that would have kept any onlookers from peering into the high security floors run by Kiesling's special project division. Not that they had many onlookers there on the 71st floor, outside of a few ratty pigeons and the odd news chopper that would buzz by on one breaking news story or another.

No surprises were revealed to Kiesling by the first pair of folders; they contained basic background information on Malcolm Weir, the man now referred to as 'Designate Cestus' there at Project: Hardwired: standard bio, exemplary service record, medical files from when he was first brought in eleven months earlier and so on. As executive director and sole head of the division, Kiesling was intimately familiar with the background files of all twelve of the Project: Hardwired Prime units. After all, he had been the one who approved the addition of each of the men long before they were eventually brought under the project's aegis.

Weir had been the perfect Hardwired candidate and a model operative. The second batch of files, bound with "Eyes Only" tape and covered in "Top Secret" stamps, ran through each of the nineteen missions he'd undertaken in the nine months since he'd been on active duty—nearly double the assignments of any other unit.

Kiesling whistled in admiration as he flipped through pages upon pages of mission logs, photos, maps and more from the Weir's time out in the field, and wished he had the budget to build ten more like the soldier.

The final folder, labeled "Under Review" across its cover, was what Kiesling had been searching for: the incident report and follow-up from Kabul.

According to the documentation, Cestus had been operating at peak performance for a Prime unit prior to the operation— above peak if his team's reports were accurate. Hell, he even exceeded Gauss's results in every joint excursion they were tasked to. It was the reason Dr. Ryan had pushed so hard for Weir to be upgraded with the new nano-tech. The reactive A.I. of the nano-drones made the "living" metal of the soldier's arms into some of the most deadly weapons on the planet for the types of covert missions he specialized in.

Before he received them, the man had been a beast, thought Kiesling. With them, Designate Cestus had become Goddamn Death incarnate.

The comfortable office chair creaked with Kiesling's 185 pounds of muscle and slid a bit on the clear plastic floor protector it rested on as he leaned forward to rest his elbows on his cluttered desktop. One hand shifted a black wireless mouse back and forth, causing the large flatscreen monitor nestled on one corner of the workspace to flicker on, while the other smacked the folder down and quickly turned to the next page.

"Twenty kills within one minute of insertion," marveled Kiesling. He wanted to view POV footage from Kabul to see the "complications" in real time, but was dismayed to have a blue error screen staring back at him from the glowing monitor. Intercom button tapped quickly by his long, tapered middle finger, Kiesling leaned back in his chair and asked aloud, "Melissa, something's wrong with my computer. It's telling me the system is down. Can you please tell me how it is possible for a billion dollar quad-redundant computer system to be 'down?' Is there maintenance I wasn't informed of?"

A long silence was the only answer that came back over the intercom. After a moment of drumming his fingers on the highly lacquered wood of his desk, Gordon Kiesling became agitated. Melissa knew how much he hated to be kept waiting… for anything!

"Melissa," the volume of his voice rose just as its octave dropped in annoyance.

"I apologize, Executive Director. Reports are coming in from all over. The system has been breached and everything has gone offline. Word from all remote sites are in agreement-Chicago, Houston, Poughkeepsie…even the redundancies in Cardiff and Hong Kong, all report connection to the Brain Coral has been lost, sir."

The nervous tic he'd been working on to rid himself of for years returned and caused a vein to twitch angrily on the left side of his forehead, just off-set of his brow line. "Now, Melissa," he forced the words through clenched teeth, "you know I find that particular nickname for the Abraxas-configuration to be inappropriate."

"Sorry, again, sir. I-Oh, my God!"

An explosion rocked the building and plaster snowflakes covered Kiesling's immaculate suit and perfectly coiffed hair. He sprang to his feet, chair spinning chaotically away from his desk before collapsing to the ground, as he heard the shock in his assistant's normally calm voice.

"Melissa?!" yelled Kiesling as he jogged for the door, which was thrown open just as his hand, shaking with adrenaline, reached for the handle.

Obviously shaken, Ms. Roslan stood in the entrance, glasses slightly askew and a strand of hair uncharacteristically bouncing down in front of her face. Kiesling read the concern in her eyes.

"Sir, you're going to want to see this."

Standing in at the center of a group of scientists, engineers and security officers, Gordon Kiesling couldn't believe what he was looking at on the small, silent black-and-white security monitors Melissa had ordered dragged into his office. It was unbelievable.

No, impossible. It was impossible.

But there it was: one of the most lethal weapons on the planet, a weapon HE was responsible for creating and overseeing, had gone rogue.

The Cestus unit, Malcolm Weir, had somehow taken out their entire computer network, killed at least three of Kiesling's operatives, including a pair of the earlier GMR base-infantry units, and was now attempting to escape the facility. The renegade cyborg had to be stopped before he could make off with billions of dollars in US government research and development attached to his body.

He had to be stopped.

Kiesling snatched a communications unit from Larry Doherty, the beefy security chief from New Hampshire, startling the man with the sudden movement.

"Can Gauss hear me on this thing?"

Seeing Doherty's nod, Kiesling held the earpiece in place with one hand and brought the unit's microphone up to his mouth with the other.

"Designate Gauss," he paused to allow the operative to acknowledge he was receiving. "This is Executive Director Gordon Kiesling, clearance omega-nine-aught-seven-three-nine-five. Unit Cestus has gone rogue. You will stop him at all cost: use of deadly force authorized. Confirm?"

The ten observers watching the closed-caption monitors saw Gauss look up into the security monitors, nod and smile as his voice came in over the headset in their boss's hand, "Confirmed."

In black-and-white, a miniature Gauss launched into battle against Cestus, wreaking havoc on the entire floor just above where they were being scrutinized. Kiesling groaned inwardly as walls and fixtures were annihilated by the battling duo: the damage would easily run into the millions when all was said and done. He was going to hate having to explain that to the Senate oversight committee.

While the battle continued above in real life and below on the screen, Kiesling asked Carl Anderson, the short, slightly rotund IT technician what the state of Project: Hardwired's computer system was. The answer filled him with dread.

"Gone," responded the small man, his greasy light blond ponytail bounced about the back of his head as he did. Kiesling hated that nasty bit of horsehair almost as much as he hated the man's ratty goatee, which always seemed to be shaved asymmetrically. "It's all gone."

Forcing himself to take a deep breath to keep from tearing the tuft of hair out by its roots, Kiesling said as calmly as his building rage would allow, "What do you mean by 'gone?' You're talking about ten years of research…millions of man-hours. Can you recover it from the system?"

Anderson shrank down into himself as his boss loomed over him, fists clenched and fuming. He licked his lips and looked around the room for someone, anyone to help. Finding himself alone in Kiesling's sights, Anderson finally stuttered, "G-gone. As in gone. There's nothing left. The system is blank… reformatted and gone. Just gone."

"If you say 'gone' one more time, I'm going to have Mr. Doherty shoot you in the back of the head," Kiesling nodded over to his now shocked-looking head of security. "Please, explain."

The terrified computer technician flipped his laptop around to reveal its screen, which seemed to show an ever-increasing line of numbers and letters scrolling down its face. "See here?" asked Anderson, "The system is showing a clean wipe of everything. Whatever Designate Cestus did while he was plugged into the system, it took down everything: active data, back-ups, programs…hell, he even took out the base operating system. Everything is go…deleted. But that isn't the worst part."

With a headache of biblical proportions building just behind his brow, Kiesling clenched his eyes and waved for the tech to continue. "Go on."

"The server logs show a massive download of information occurred right before the system died. Zettabytes of data were copied. Everything was taken."

"Taken by whom?" quizzed the increasingly worried Kiesling.

"Designate Cestus."

"That's impossible," interrupted Melissa to the man's left, causing both Kiesling and Anderson to jump. "Cestus may have had the most advanced wetware we've ever integrated into a biological unit, but that amount of information is magnitudes beyond what he is capable of storing."

Everyone stared at the woman in amazement. A tiny grin tugged at Kiesling's lips. It might be time to give Melissa a raise.

"Well," started Anderson, insecurity oozing from every pore of his body. "Normally, you'd be correct, Ms. Roslan: the base system Cestus had been operating with would have been unable to process, let alone store that amount of data. It would have fried every synapse in his brain and shut him down; maybe even killing him in the process."

Melissa looked down on the man, smirking.

"However," he continued, "With his upgrade last month, we gave him tens of millions of tiny computers to add to his network…"

"Oh, my God," realization hit the executive assistant's face before anyone else realized what Anderson was saying. "The nano-drones…"

"Exactly," returned Anderson, shifting his attention from his boss to the only other person in the room who seemed to understand what he was saying. "All of those microscopic drones are tiny computers, all slaved to the one in the head of Designate Cestus. It's possible they're operating as a cloud-processing network—each nano-drone carrying and managing a small piece of the information and taking some of the lode off of his core-system. He may not even realize what he's got—the download may have fried his governing AI…"

"Which is what caused him to go rogue," finished Ms. Roslan.

"Precisely! With his AI gone, the original personality construct resumed control."

"Wait a minute," Kiesling jumped in as he finally processed the information. "You mean our entire project is stuck in Malcolm Weir's brain and I've got Gauss down there trying to kill him?"

Every head in the room snapped back to the events playing out in monochromatic gray on a tiny Sony brand monitor. Kiesling pushed Anderson out of the way as he started screaming into the tiny white communications unit security chief Doherty had given him, "Stand down! Stand down! Gauss, abort!"

Kiesling was too late as an irresistible force slammed into an immovable object, and the explosive result shattered windows in the top twenty floors of the US Bank Building, throwing the heads of Project: Hardwired to the floor.

He had recovered just enough to see a very naked and very unconscious Malcolm Weir falling past his office window, surrounded by a rain of broken glass and wreckage.

With his once promising future political career flashing before his eyes, Gordon Kiesling rushed for the most powerful weapon at his disposal, the telephone, and began the most important case of damage control in his life.

"Get me the Secretary of Defense…"

CHAPTER 4

Falling to his death from the seventy-second floor of the tenth tallest building in the United States resulted in a not-so-surprising epiphany about himself: Malcolm Weir hated heights.

The only thing Mal hated even more than heights at that particular moment was the fact the new computer he found himself implanted with was informing him that he was currently traveling at nearly 80 miles per hour after approximately five seconds of falling; that he had already fallen about one hundred and fifty feet, give or take; and, finally, that he would reach terminal velocity right as his body impacted, leaving what he could only assume would be a rather messy smear on the immaculately kept gray stone tiled courtyard just outside the US Bank Tower's main entrance.

Being nude was, of course, just icing on the cake.

Recognizing no amount of cybernetic enhancements were going to allow him to survive a seventy-two story fall, being too far away from the structure of the building to even attempt to grab on to the ledge and realizing none of the magical flagpoles Daredevil or Batman used in the comic books were going to materialize and save him, Mal angled his body towards the ground and used it like an airfoil in an attempt to make it into one of the windows. While the action would increase his airspeed and decrease his time to ground impact, and a collision with the side of the building in excess of 100 miles per hour would probably kill him just as quickly, the battered and bruised Army Ranger saw no other options.

Hurricane winds tore at his flesh and made his eyes tear up. The wind-induced blindness threw off his aim, caused Mal to miss a 30th floor bank of windows and slam with sense-shattering force into the concrete and steel outer wall instead.

Mal was sent spinning uncontrollably out into the abyss between buildings, but was able to stay calm enough to correct his course and try again.

As the man approached the building's side once again, his mind fired off a prayer and reached out with the segmented chrome weapons that now replaced his arms.

The ground rose up quickly to meet him and Mal knew this was his last chance and his only hope of survival.

"No!!" screamed Mal as his right hand missed a lip by mere inches. He instinctively reached out with his left arm in a reflexive attempt to grab on, knowing full well he was still too far away.

A fire in his shoulder and chest caught the man by surprise. The electrical hum that had been present in his new limbs increased to painful proportions and Mal's eyes went wide at what he saw happening.

Within the blink of an eye, his left arm shot out, elongating to nearly 6 feet in length and caught the ledge, which had been rushing out of sight an instant before, titanium-steel fingers digging deep into the hard shell of the US Bank Tower.

Mal was never so relieved to have his nose broken from the momentum of being thrown into the side of a building. His relief, however, was short lived as the lip his claws held onto disintegrated under his weight, sending him falling once more toward the pavement hundreds of feet below.

This time, Mal was close enough to jam both arms into the pale gray skin of the building to slow his fall. Ten gouges ripped through stone and steel and glass as Mal's descent continued, destroying the once pristine face of the skyscraper.

Mal kept his head down to keep his face safe from deadly debris as he fell and forced back the pain of having his shoulders nearly ripped off in the process of saving himself. Silently, Mal thanked whoever made his new arms even as he cursed them for what they had done to him.

Twenty feet above the ground, the regular construction of the building halted for the vaulted ceilings of the first floor and

Mal found himself in a short free fall once more.

Mal landed harshly, skidding to a halt just outside of the giant glass entrance of the building. The rough stone of the pavement shredded the skin on his left leg and re-aggravated the semi-healed bullet wound in his thigh as he vaulted to one side to dodge the dagger sharp shards of glass and brick the blades of his fingers had torn free during his escape.

A businessman in a four thousand dollar charcoal-colored H. Huntsman Super 100 wool suit and fifteen hundred dollar John Lobb shoes, shocked by the sight of an incredibly muscled, naked man with metal arms dropping out of the sky, barely noticed the four foot tall brass and aluminum "3" crashing into the ground mere inches from his body as he about-faced and hurried back inside through the nearest set of revolving doors.

Mal inhaled deeply and let it out slowly to try and calm the jack-hammering of his heart. Easing slowly to his feet, the battered, bruised and bloodied man took inventory of his wounds: three broken or cracked ribs, broken nose, a bullet hole in his upper thigh, skin scraped almost entirely off of his left side, glass embedded in places he didn't want to think about and a bruised tail-bone from dropping onto his butt after a nine hundred and sixty plus foot fall.

Oh, that and he seemed to be missing two arms, his pectoral muscles, most of his back and all of his clothing.

All things considered, he was lucky to be alive at all.

Bare feet slapped pavement warmed by the hot summer sun of Southern California. Mal headed for the large, briskly moving street out in front of the tower. He was completely unsure of where to go or even how to get there in the middle of downtown Los Angeles without any clothing. Before he discovered an answer to either of those questions, a third problem arose when a shrill alarm sounded from somewhere in the depths of the US Bank Tower.

Damn it, thought Mal to himself as he continued towards the street in hopes of a solution to his dilemma would fall out of the sky the same way he had. He figured it would take them— whoever 'them' was—a few minutes to get any sort of response team together and down to street level.

At least no one has noticed me, was Mal's thought as he looked around and noticed a crowd gathering on the street nearby.

"Surveillance devices detected," announced the computer voice from within. "Executing countermeasures."

Frustration consumed Mal as he bolted towards a mixed trio of a large, balding man with sweat stains on the armpits of his long-sleeved blue dress shirt; an elderly Korean woman with a small push cart full of grocery bags; and a tall man dressed in denim jeans and a stark white wife-beater, half astride a still-idling black-and-green Kawasaki Z1000 motorcycle. A black, full-face helmet and leather jacket sat on the seat in front of the man.

They were all staring at him through the cameras in their cell phones.

"That's just superb," spat Mal as he neared the group and gave them some excellent footage of 'Little Mal' flapping in the breeze. "I hope those bastards on YouTube aren't mean!"

All three onlookers dropped their phones as the tiny devices shot sparks almost simultaneously. The silent electronic voice informed Mal that all mobile devices within 30 yards had been disabled, but that there were a series of traffic and other cameras observing him. It instructed that he vacate the immediate area before local authorities or Project: Hardwired units arrived.

The fat man and old woman dove out of Mal's path as he aimed for the biker, head down and eyes glaring, "I'm taking your bike, your jacket and your pants!"

"Dude I-" was all the red-goateed man got out before he was laid flat by a steel-fisted right cross. Mal caught the man before he hit the ground and quickly stripped off his old tan work boots and jeans.

Probably not the most sanitary of shopping methods, but beggars can't be choosers, thought Mal as he dressed at near light speed. His metallic arms, filled with strange plates, spikes and weird angles, fought the jacket, but finally went in with one last shove that popped a few seams. The crowd around the building was growing, and he'd need to hurry before…

"Multiple hostiles approaching."

Looking up to see a gang of men dressed in tactical gear similar to what he had encountered upstairs, Mal groaned and asked his "other" self for the number of hostiles incoming.

"Ten standard humans bearing large caliber weapons."

"Not too bad," he responded aloud. "It could be worse."

"One shoulder-mounted rocket-launcher."

Mal was really starting to hate the voice in his head.

The motorcycle's engine revved, buzzing like the world's largest hornets' nest, the sound echoing madly between the towering high rise buildings filling the tight area of downtown Los Angeles. Mal let go of the brake and caused the super bike to pop up into a wheelie, barely getting out of the way as automatic gunfire ripped into the asphalt where it had been parked.

Fifth Street was a one-way street, heading northwest. With a red light formed pocket empty of traffic, Mal assumed he'd be able to go full throttle and get far enough away from the gunmen to avoid taking a bullet up his tailpipe.

The scream of sirens and six black and white police vehicles blocking off the road's intersection with South Flower Street, their harsh red and blue lights bouncing off of every reflective surface in sight.

Mal knew, between his military training and the living metal of his arms, he could fight his way past the cops, but the thought of harming or even killing police officers out doing their jobs caused Mal's stomach to fill with knots.

No way, he thought to himself as a sneer ripped across his bloodied face. Maybe they'll listen to my side of the story?

The sound of an authoritative voice crackling over a car-mounted loudspeaker gave him hope.

"You, on the bike, pull over and place your hands where we can see them!"

His hopes were shattered as a well-placed shot from behind tore through his coat and punched through the window of the cop car directly in front of Mal, killing the officer with a high-powered bullet to the forehead.

From the oncoming cops' perspective, it appeared as though Mal had fired the round.

"Those bastards!" Mal snapped again as the blood in his

veins pumped so loud he swore he could hear it. He leaned the bike over, planted a steel-toed boot onto the ground and slammed the front brake as hard as he could, which sent the vehicle's back wheel into a spin. Only his enhanced strength and reflexes kept the motorcycle from crashing and allowed Mal to change directions at just under 50 miles per hour to go rocketing back towards the men who turned his life upside down.

They're dead, was all that went through his mind as the bike leapt the curb onto the sidewalk, heading straight for the loosely grouped team of men.

Bullets hammered into the front of the bike, obliterating its front end, but Mal didn't notice. Head down, arms extended forward, Mal paid even less attention to the few bullets that impacted him—tearing his new coat to shreds and glancing off his armored body.

If the sight of one of the mercenaries kneeling down and bracing a small self-propelled rocket launcher on his shoulder worried him, it didn't show in the rider's eyes so intent was his purpose.

At approximately fifty feet away, the thug squeezed hard on the weapon's trigger and let loose the weapon directly into Mal's mad rush on the quickly disintegrating product of Japanese motorcycle engineering.

A split second before the tiny white and red missile blasted into the steel, aluminum and plastic form of the Kawasaki, Mal launched himself into the air with a thrust from his inhumanly strong arms and legs. Mal's momentum, aided by the concussive force of the bike exploding into a ball of yellow flame, carried the man the final few yards into the midst of the men who were the focus of his own burning rage.

The Project: Hardwired security force was made up of some of the top soldiers recruited from all across the United States military and all of its branches, and, in some cases, outsourced from other countries. The force was a team of men who lived, ate and breathed combat. Killing was their stock-and-trade, and between them, the group of ten men standing toe-to-toe with Malcolm Weir had decades of experience. They were killers in every sense of the word.

They didn't stand a chance, caught in the razor-edged whirlwind of Mal's fury and rage and hatred. The carnage lasted less time than it took for a man to fall from a seventy-two-story building.

Mal gave himself completely over to his reflexes and his pain and anger clouded instincts, barely noticing as bladed ridges grew along the living metal of his arms, spikes covered his back, and men fell before his unquenchable desire for blood.

Arms were sliced from shoulders, legs hacked from torsos, heads chopped from necks and none of it mattered to Mal, engulfed by the urge to have his tormentors dead. Their screams failed to reach his ears as one and all lost lives at his cruel touch.

When all was said and done, ten men lay dead, although from what was left of the men the LAPD's coroners would have trouble confirming that count, so mangled were the bodies.

Not a single intact corpse remained and the pieces of once-living men were spread out at the feet of a shaking and weeping Malcolm Weir, arms glistening moistly with the product of his unstoppable attack. Blood soaked the air in a fine cloud of mist, covering the entire area and leaving a hot dampness across Mal's body, soaking his clothes through to sweat-drenched skin.

So disturbing was the scene that Mal, once the red heat of the berserker fury had dissipated from his eyes, vomited at the sight of what he had done. With the sounds of police sirens quickly approaching from the street, and another group of heavily armed government soldiers running towards him from the entrance to the US Bank Tower building, Mal dropped to his knees, hands hung limply to his sides as his fantastic, seemingly inexhaustible stamina finally evaporated, leaving him a spent husk.

"Take him down!" commanded one of the approaching soldiers from behind the mirrored visor of his helmet.

Every remaining flesh-and-blood muscle in his body locked up in a painful, twitching cramp as a swarm of what seemed like a hundred taser darts peppered Mal's body. Although Mal's living metal arms seemed to absorb the majority of the incapacitating charge, enough juice remained to render him nearly paralyzed and cause his body to face-plant into the hard stone tiles of the blood-soaked courtyard, further shattering his nose with a sickening crunch.

"Yarges, Silva: get the adamantine cuffs up and lock those arms down," ordered the officer who called for the taser attack. "Teran, Volante: put a restraining bolt on his rear power core, ASAP. I don't want any surprises while we talk to the local cops."

A hard-soled boot slammed down on the back of Mal's neck, grinding his broken nose once more into the rough ground. The pressure of the restraints kept Mal from struggling as two pairs of hands clamped cold, smooth casings of metal over his hands, covering from fingertip to just over his elbow. He was trapped and his movement limited, with his arms drawn tightly behind his back and unable to bend or rotate except at the shoulder.

Mal could hear the squeal of brakes and the smell of burned rubber that announced the LAPD's arrival at the location. Movement out of the corner of his eye showed the military man in charge of the operation striding out to meet the police officers...probably to try and keep them from getting involved and taking their new prisoner away.

Car doors were thrown open and the thud of what seemed to be a hundred feet hitting the ground almost simultaneously. The cacophony was quickly followed by the popcorn-like sound of a multitude of rounds being chambered into weapons. Mal's inner voice told him the "multitude" was actually 12 rounds, but he stopped listening as it started to drone on with the specific breakdown of what those rounds and weapons were. He'd lost the ability to care.

"Drop your weapons and place your hands where we can see them!" screamed one of the cops—ten meters behind him at just over twenty-seven degrees off-center, quipped the voice. Mal was yanked to his feet from behind and hidden from view by the thick bodies of the men who had captured him.

"Officers, this is a government-sanctioned operation," started the head soldier. Mal lost whatever the man said next as he was distracted by an incredibly ugly, incredibly boxy, off-white car hitting the curb nearby and launching itself a few inches into the air with a shower of sparks and tremendous grating noise.

Glare from the setting sun kept the driver hidden behind the car's windshield, but Mal was convinced the man was grinning evilly as the vehicle's brakes shrieked violently, sent up a blast of smoke and the entire thing fishtailed toward him.

The only thing that saved Mal from being crushed by two-and-a-half tons of a Nissan Cube, spinning nearly out of control, were his supernatural reflexes. Unfortunately, the group of government agents standing in a very tight group around him was not quite so lucky.

Bodies went flying as the fiberglass frame of the Cube slammed into the men at high speed—the one identified as "Yarges" took a header across the hood of the car, snapping off its radio antenna before he disappeared over the opposite side.

Injured men fell all around as the car shuddered to a stop, its passenger's side less than an inch from Mal's startled face. He had to snap his upper torso backwards and flop onto his side to avoid the Nissan's rear door as it was thrown open.

Mal looked into the car and saw a man in his mid-forties, head completely shaved of hair, and a salt-and-pepper goatee encircling his frantically moving mouth. The crazed man looked familiar, but Mal couldn't quite place his face. The man's arms waved about insanely. It took Mal a couple of seconds to realize the man was yelling at him.

"Get in, Mal! They've got your face all over the TV!"

I've got it, thought Mal, grinning stupidly as he finally recognized the man. David Zuzelo—Zuz to his buddies—had been a friend of Mal's back in college.

"Zuz! Man, what are you doing here," babbled Mal, trying and failing to stand up.

The vehicle's tinted rear windshield exploded as bullets blasted into the car. A line of bullet holes appeared in the car's side panel next to the dazed Mal, as if by magic, causing the man to chuckle.

Another window shattered and sent glass flying.

"Get in, you asshole, before they kill us both!" bellowed Zuzelo in his heavy New England accent, scrunching down his head behind the steering wheel in a vain attempt to avoid being shot.

Mal didn't know what to do. Why was Zuz here...of all places? Was it his imagination?

"Withdrawal advised. Hostiles closing in on foot," chimed in the computerized voice of the hitchhiker in Mal's head, snapping him back to reality.

Mal made up his mind as he looked around to see some of the soldiers getting back to their feet and going for their weapons. Arms still cuffed with heavy metal manacles behind his back, Mal dove through the open passenger's side door even as the ungainly vehicle started to pull away, barely making it into the backseat.

From his stomach-down position on vinyl seats covered in discarded soda cans and fast food wrappers, Mal braced himself as best he could as the driver leaned into the wheel, sending the vehicle into a hairpin turn, nearly slamming the opened door onto the hog-tied man's flailing feet.

Zuzelo looked back with a wide, half-insane smile splitting his face and belched out, "Keep your head down...I'll have us out of here in no time flat!"

A long, weary sigh escaped through Mal's half-clenched teeth as he allowed his face to sink down onto the fuzzy, dark-gray seats of the Nissan Cube, eyes already closing as the unwanted passenger in his head stated without passion, "Commencing self-repair. All system shutting down."

The last thing Mal heard before the comforting oblivion of exhaustion took him was his old friend belting out 'Firework' by Katy Perry at the top of his lungs. Mal thought the sound of distant sirens provided a rather fitting melody as he passed out.

CHAPTER 5

The sounds of screeching tires and an automobile engine being pushed to the max, somehow transformed into the high-pitched whine of a UH-60 Black Hawk in hard flight. Malcolm Weir recognized the sound instantly. It had been an almost everyday part of his life for the better part of a decade. There were times he swore he'd spent more time in the belly of a chopper than most pilots clocked behind the flight stick.

The familiar bumps and jostling of his bolted-down seat in the main cabin, something that had made him violently ill during training, were a soothing massage to his strapped-in body.

Mal allowed his head to lie back so he could feel the cloth covering on his ACH butt up against the hard metal frame of the helicopter. The ranger had to suppress a chuckle as he felt the sock he kept taped to the inside of his helmet out of nostalgia for basic training tickle the back of his neck.

This is how things are supposed to be, he thought to himself as he finally let the other voices in the cabin break through his bubble of government-issued comfort.

"I cannot believe yuh finally doin' it, El-Tee," boomed a deep bass voice in the worst attempt at a whisper Mal had ever heard. Corporal John Narcomy was a big man from Houston, Texas, and clocked in at somewhere in the neighborhood of three hundred and fifty pounds of solid, good-hearted muscle. "It ain't right!"

Staring at the dark-skinned man barely contained on the flight bench by straps pushed well beyond their limits, Mal was convinced the Black Hawk was buckled to Narcomy for safety and not the other way around. The ACH cinched onto his head seemed too small to contain it.

"Got my acceptance yesterday. After we get back from this jaunt, I'm going back to school and then to JAG," responded a smooth voice seated directly across from Narcomy and to Mal's immediate left. Tilting his head allowed the young, brown haired Lieutenant Chris Donlin to come into view out of the corner of Mal's eye. "But don't worry, old son, I won't forget the "little" people after I'm gone."

A general round of laughter erupted from the six men seat belted into the chairs of the chopper: the men of Mal's special response unit.

Technician Third Grade James "Jimmy" Jay, the round-faced ex-baseball player from San Diego sitting on Narcomy's left, chipped in, "I was going to join up with JAG, but I'd miss the food at Fort Benning way too much."

"Yeah and we can tell you ain't missed food in your entire life, lunch box," added Sergeant Steve Douros in a thick Philadelphia accent.

"It just ain't right, I tell ya," grumbled Narcomy, visibly upset by the news. "Yuh momma didn't send yuh to ranger school just to go an' become a lawyer. Whatta we need lawyers for anyways?"

Mal laughed out loud, enjoying the banter even if he had heard it all before.

"If people were honest, we wouldn't need lawyers, Narc'," counseled Lieutenant Donlin, grinning from ear-to-ear.

"And what would we do if lawyers were honest, LT?" Mal quipped at the exact same time the words spilled from Sergeant Douros's mouth.

Mal's eyes went wide even as the rest of the US ranger unit burst into uncontrolled laughter.

Something was wrong.

He HAD heard it all before.

Oh, no, Mal thought to himself, panicking. And I know what happens next!

He tried to scream, tried to tear the straps from his chest. Mal found himself unable to move, unable to speak, his face locked into a smile that fit in with the joviality of the men around him. They had no idea.

They were all going to die.

The laughter was interrupted as the Black Hawk jerked to one side and the static-filled voice of the co-pilot shrieked over their helmet communication systems.

"Incoming! Starboard side!"

It was too late.

An explosion rocked the chopper, shredding one side of the craft and filling the cabin with fire. All Mal saw before the entire world seemed to spin out of control was big John Narcomy vaporized in a flash of blinding white light.

CHAPTER 6

Malcolm Weir woke himself screaming, entangled in ragged strips of linen from the small cot he had been lying on, and covered in a fine dusting of what appeared to be goose down. For some reason his left arm was lodged in the middle of the bed, clean through mattress, metal springs and into the wooden base the entire thing rested upon.

It took Mal a moment to realize he was the perpetrator of the mattress-cide. His new body must have responded to the highly emotional state the nightmare had evoked in him and reacted accordingly. The hand Mal pulled up to inspect had formed the razor sharp knife-fingers he had seen during his escape from the Project: Hardwired labs, and a quick look at his shoulder revealed the defensive spines and plates had emerged as the living metal quickly adopted a more aggressive profile.

Standing up and disengaging himself from the tattered mess of the tiny bed, the smells of old laundry, dust and papers left too long filtered to his nose.

"Where am I?" muttered Mal to himself.

Mal let his gaze wander slowly. A cramped back-office somewhere was the answer he received from the rickety Swedish-made desk with an old computer monitor and phone resting on it, piles of white copy paper boxes over-flowing with old paperwork and invoices of some kind, and coat rack with a pair of dirty overalls he found during his search. The walls were off-white with a band of ugly gray coloring them for a foot up from the floor. A single spiral energy-saver bulb was stuck into the double light fixture overhead - Mal noticed the glass covering for which sat dangerously close to the edge of one stack of boxes - although the light was off and the room almost pitch dark. A tiny, curtainless window on the wall above the destroyed cot, and a half-opened door on the opposite side were the only exits from the space.

A spear of light from the open door seemed to bring with it the smell of old oil, gasoline, rusted metal and rubber.

A garage?

"Better go see where I am."

Blowing a stray feather from its ticklish perch on his upper lip, Mal's head snapped to attention, the spines on his arms flexing. Heavy boots on concrete. Someone was coming.

As if in answer to his next unasked question, the computerized voice announced, "Inbound target identified: David Anthony Zuzelo. Arrival in ten point two seconds. Target unarmed."

"What's going on in here?" came Zuz's voice from the hallway, "I'm armed!"

When Zuzelo pushed the door open Mal had already visibly relaxed, and his malleable metallic arms had returned to their normal, more human-looking, state. Although, Mal had to admit, neither 'normal' nor 'human-looking' were the best way to describe the transforming weapons that had been grafted onto his body.

"So am I, Zuz," smirked Mal at his friend.

"Yeah, I guess you are, Mal," Zuz's said without the hint of laughter in his voice. After a once over of Mal to make sure the soldier was OK, Zuzelo's eyes went wide at the disarrayed state of the bed. The man rubbed a hand nervously through his goatee and pushed the door open wide behind him, nodding for Mal to follow him, "I'm not going to ask you what happened with the bed, but maybe we can sit down and you can tell me what the hell happened to you."

"As soon as I figure it out, I'll let you know," sighed Mal as he followed his friend out the door.

The two men sat across an ancient iron work table cluttered with what must have been years' worth of unsorted tools, pencils chewed down to nubs, presumably empty pizza boxes from some place called 'Hungry Howie's Pizza,' dirty rags and the general clutter of a working man's garage. Although, this 'garage' was actually a ten thousand square foot warehouse in the heart of a monstrous salvage and junkyard that David Zuzelo had converted into his workshop.

Zuzelo informed his friend that he'd purchased the location a few years back when he'd finally had enough of the government. They were surrounded by two hundred tons of steel, aluminum and various other radar and satellite-blocking materials. In fact, the main building was now located nearly fifty feet underground. No one would be able to find them there. The man's talk of hiding from the government and keeping 'off the grid' amused and relaxed Mal; his old friend hadn't changed one bit. Zuz had always been about two steps from starring in his own version of 'Conspiracy Theory.'

Two banks of fluorescent lights, mounted some thirty feet up in the cavernous ceiling, shone down on the immediate area, illuminating the table the men were talking at, a workbench running along at least forty feet of the nearby wall and covered in more junk than Mal had ever seen jammed into one location and a number of burned out and rusted hulks that had once belonged to cars, tractors and other vehicles. It was a smorgasbord of scrap metal. Mal swore he saw the stripped down frame of an armored personnel carrier off in the shadows that covered most of the huge building.

Mal's computerized friend blandly informed him of the presence of forty-nine heartbeats in the vicinity: Mal's, Zuzelo's, forty-five rats and a pair of large cats. The voice also laid out the floor plan of the building, located in the City of Industry, California, as had been filed by its original owners when it was built in 1952, and had identified no less than thirteen potential egresses from the building in case of an emergency as Mal gave his friend a full rundown of the events of the last few hours of his life.

Annoying as it was, Mal was beginning to appreciate the strategic value of the system.

"And that's all you remember? Waking up with a scalpel in your face?" Zuzelo had listened to the story without moving or speaking for almost ten minutes, completely enraptured by Mal's telling.

Mal shot Zuzelo a sideways glance at the comment, "It wasn't exactly a 'scalpel in my face,' man. I did have to yank something out of the back of my head, though."

Mal reached around to where the wires had been plugged into his skull.

"There's something over it now, but when I first woke up there was a huge hole at the base of my skull with cables coming out, covered in a gel of some kind."

With an eager look on his face, Zuzelo moved around the table to stand next to Mal, and pushed the soldier's head down, almost slamming it into the tabletop. "Let me see!"

After a moment touching and, to Mal's discomfort, caressing the area, Zuzelo moved back around to his seat. "Wow. They did a number on you. That thing, it's a port of some kind…and it goes deep. Looks like it goes directly into your brain, and I can see filaments just under the skin that lead down into your spine and to the arms. At first, I thought you were wearing some kind of high-tech armor, but those things are part of you."

His lips tightened into a severe line on his tanned face and pulled a hard line between his brows, as Mal nodded grimly. In his heart, he had already known what Zuzelo was saying, but hearing it out loud from someone else caused it all to finally hit home. He dropped his head into the oddly warm metal of his hands, unable to speak.

Quietly, Zuzelo asked, "What's the last thing you remember before today?"

"Before today?" Mal thought hard; a metallic finger traced a wrinkle down the center of his cheek, scratching over the beginnings of a five o'clock shadow forming on his chin. "We were on maneuvers in the mountains just north of Dahuk in Iraq. Everyone in my unit was…"

The rough emotions, still fresh for Mal, welled up in him, choking off his voice. His heart raced so fast he thought it was going to punch through his chest.

"It's ok, Mal, man…you don't have to finish." Zuzelo's

voice softened, unused to seeing the Army ranger in such a vulnerable state.

Mal continued, ignoring the pause, unable to stop now that he had started, "It was a night op and we were flying low over the hills in a chopper, there were six of us. We were hit by something and the chopper went up like a roman candle. I must have blacked out in the crash."

"We went down in a ball of fire...I wasn't sure any of us would make it out alive," standing, Mal gestured at his sides and chest. "By the looks of things, I'm not sure I did."

"If that's not a mind-fuck, I don't know what is. How long do you think you were out?"

"Beats me. What day is it?" Mal replied with a baffled look on his face.

Zuzelo had to think for a moment: keeping up on 'trivial' things like the date had never been his strong suit. "I dunno, man. March 25th...26th?"

"March 25th...?" All the blood rushed from Mal's face.

"Yeah. Or 26th."

"The mission was April 3rd," realization hit Mal right before horror swooped in and took control. "What year is it?"

Zuzelo told him.

"A year...I've lost a year."

"My, god," Zuzelo reached out to put his hand on Mal's shoulder and shied away as his fingers brushed the cool metal surface.

Head down, arms limp at his sides, Mal didn't seem to notice the uneasiness in his old friend's actions and pushed past him. The sound of metal on metal echoed through the empty space of the warehouse, bouncing off of the wreckage before disappearing into the distance as Mal leaned down onto the half-rusted table, bracing himself on widespread hands.

"Mal...if there's anything I can do..."

A thunderous boom and the sound of shrieking, tearing metal interrupted David Zuzelo's attempt to comfort his friend. One moment, his forty-year-old solid steel work table had been whole, the next it was dented nearly in half by a single blow from a gleaming metal fist. The force of the blow was so great, its reverberation so powerful, it knocked Zuzelo off his feet and painfully onto his rear end.

The pure fury of Malcolm Weir was visible to his friend, even from behind, and five more titanic blows reduced the half-ton table to a demolished ruin. Each blow sent another spider web of cracks streaking out in the concrete floor from beneath the mess of tortured iron.

Before his anger was spent, Mal gripped two sides of the bent and ruined six hundred pound tabletop in his mighty hands and, straining, tore the piece from its welded mountings. With a primal scream he threw the unwieldy projectile with enough brute force to obliterate the burned out Volkswagen frame it slammed into at nearly sixty miles per hour.

Scrambling to his feet, Zuzelo dove behind the poor cover of a rolling tool rack for safety.

"Dude, Mal! I think you skipped a couple of grief stages and went right to 'pissed off!' I know you're mad, but don't destroy my home, man." Zuzelo's voice leapt five octaves as he yelled at the maddened cyborg. "Stop!"

The hammering fists stopped their relentless assault on the now nearly formless lump of steel, seemingly halted by Zuzelo's plea. Shoulders shaking from the adrenaline shooting through his veins, Mal bowed his head for a moment and replayed the day in his head, analyzing every second that had gone by with a microscopic gaze.

He had missed something and it was nagging at the back of his mind.

"How did you find me?" he finally said, in a voice far too calm to be natural, or safe.

From behind his shield of plastic and nylon, David Zuzelo responded meekly, "Excuse me?"

Mal shot a glance at Zuzelo over his shoulder; eyes alight with a rapidly rekindled fire. "I disappeared for a year—you haven't seen me in five years—and you knew right where to find me. How did you know, Zuz?"

"Mal, I...you..." before Zuzelo could finish, Mal had moved across the floor with the speed of a serpent's strike, covering the twenty foot distance between them in the blink of an eye.

The cyborg sent the protective chair spinning across the floor with a backhanded blow, and jerked the nearly two hundred and twenty-five pound man to his feet as if he weighed nothing at all. It took every ounce of control Zuzelo had to avoid soiling himself in response.

"How did you find me? Answer me!" Mal raged, spittle flying as he shook his friend like a rag doll, lifting his bulk four inches off the floor. "Did they send you?! Tell me! Tell me! How did you find me?"

"I...ack..."

Unable to speak as he was being manhandled by his enraged half-machine friend, David Zuzelo reached into the inner pocket of his worn denim jacket and pulled something out. Mal saw the movement and responded with all the inhuman speed his living metal implants had given him. He locked one hand around the throat of his supposed savior, suspending him in the air with the sheer power of his arm, and caught the man's hand in a crushing grip with the other.

"You..." choked Zuzelo as unyielding metallic fingers cut off his oxygen.

"Not so fast," spat Mal, barely contained fury threatened to bubble over into more violence. In his grip, Zuzelo choked and sputtered and squirmed, trying to free himself. Mal sneered to himself as he flipped the man's hand over to see whatever weapon he had hidden. All that greeted him was the sight of a thin black cellphone, clutched tightly in a hand rapidly turning purple from the loss of circulation Mal was inflecting upon it.

"Aw, shit, Zuz..." Mal released his hold on the nearly unconscious man and tried to help him to the nearby water cooler for a drink. Zuzelo was having none of it and slapped the cyborg's offending hand away and stumbled his way to snatch a tiny paper cup from its receptacle and pour icy liquid down his half-crushed throat.

After a moment of sputtering and coughing, Zuzelo barked, "You've got a funny way of thanking a guy for saving your bacon."

Fists thrust hard into his sides and still far from trusting, "How did you find me, Zuz?"

"I got your damn text, you douche bag."

"What the hell are you talking about, Zuz?" Mal's eyes turned to slits as he watched the man warily.

"Your text came through...you told me where you were and when to get you," seeing Mal's quizzical look, Zuzelo tossed his cellphone to Mal and added, "Take a look for yourself."

With a quick flick of his wrist, Mal caught the phone and brought it up to his face for a closer look. Still unsure of his newfound strength, he delicately pulled open the phone's history and saw a series of messages sent from his cellphone. Zuzelo had even programmed it to display an old, drunken college picture of the two of them whenever Mal called.

There were three messages in total, giving the address where Mal had woken up, the request for a fast car, and a demand for Zuzelo to hurry. Looking at the time stamp for the first text, Mal saw it went through at almost the exact same time he came to in the operating room.

He had no idea what was going on, but Mal knew those messages weren't his. Hell, he didn't even know where his phone was.

"They're not from me, Zuz. Someone else sent them." Seeing the confused look on his friend's face, Mal told him about the time stamps on the messages and that there was no way he could have sent them.

"You've got yourself into some deep shit," whistled Zuzelo in astonishment.

"Yeah, I guess I do. I've got no idea who had me or why, and I have even less of an idea of who called you. None of it makes any sense."

"I still can't believe it, Mal...gone for a year and waking up with metal arms. It's like everything we talk about online is true—abductions, conspiracies, cover-ups—and all of it's happening to you. Oh, shit," eyes wide, a pained and worried look formed on Zuzelo's rather expressive face. "You weren't... probed were you?"

Mal looked at his friend, taken completely by surprise. Then, over the course of two heartbeats, a giant smile split his face from ear to ear.

"You're a nut, Zuz," laughed Mal. "You're crazy."

"I'm crazy?" retorted Zuzelo from behind an incredulous smirk. "Says the man who just tore a bunch of rent-a-cops to shreds with his freaky metal arms...yeah, I'm the one with issues here."

Mal let loose with a great belly laugh and clapped his friend on the back, causing Zuzelo to cringe a bit from the impact. The recently awakened cyborg still didn't have a handle on the extent of his new strength. He would have to walk on eggshells when interacting with normal people for a while.

"Sorry...still getting used to these things. It's not every day a guy wakes up with stainless steel arms, right?"

"Speaking of which..." Zuzelo said from beneath a bushy graying eyebrow, intrigued. "Let's take a look at those things and see what's going on. See if we can figure out exactly what those jack-booted pawns of the imperialistic establishment did to you"

Mal stared back at his friend, completely unconvinced.

"C'mon, let's check those puppies out!" David Zuzelo tapped his teeth for a moment while he stared intently at the gleaming metal of Mal's arms and chest. Mal could almost see the man thinking.

Face brightening, Zuzelo shouted, "Got it!" and bolted for a darkened corner of the room.

Although Zuzelo had disappeared into the shadows, surrounded by steel frames, piles of rubber and God knows what else, Mal found himself able to follow the man's progress in spite of the lack of light. It seemed his upgrades included some sort of night vision along with everything else.

They've turned me into a living weapon...some kind of ultimate soldier.

Mal shuddered at the thought, watching Zuzelo find whatever it was he was looking for and move back towards the light of the work area carrying something that turned out to be a rather vicious-looking sledgehammer with an enormous head and four foot long haft.

"And what the hell are you going to do with that?"

"We're going to perform a series of scientific experiments to determine the make-up and capabilities of your new prosthetics," Zuzelo dropped the head of the hammer down onto the concrete floor with a thud that caused Mal to grimace. Spitting in to his hands before taking up a baseball like grip on the tool's handle, Zuzelo added, smiling wickedly, "Trust me. I'm a professional."

"Trust you?" repeated Mal as he widened his stance and lowered his center of gravity in preparation. "This is payback for the choking thing, isn't it?"

Zuzelo's only response as he started his swing, "No comment."

The hammer slammed into Mal's braced right arm, just above the elbow. It should have pulverized every bone in the area. Instead, the force of impact knocked Mal from his feet and sent him bouncing roughly across the dirty, oil-covered floor to slam into, and knock over, one of the rusted steel art pieces Zuzelo had created from the salvage.

Mal slowly pushed himself up to a rather unsteady standing position, teeth still vibrating from the blow. Looking down, the cyborg noticed the living metal of his arm was unmarked, completely unblemished from the hammer strike. His eyes went wide and met with Zuzelo's own astonished orbs.

"Holy shit."

"Yeah," agreed Zuzelo, resting the hammer's shaft on his shoulder. "Do you know what just happened?"

"You hit me with a sledgehammer?"

"Besides that, Mal. Don't you understand?"

Mal's eyes bunched together and their lack of realization made Zuzelo shake his head in frustration.

"The amount of forced delivered by a sledgehammer is one half the mass of the hammer's head times the square of its speed at the time of impact."

"...and that is?"

"It's approximately..." Zuzelo's face scrunched up, eyes gazing towards the ceiling, and mouth silently working through what seemed to be a rather intense equation. Nodding, the engineer answered, "...a shitload."

"A...shitload, you say," grinned Mal. "Is that a technical term?"

"Yup," replied the man, mirroring Mal's smile as he dropped the heavy tool back to the ground and used its shaft as a cane to lean on.

"So what, pray tell, did you learn from that shitload?" requested Mal.

"Quite a bit, actually. You see this?" Zuzelo flipped the sledgehammer back up for the cyborg to examine. "It's got a tungsten-alloy head. One of the hardest metals around—it'll dent, even punch through solid steel."

Mal gripped the hammer's head in his right hand to examine it. He hardly felt its 35-pound weight in his hand.

"Go on."

"The tungsten-alloy has a Mohs hardness rating of about nine—diamond has a ten."

"So?" Mal responded, unsure of what Zuzelo was trying to say. Unconsciously, his finger had begun to gouge thin strips of material from the side of the sledge's hammerhead.

"Look at your arm...I hit it full on with a sledgehammer made of one of the toughest substances around. It should be dented. Crushed. Damaged in some way."

They both stared hard at the gleaming, unblemished surface of Mal's living metal arm, stunned.

"It's not even scratched..." came Mal's voice in a half-whisper.

"Not even scratched," repeated Zuzelo, knowingly. He grabbed Mal's arm and pulled him over to an open area of the workroom that contained a dark metal worktable nearly 10 feet long, a number of dark red gas canisters, each standing nearly five feet in height, and a welding set-up of some kind. "Come over here. Let's try something."

Zuzelo popped on an old welder's goggles and a pair of thick, dirty brown gloves. After a moment of fiddling with the machine's controls, a bright white light emerged from the tip of the welder, and the engineer moved towards Mal.

"What the hell are you doing?" gulped Mal as he shielded his eyes with one hand.

"This is a gas tungsten arc welder. It burns at just over 3400 degrees Fahrenheit and slices through reinforced-steel like butter," Zuzelo grabbed Mal's hand dramatically, pausing for effect. "I'm going to try cutting your arm off, Mal."

Mal found himself unable to move as Zuzelo jammed the pulsating blue-white flame of the GTA welder to the top of his forearm and slid it around. He could feel his mouth drop open, eyes tearing up as he stared a bit too long at the painful light of the high-powered torch.

"Surface temperatures have reached thirty-four hundred and twelve degrees," came the until-now silent computer voice in Mal's head. It felt almost reassuring. "Nano-drones affecting cool down. All systems within normal operating parameters."

The metal 'skin' of Mal's forearm began to move under the heat in the same way muscles move beneath normal skin, but the arc welder seemed to have no other effect upon it. No burns. No oxidization. No damage or carbon scoring at all. If anything, Zuzelo's ministrations seemed to do nothing more than clean the dirt, blood and grime Mal had collected during his escape, and shine the metallic surface to an almost mirror-polish.

"Holy..."

"...shit!" finished Mal as his friend pulled the welding apparatus away and shut it down.

Licking his lips, eyes glittering darkly, Zuzelo set the welder down and strode back over to Mal's side with purpose. He dropped both gloves to the ground at their feet, took a deep breath and grabbed on to the gleaming chrome lower arm. Both men gasped out loud at the action.

Zuzelo's eyes went so wide Mal was afraid they were going to pop out of the man's head. "It's cool to the touch."

"What?!"

"Yeah, it's not even warm," replied Zuzelo as he ran his hand up and down the arm, tracing it's every nook, cranny and groove. "It feels cold."

"That's my arm you're molesting there, Zuz."

Realizing what he was doing, David stopped and thought for a moment; staring hard at the man he rescued a handful of hours earlier.

After a few long moments of silent analysis, Zuzelo spoke, a seriousness Mal had never heard before filled his voice, "I don't know what they did to you, Mal, but that is some top secret government researched alien shit going on there. You're an X-file."

Mal nodded.

"So what should we do now?"

"I have no idea," the bald man answered, calloused fingers stroking his goatee thoughtfully

"Big help you are, Zuz."

"What did you expect?"

"Well, I was kind of hoping you had something in mind more technical than just hitting me with things to see if something breaks," spit back Mal.

"Like what?! You're the first government cyborg I've ever run into, my friend."

Mal slumped down to the floor and held his head in both hands, weariness and frustration finally getting the best of him. He looked up at his friend and pleaded, "I don't know what to do. They've taken everything. Help me."

Sighing, David Zuzelo scratched his head and nodded.

"Let's go up to the computer bay and see if we can't access whatever internal systems you've got going on there. There's got to be something in there making everything tick, and maybe, just maybe, we can hack into it."

Zuzelo extended his hand down to his weary friend and backed it with the familiar, warm smile Mal had known for more than a decade, "C'mon."

As the pair headed upstairs towards Zuzelo's computer room, he asked, "By the way, what do you think your fiancée is up to?"

"Oh, shit...Kristin!"

CHAPTER 7

Seated at the head of a large conference table, Gordon Kiesling was already three Vicodins into his headache by the time Representative Michael Fountain had arrived from Washington, DC. Stroking the bottle in the pocket of his still crisply-pressed pants, Kiesling felt the need to increase that number every time the Congressman interrupted the meeting with one his snide little comments. He may have been Washington's liaison with Project: Hardwired, but Fountain's attempted Columbo act was getting on the director's nerves almost as much as his cheap gray Men's Warehouse suit.

Seriously, thought Kiesling to himself. Brown shoes with a gray suit? They should be allowed to kill the man on principal alone.

"...is beyond me," cut in Fountain's voice, snapping Kiesling back to reality with its over-excitable San Diego cadence.

The last time Kiesling had heard a bass voice as whiny and annoying as the Congressman's was from Darth Vader at the end of *Revenge of the Sith.*

"Are you listening to me, Director Kiesling," came Fountain's poor attempt at gravitas.

"With rapt attention, Representative Fountain," replied Kiesling, his smile filled with the whitest teeth this side of a Hollywood blockbuster. "As to why we haven't been able to locate Designate Cestus, I'll leave that answer to our head tech on the project."

Chair half spinning far enough around to get the politician's face out of his peripheral vision, Kiesling gestured to the now sweat-drenched Carl Anderson. "Please explain to the

Congressman and to all of us, Mister Anderson, why we are unable to locate the prodigal Captain Malcolm Weir? If my memory serves me correctly, and I have Ms. Roslan there to ensure it always does, the first thing Doctor Ryan's lab boys do with every single Project: Hardwired recruit is surgically implant a sub-dermal tracking device. Beyond that, I've seen POV video from Designate Cestus in his mission logs. Shouldn't we be able to access his cameras by now?"

To say Carl Anderson shrunk beneath the withering gaze of his boss and his boss's boss would be an understatement. His entire body seemed to go flaccid and threaten to collapse in on itself. For several excruciating seconds, Anderson was unable to speak. The perspiration stains beneath his armpits grew to engulf his entire Wal-Mart purchased pale blue polo shirt, and Kiesling was convinced the man's breathing had stopped altogether.

"Mister Anderson?"

A hand on Anderson's shoulder and the sultry voice of Kiesling's executive assistant brought the man back to life. "Tell them what you told me, Carl. It's OK."

Smiling up at the lovely Ms. Roslan, Anderson exhaled a deep breath, turned to lock eyes with his boss, and launched into his explanation

"You're one-hundred percent correct, sir. We should be able to track Designate Cestus up to within six feet of his location—closer than that when we've got one of the Sentinel-class satellites keyed into his signal and located in geostationary orbit. And you're right again about the point-of-view camera systems installed in the occipital lobe of each of the prime units, such as Designate Cestus or Gauss. We viewed footage from Designate Gauss earlier—watched his fight with Cestus upstairs…"

"Yes, yes! I know all of that, Mister Anderson," interrupted Kiesling, growing increasingly annoyed with the little engineer with each passing second he rambled on. "Now tell me something I don't know. Tell me why, with all the little toys you tech boys love so much, we cannot locate the damned Cestus unit? Tell me."

Kiesling's voice nailed Anderson to place. The poor man's

eyes darted to each face in the room, trying to gain some sort of support or sympathy from those present. Unfortunately for Carl Anderson, none of the thirteen people seated around the large mahogany table would hold his gaze—not Security Chief Doherty, nor the May Brothers from the weapons lab with their matching goatees, or even Anderson's best friend from the computer lab, Hal Hefner. No one met his pleading, desperate eyes. The only thing that held him in place, kept him from bolting from the room in terror, was the firm, reassuring grip of Ms. Roslan. The feel of her nails, polished a deep red, sliding along his shirt, and the intoxicating smell of her perfume wrapping Anderson like a warm, protective, lavender-scented blanket, helped him press on in the face of his employer's anger.

"Um...right, Kiesling, sir. Director Kiesling, sir, that is," Anderson cleared his through and jumped head first into the rest of his debriefing before the head of Project: Hardwired allowed the obvious range in his face to explode. "With the Abraxas Hub still down, we can't see anything. We couldn't find the man if he were standing on the other side of that door there."

"When our network goes down in Washington, we just have someone in IT reboot the system," chimed Fountain. "Can't someone just flip a switch and turn the computer back on?"

Ms. Roslan jumped in to cut the Representative's line of thought off, "The Abraxas-configuration is infinitely more complex than your little office PC, Congressman Fountain. The secondary node here in the building takes up an entire floor, and the main Abraxas Hub in Houston covers a city block. It'll take a near army of technicians three days to get the system back up, and a week before it's running at full capacity."

"They have twelve hours," ordered Fountain, with crossed arms and as commanding a scowl as he could muster.

"Twelve..." started Anderson, stunned.

"Hours...?" finished Ms. Roslan, furious. "Are you insane, man? This isn't the Enterprise and he's not Scotty!" she spat, jerking her thumb down at Anderson.

The little engineer shrunk down again, uncomfortable at being the focus of everyone's attention once more, and a tad hurt by the sexy executive assistant's comment. Anderson knew he wasn't a Kirk, a Spock, or even a Sulu, but had always pictured himself as the 'Scotty' of the team: often being able to beat even the most insane of deadlines imposed upon him by the powers-that-be. If he was forced to be a 'red shirt,' he wanted to be the one that survived.

Fountain interrupted Anderson's Roddenberry-dreams.

"Best put your little bitch on a leash, Kiesling, or I'll have her put down," working himself up to a self-righteous froth, Fountain continued, "I'm of the mind to have this entire operation shut down for all your incompetence."

"Shut up," came Kiesling's voice from beneath lowered eyebrows.

"What did you say to me?" gasped the gray-haired politician, unsure if he had heard the man correctly.

"I said: sit down and shut up before I have you thrown out of my building. Or shot. Or both."

Standing up and stalking over to the seated Kiesling, Fountain nearly popped in anger, as all the exposed skin from the rim of his cheap buttoned-up collar to the top of his thinning steel gray perm turned beetred.

The man was so furious he was almost unable to get words to form on his saliva coated lips.

"I'll have you all fired!" Fountain showering everyone in his vicinity with rage-fueled spittle as he worked himself up. "Do you know who I am?"

"Yes," inserted Kiesling flatly. "You're the third liaison we've had from the capitol in the five years since we began."

The director of Project: Hardwired stood up so he could stare down at the much shorter, slighter Representative from California.

"The first, Representative..." Kiesling looked over at his assistant for back-up.

"Robert Liefeld," completed Ms. Roslan, smiling at Fountain with all the warmth of a piece of maguro at a sushi bar.

"Yes, Liefeld. Thank you, Ms. Roslan. Representative Liefeld, died rather suddenly of heart failure, I believe," behind him, Ms. Roslan nodded in confirmation, and Kiesling continued, never removing his eyes from the Congressman. "The second, Representative..."

"Jacob Kurtzberg."

"...Kurtzberg. Boring little man, originally from New York. The Bronx, I think," another confirmation from his assistant kept Kiesling going. Unnoticed in the background, Carl Anderson smiled to himself, pleased to be free of the director's attention. "Died in an arson fire at his lovely home in Encino, along with his wife of forty years and their dog, Kirby. It was a terrible tragedy. Did they ever catch the man who did it, Ms. Roslan?"

"No, sir."

"It would be a shame if something happened to you, Congressman Fountain."

The two men locked gazes, eyes drawn tight, each fighting for dominance.

Fountain blinked first. "Are you threatening me, Director Kiesling?"

With a smile as real as that of a leading man posing for pictures on a red carpet splitting his perfectly chiseled features, Kiesling responded, eyes never once leaving the politician's face, "No, Congressman Fountain. I'm just explaining who you are and what your importance is to this project. The latest in a line of easily replaceable little men."

A quick shift in his glaze was all Kiesling needed to do to signal his security chief to move behind the now shaking Michael Fountain.

"This isn't over, Kiesling," stammered Fountain. "Not by a long shot."

Dismissing the man with a wave of his polished right hand, Kiesling fired back, "It is for now." Then, to Security Chief Doherty, he finished, "Mr. Doherty, please make sure Congressman Fountain gets back to his hotel safely. We'd hate for anything to happen to him before his flight back to D.C. tomorrow."

Kiesling strode confidently over to stand next to Ms. Roslan as Doherty exited the well-lit conference room with the skittish politician in tow.

In a low voice only she could hear, Kiesling whispered to

Roslan, "Get a unit to keep an eye on the good Congressman Fountain. Set up a phone trace and monitor anyone he speaks to. It'd be a shame if he decided to make any sort of rash decisions with regards to our project."

Nodding, Ms. Roslan disappeared in a cloud of clacks from her high heels.

Carl Anderson almost voided his bladder as his boss's firm hands clasped down on his shoulders, voice prodding him on, "Please continue, Mr. Anderson."

Knocking out a lump in his throat the size of a large cat, Anderson closed his eyes and continued.

"With the system still down, we're blind on our own. If we can get clearance from the FCC to commandeer a few satellites, we could scan for the power core located at the base of Designate Cestus's spine," Anderson ventured a quick glance back over his shoulder when he felt the pressure of Director Kiesling's powerful grasp disappear. Seeing that his boss had stepped back a couple of feet, Anderson spun in his chair and continued, "The core gives off a large enough radioactive signal that we'd be able to track him pretty easily. I've got a work up of what we should have the eyes in the sky look for."

For the first time in hours, a genuine smile crossed Kiesling's face as he took in the tech's information.

"Good work, son. Great work," grinned Kiesling. "Hefner," bellowed the director of Project: Hardwired in order to get the computer tech's attention off of whatever he had on his computer screen. "Get the information from Carl here and take care of the satellite situation yourself. We don't have time to ask for permission." To the two May brothers, TJ and Jason, he added, "Mr. May. Other…uh, bald, Mr. May. Put together a briefing on all the improvements from the nano-tech upgrade Dr. Ryan did to Designate Cestus. We need a plan of attack for taking down one of the deadliest weapons on the planet without destroying the information in its head."

"Yes, sir," responded the good-looking Jason May as his bald brother, TJ, grabbed a thick folder from Anderson and passed it to the effeminate Hefner. The trio quickly hurried out the same doors recently vacated by Doherty, Roslan, and the Congressman.

"What else have you got for me, Carl?"

Spinning back to the laptop resting on top of the dark wood table, Anderson quickly tapped through a series of commands, pulling up a series of grainy images on the large flatscreen monitor mounted in the rear wall of the conference room.

"If you'll take a look at the screen, I've got some footage from the external security camera feed."

Dropping down into the seat next to the computer tech, Kiesling tapped his large Harvard class ring on the varnished table top, indicating Anderson should start the show.

For a few absolutely silent moments, the pair of men watched the events of Malcolm Weir's escape play out on the high resolution TV monitor.

The image of the off-white car leaping into frame before them caused Kiesling's ice blue eyes to go wide in surprise.

"Stop," commanded Kiesling. "Who is the man in the car?"

Already ready for his employer's question, Anderson removed a series of images from a manila envelope and slid them over. A number of the photos were obvious print-outs captured from the cell phones of onlookers on the street, but one was a blow-up of the driver's license of a rather intense-looking man with a beard and shaved head.

"David Anthony Zuzelo," Anderson read from a piece of stark white paper.

"That's just a name. Who is he?"

Anderson went down his checklist.

"David Anthony Zuzelo. Born in Lowell, Massachusetts. Age thirty-four."

The name still meant nothing to Kiesling. "What is his link to Designate Cestus?"

Getting excited, Anderson slid over another folder, this one containing college transcripts and a yearbook from the University of Boston.

"That's where it gets interesting. Zuzelo was college roommates with Malcolm Weir," getting an annoyed look from Kiesling, Anderson quickly corrected himself. "With Designate Cestus. From all indications, the pair were inseparable up until Cestus enlisted into the army. But they continued to keep in touch until about five years ago."

"What happened then?" Kiesling's curiosity was piqued.

"We don't know. Zuzelo vanished. Fell off the face of the earth. He hasn't popped up anywhere since. The guy's a bit of a nut-job. A conspiracy theorist. He follows UFOs, hates the government. Real paranoid type."

A baffled Kiesling quizzed, "How did this 'paranoid nut-job' know where to find us? This base, Project: Hardwired, even Cestus's existence, it's all top secret."

"Phone records show he received a call about fifteen minutes before Designate Cestus went rogue and made a beeline for our location."

"Who made the call?"

Taking a second to grab a slip of computer-printed paper from one of the stacks in front of him, Anderson leaned over and handed it to Kiesling timidly.

Confusion played across the director's face as he read the contents of the sheet. "This says the call came from a cell number registered to Malcolm Weir."

"Yes, sir," replied Anderson. "A number disconnected a year ago at the time of his acceptance into Project: Hardwired."

"Do you know where the call came from?"

"Six thirty-three West Fifth street."

The need for another Vicodin screamed from the back of Kiesling's head as realization hit him squarely between the eyes. "That's our location…"

"Yes, sir."

"What's going on here, Anderson?" asked Kiesling quietly, his famed confidence shaken to the core.

"My best guess is that somehow Designate Cestus's original personality construct, that of Captain Malcolm Weir, has been restored," Anderson flipped an old photograph of Malcolm Weir dressed in his US Army Ranger's uniform to over to Kiesling. "Weir is back, and he reached out to someone he thought could help him escape."

Nodding grimly, Kiesling ordered, "Locate Zuzelo. Do whatever it takes. Co-opt whatever resources you need. Ms. Roslan will help you. Find the man and bring him in."

Bolting up from his seat, Anderson gathered the paperwork and materials scattered across the table. Excitement bubbled up from deep within his belly—this was going to be his big break.

"Yes, sir. I'll find him."

Leaning back in his chair, Kiesling called out to the ratty little computer engineer, "Any ideas where Designate Cestus… where Malcolm Weir might go now that his original personality has returned?"

"Weir had a fiancée before he joined the program, but no other immediate friends or family to speak of."

"Get a GMR team out to keep an eye on her, just in case," called Kiesling as Anderson headed for the door. "And, Mr. Anderson…"

"Yes, Director Kiesling?"

"Make sure to use Designate Gauss. I'm sure he'll be itching for a rematch with Cestus after their little tussle. Just make sure he keeps Weir's head intact for the good Dr. Ryan to take apart."

CHAPTER 8

One of the things Malcolm Weir had always hated about Southern California was that even in mid-Spring the weather was hot. It was only 6:30 a.m. and the sun was already beating down relentlessly from its position high in the cloudless, clear blue morning sky. While the Southern-grown Mal absolutely adored a good hot day, nothing messed him up more than warm morning.

And this morning, deep within the suburban setting of Thousand Oaks, California, was going to be a very warm one. Much to Mal's distress.

Crouched down low in the passenger seat of Zuz's half-wrecked, barely running Nissan, Mal quizzed in a voice not quite as hushed as he had intended, "Are you sure this is the place?"

Waiting for his friend to respond, Mal took another look at the ranch-style home just down the block from where the car was parked. His human eyes could tell nothing about the house, aside from noticing it had a well-manicured lawn with sprinklers that had gone off at precisely 6:22 A.M., and excellent curb appeal. Mal could also see a large red SUV parked off to one side of the two-car driveway, with a small oil stain hinting that a second car with some minor transmission issues normally sat next to it. Very little set it apart from the 8 other homes on the block that contained it or from the one hundred other ones that had sprung up in the surrounding development.

His "other" eyes revealed quite a bit more.

The house had been built ten years earlier, having been sold off by its original owners, Sara and Roy Zamora, nine months ago. The new buyer, and current resident, was one Marc Morrell.

Architect's plans, electrical diagrams, building permits, and other information were all relayed to Mal by his inner voice, but none of that was as interesting to him as the name on the cable and utilities bills: Kristin Meyer-Morrell.

Mal grumbled mostly to himself as he called up marriage records for the couple, confirming that his former fiancée did, indeed, live at the residence.

With her new husband.

"Aw, hell."

Before Mal realized it, his right index finger elongated into a rather nasty spike and, somewhere in his distress-caused distraction, he'd unconsciously carved a series of deep scratches and grooves into the hard plastic covering of the car's dashboard.

Scooting a stack of forgotten papers and discarded fast food wrappers, the cyborg hid the wounds he'd inflicted on the vehicle. A quick glance at the opposite side of the interior showed Zuz, so caught up in examining the laptop he had propped up against the leather-wrapped steering wheel, he was completely oblivious to the maiming of his sole mode of transportation.

Mal looked at his friend for a moment, watching his eyes dart back and forth as a seemingly endless array of information scrolled across the screen in front of him, the harsh light reflecting off of the thick glasses he continually had to slide back up his nose and illuminating his face in a sickly glow. The man hadn't looked up once in the entire time they'd been sitting and watching the house.

Heck, once he figured out how to pull down information from the computer system inside Mal, it had been almost impossible to get Zuz to focus on anything else. Mal had been convinced they were going to crash numerous times on the nearly two hour trip out from the warehouse.

The man was like a fat kid in a candy store and Mal couldn't completely blame him. It wasn't every day that one of your oldest friends called and asked you to pick him up from out front of a top secret government agency and help him escape from the aforementioned agency after it had turned him into a killer cyborg. Heck, even trying to put that sentence together correctly was more than enough to crash Mal's newly computerized brain.

It reinforced every hair-brained anti-government theory David Zuzelo had ever come up with, and finally being able to see hard data proving him right had the man absolutely giddy.

Mal turned back to stare at his right hand with its knife-like finger still extended. Concentrating, a warm pulse moved down his spine and into his arms, and the finger shrank back down to normal.

Well, thought Mal, normal in only the most relative sense.

Watching the morning sun reflect off of the highly polished metallic plates of his arm, Mal wondered what Kristin would say when she saw what had happened to him. Had she even wondered what happened to him, or had she just run off and married the first guy she met with good enough credit to buy a house in the well-to-do Valley neighborhood?

Anger spilled from Mal as he slammed his hand down on to the dash, sending spiderweb cracks throughout its length.

"It just ain't right!"

"You're telling me," Mal was surprised at Zuz's response, sure his friend hadn't been paying attention—even his internal voice had revealed the vital signs of someone deep in concentration: deep steady breathing, delta brain waves at an even four cycles per second, heart rate at forty beats per minute. Mal made himself vow to forget the indications of increased blood flow to certain unmentionable areas of Zuz's anatomy.

"Excuse me?"

Middle finger pushing his glasses back into place, Zuz continued without allowing his eyes to stop skimming the information steaming in front of them, "Yeah, No. You're totally right. It ain't right, man."

Mal turned to face the man, a puzzled look on his face. "What 'ain't right,' Zuz?"

Zuz looked up, finally realizing he was part of a conversation, "You know, what you were talking about. What the government did to you. I mean, most of the stuff I pulled out of your head is encrypted beyond anything I've ever seen, but what I can make out is nuts. Human modification, hit squads. It's insane. I knew it, but I didn't, you know, KNOW it. You know?"

"I was talking about Kristin, Zuz," sighed Mal, head drooping in slightly exaggerated melancholy. Sure, he was a billion dollar cyborg killing machine now, but that didn't mean he didn't need a little compassion every once in a while.

"Oh, right," said Zuz, still clueless. "Wait. What about Kirstin?"

Staring out through the dirty windshield at the home of his ex-lover not fifty yards distant, Mal stated flatly, "She's married."

"Aw, hell," repeated Zuz, watching Mal fidgeting restlessly in the passenger's seat. "What should we do now?"

Mal continued to stare at the house, ignoring the question posed to him. Ten seconds of silence passed. Fifteen. Thirty. The newly awakened cyborg soldier seemed frozen in place, locked on Kristin's home just across fifteen feet of freshly swept asphalt road and three meticulously manicured front lawns.

Zuz grew increasing worried as his friend's silence continued, with no signs of stopping. "Do you want to go to Denny's and grab some chow? You haven't eaten in God knows how long."

No response.

No movement.

Sliding the laptop onto the dash, Zuz reached out with his right hand and gripped the warm metal of Mal's organic metal shoulder, "Mal?"

Without turning his head, Mal spoke, "I have to see her."

"Are you sure that's a good idea? You know. Looking like," Zuz gestured wildly at Mal's new appearance "…that."

Mal spun around in the seat, doing a quick once over of the hoarder's wet dream that was Zuz's Nissan, and then smiled as his ran a nearly leering eye up and down the smaller man's loose, gray sweatshirt that declared he was a "one man wolf pack."

Fingers wagging, Mal ordered, "Give me your hoodie."

The cyborg exited the car a few minutes later, living metal arms now covered to the wrist by the thin gray material of Zuz's long sleeve shirt. Mal flipped up the hood to hide his face from any of Kristin's nosy neighbors who might be out and about doing early morning chores. There was no need to bring attention to his visit to his ex-fiancée if he could help it—there was no telling what kind of trouble it could get her into.

"Stay low and keep an eye out for anything suspicious," said Mal, shutting the car door as quietly as possible behind him as he began what felt like the longest walk of his life, forcing himself to walk slowly across the street and up to the front porch of the house the pair had been staking out for more than half an hour.

Standing in front of the large dark green door, Mal was done waiting. He had to find out what had happened in the year he had lost. He had to know why Kirstin had left him. Inhaling deeply, Mal rang the doorbell and tried to control the excitement and anxiety building in his gut. Listening to the sound of footsteps approaching the door had Mal convinced his living metal palms were sweating.

The sight of a female figure through the faux stained glass window of the door had him gulping out loud.

The door swung open on silent hinges and Mal's breath was taken away at the sight of the only woman he'd ever truly loved. Kristin Meyer, now Kristin Meyer-Morrell, stood before him, half-awake, long blond hair still mussed from sleep, dressed in a comfy deep burgundy fleece robe that ended just high enough on her thigh to get his blood racing.

"Can I help..." recognition hit Kristin with the force of a hurricane, jolting her eyes from sleepy boredom to horrified shock to straight up fury in a heartbeat, "...you!"

Mal used the time to try and decide what the best way to greet his long-lost love would be.

"Hi, honey, I'm home," was his final decision.

It wasn't the wisest of choices.

Mal's computer warned him of the spike in Kristin's pulse rate and the rush of blood to her arm in more than enough time for him to block the jaw-rattling punch she threw at him, but better judgment prevailed and he let it connect.

"You bastard!" the pretty blond bellowed, crossing her arms tightly just below her rather ample bosom. "How dare you show your face here!"

Rubbing his chin where a decent-sized bruise was already forming from her fist, "Nice to see you're still packing a mean right cross."

Kristin cinched her robe tighter around her body and shot daggers at the cyborg. Even scrunched up in rage, Mal thought she had the most beautiful green eyes he'd ever seen.

"It was a left hook," she corrected. "What do you want, Malcolm?"

This was going to be harder than he thought. She only called him "Malcolm" when she was getting ready to start throwing things or exile him out to sleep on the couch.

Mal decided to try his serious voice to help get things on the right track.

"Something's gone wrong, Kris...I'm in trouble and I need to talk. I need to get some questions answered," Mal said as earnestly as possible. "May I come in?"

Kristin moved to block his entrance to her home.

"You're fine out here," she glowered and gestured for him to get on with whatever it is he needed to do.

"Fair enough. I'm having trouble remembering things," he began. "Trouble remembering about us and what happened last year."

"Go on," Kristin's foot started tapping impatiently. She wanted Mal to get to the point and get out.

"Why were you so startled to see me standing at your door?"

"To be honest, I half-expected you were going to find some way to kill yourself in the hospital after you broke off our engagement," Kristin responded, her annoyance growing with every passing second.

"I broke up with you?" Mal spat out the words, unbelieving them, and grabbed his ex-fiancée tightly by the tops of her arms. "You're lying! I loved you—I still love you, Kris. I'd never—!"

"You left me, Mal. YOU left me," she snapped, her voice filled to overflow with venom and anger. "Let go, Mal—you're hurting me."

The dark red imprints of cruel organic metal fingers remained behind long after Mal removed them. He couldn't believe what Kristin was telling him, but the look in her eyes confirmed it was the truth and the realization sent him to his knees.

"Why can't I remember?"

Mal started to drop his head into his hands—until he caught sight of them as the rising sun's light hit their strange, moving metal bands and twisting cables and rage erupted.

Lighting fast, Mal's arm whipped out and tore through the red brick planter lining on side of Kristin's tiny porch, pulverizing it to powder and cleaving a tiny plumeria bush in half.

Seeing the fragile state her former lover was in, Kristin's voice reached out tenderly, "My God, what happened to you?"

"Tell me," Mal's voice was a ragged whisper, barely audible. "Tell me, what happened."

Kristin's eyes narrowed, anger still welling up behind them. Mal caught her gaze and his eyes plead for her to help him. She signed and her face softened in resignation.

Pushing the door open behind her, Kristin gestured for Mal to follow her inside. The pair made their way to a bright kitchen, covered in pastels and light-colored wood fixtures, and sat down at a small table set back in a breakfast nook. The aroma of freshly brewed coffee filled Mal's nostrils, but Kristin disappointed his taste buds by not offering him a cup.

Instead, she sat shock upright in the pale yellow chair across from him, hands placed flat on floral table cloth.

"You stopped writing me," Kristin began slowly, unsure of what to say to the shadow of the man she once loved. "Just after you went overseas—to Iraq. You stopped writing, and I didn't know why. I sent letters, it felt like a hundred of them, trying to get you to respond. Begging you to write me back."

A single tear wound its way down the side of her face causing Mal to reach out to comfort her. Kristin shied away, but he wasn't sure if it was from his inhuman hand or from an old pain re-aggravated by his presence.

"I called the army, but they were no help," she continued a bit stronger than before. "You were too busy protecting my freedoms to practice your penmanship, they said."

"My unit was shot down over…"

"I know...now," Kristin cut him off, her fist clenching at her side let him know it was her time to speak. "A month or so later, men from the government contacted me and said you had been brought home—that you were in the hospital. In critical shape, they said. I rushed down to the base to see you."

She leaned back and closed her eyes, remembering.

"They took me to your room in the ICU...it was terrible. Your arm..." her eyes fluttered open and she paused, staring intently at the gleaming cybernetic replacement mounted to his left shoulder. "Your arm was gone. There were three men in suits with us in the ICU, they told me your helicopter had been hit with a surface-to-air missile—that you were almost killed. You'd lost your arm in the attack, suffered massive internal injuries. Wires and tubes covered your body, and a machine was keeping you alive. I hated the sound of that machine."

"The government men said you were conscious and had asked to speak with me," Kristin scowled. "They wouldn't leave—they barely gave me room to stand next to you. They smelled of too much aftershave and cigarettes."

"The men...do you remember their names?" Mal asked, intrigued at her mention of government suits.

Kristin rubbed her temple and Mal noticed a small scar just to the left of her eyebrow and her hair was a couple of shades lighter, and far shorter, than he remembered. It ate him up that she'd been forced to go through so much without him.

"I don't remember their names," she admitted. "But the tall one—the one in charge, I think—he had the palest blue eyes."

Mal filed the fact away, for whatever good it would do him later, and told her to go on.

"When they finally let us talk, you told me we were through, that you didn't have the time or patience to deal with my trivialities anymore and that nothing mattered anymore," her voice finally cracked. "That I didn't matter anymore."

Kristin looked at Mal in the way only a wronged woman could. It'd been a year and she was still pissed off.

"And that was it. They escorted me out and a group of soldiers from the army came and removed your things from our loft. I never saw you again...until this morning."

Mal nodded and looked around the room, trying to avoid her accusing stare. His eyes fell on a wedding picture held to the stainless steel refrigerator nearby. A man in a military dress uniform stood behind Kristin with a huge smile on his face.

"Is that your husband?" Mal asked.

Kristin was confused for a split second until she followed Mal's gaze to the photograph. Her face brightened considerably as she looked at it.

"Yes. That's Marc," she replied. "We met a month or so after you vanished. It was love at first sight."

"Fantastic," Mal had problems hiding the sarcasm in his voice.

"At least he was there for me," the anger returned. "He didn't run away."

The two locked eyes in a ferocious staring contest, neither one's pride allowing them to look away.

Mal caved first, realizing none of this was Kristin's fault. She was as much a victim as he was.

"I…I better go."

"Yeah, you better," Kristin's nostrils flared and she jerked her head towards the door, indicating he shouldn't let it hit him on the way out.

Mal's world was in pieces as he made his way through Kristin's home and back onto the street. Everything seemed to close in around him, blanking the world out—blanking out Zuz waving at him from the still-running automobile, blanking out the sprinklers going off all around him as he crossed a trio of lawns, and blanking out the annoying way his computerized passenger announced that Kristin dialed a cell phone registered to one Marc Morrell as soon as Mal had left. He barely noticed opening the passenger side door to the Nissan, or the way its edge dug a shallow groove into the lawn they were parked next to as he did.

Nothing mattered to the cyborg except getting far, far away.

"How did it go?" asked Zuz, already sure of the answer based on the look of utter defeat on his friend's face.

Mal dismissed Zuz's question and dropped down into the waiting car sear, exhausted.

"Let's get out of here," he barely had the energy to speak the words.

"Sure, sure, man," Zuz nodded and put the car into drive. As the Nissan eased away from the curb and rolled slowly passed Kristin's home, he asked, "Where to now?"

"It doesn't matter anymore, just drive," Mal watched as Kristin's house, and his dreams of returning to his former life, faded into the distance.

CHAPTER 9

Mal had been silent for the entire ninety-minute drive back to Zuz's garage in City of Industry, failing even to offer any sort of comment at the large sign on the junkyard hideout's rusted steel front gate warning that "trespassers would be violated."

Kristin's words and her anger had drained all life from the cyborg soldier. Mal had thought he'd find answers to what had happened to him after the helicopter crash in Dahuk—that he'd find out why his memory was gone and, more important, why Kirstin was married to another man. And she had given him some of those answers, but for each one he received, five new questions seemed to emerge.

Why had he left her? It just didn't make sense to him. Mal couldn't imagine loving anything or anyone more than he loved Kristin. She was all he thought about every day he was deployed in Iraq.

Even more puzzling to Mal was how he went from being an ICU patient missing most of his internal organs, as well as an arm, to finding himself as a black-ops cyborg super-soldier acting as an assassin for a covert agency for the US government.

If he was honest with himself, it all sounded like the plot to one of those God-awful "B" horror movies Kristin used to make him watch every Saturday on the SyFy Channel. None of it seemed real.

When Zuz walked into the main area of the garage with a pair of coffee cups containing a thick, black substance barely above room temperature (eight-five degrees according to the electronic hitchhiker in his brain), Mal waved him off, snatched the silver and black laptop out of its resting place in an old 'Super Mario Brothers' backpack, and plopped down on the old barstool positioned in front of the big iron worktable.

After banging on the keyboard for a few minutes, Mal stared at one particularly intricate set of code on the screen. Zuz took the cessation in work as an invitation to join Mal at the table.

"None of this makes any sense," groaned Mal, exasperated.

"Dude, I know," Zuz leaned forward and rotated the portable computer so he could better see what Mal was gazing at. "It looks like some sort of high end variation of the AES, probably needing a 256-bit key to access the information. Nothing I've got has been able to break it. If you give me enough time I might be able to use a quantum algorithm to crack it. Grover's might do the trick, but we could be talking days or weeks."

Zuz failed to notice the completely dazed look on Mal's face.

"It's a probabilistic algorithm, so we'd need to run it through at least a few times to verify the results."

A living metal hand reached up and snapped the laptop closed.

Shaking his head, Mal said dejectedly, "I have absolutely no idea what any of that means."

"The Grover algorithm for searching unsorted databases," Zuz saw the look of total confusion in the cyborg's eyes as his explanation continued to fly over Mal's head. "Quantum computing? Lov Kumar Grover from Bell Labs? None of this ringing a bell?"

"The only Grover I know lives with Big Bird over on Sesame Street, Zuz," sighed Mal. "And, to be honest, I was talking about the entire situation more than the mess you pulled out of my head."

"Oh!" Realization slammed hard into Zuz's brain, somewhere just between his eyes. "Yeah, that shit with Kristin was a real mind-fuck."

"What do I do now, David?" Mal leaned back on the stool, locking his fingers behind his head. "According to Kristin, less than a year ago I was confined to a hospital bed with almost no chance of survival. Now..."

Mal back-flipped off his perch, landing lightly on his feet, arms out stretched. With a casual shrug, the living metal of his arms reformed his hands into gruesome, gleaming claws.

"...I'm a God-damned killing machine."

"Mal..." started Zuz, unsure of what to say. "...I..."

Before Zuz could finish his attempt at comfort, a wave of nausea pushed through Mal as the garage lights flickered and dimmed. The feeling was bad enough to force Mal to brace himself against the dark metal of Zuz's welding table for fear of collapsing to the ancient, cracked concrete floor.

"Mal?"

Unable to respond at first, Mal rubbed his temple and tried to clear his head. Looking around, the edges of everything around him were blurry and half-formed, and he found himself unable to focus on anything. Even stranger, the background voice of the computer passenger installed in his brain was completely silent for the first time since he had awoken at Project: Hardwired, and that worried Mal most of all.

The lights continued to pulse on and off in conjunction with each beat of sickness in Mal's head.

"What's wrong?"

"Everything's gone...fuzzy. It's like I'm seeing, hearing through cotton," answered Mal, rubbing his temples. "It almost feels like something is messing with my senses. Even my tongue is numb."

Pushing past Mal, David Zuzelo flipped a series of switches, activating the security monitors he had installed throughout the junkyard right after he first purchased it five years earlier.

"Shit, shit, shit," he said as all of them filled up with the crackling 'snow' of a dead video signal. Zuz rubbed his bald head frantically and, even with his sense dulled, Mal could tell the man was on the verge of a panic attack. "Every single camera is down. The feeds are all gone...they're probably jamming you, too. We've got visitors upstairs."

"Visitors?" repeated Mal.

"Yeah," responded Zuz, "and I'm betting they're the kind with computers for brains. How the hell did they find me so fast?"

"They probably just looked for the guy with the biggest

piece of shit car on the road," Mal joked, heading for the door to the yard upstairs.

Zuz was glad to see the light return to his friend's eyes, although he did wish it was for happier reasons.

"Dude! Don't dis my ride. It saved your sorry ass downtown."

Smiling, Mal reached to open the door. "You wait here-" was all he managed to say before the ten-foot high metal and wood doors were blasted in from some force outside. Only Mal's superhuman reflexes saved him from being decapitated by the flying projectiles which impacted against the rear wall of the garage with a thunderous clang. A giant cloud of dirt, rust, and debris billowed in on a surge of warm California morning air from outside.

Mal's arms bulked up in response to the attack, a covering of six-inch long spikes covered them from shoulder to wrist, and even longer claws replaced each of his fingers.

"Computer?" thought Mal in a poor attempt at a Scottish accent. He hoped to get a response from his inner voice, but all he found was static. At least they hadn't been able to remotely shut down the systems that ran his cybernetics. If they figured out how to do that he and Zuz would both be dead men.

A quick series of hacking coughs from Zuz let Mal know his friend was still alive.

"Hey, Z," Mal whispered as loudly as he dared. "Do you have a back door to this place?"

"Yeah," coughed Zuz, rubbing thick gobs of dust from his eyes with the sleeve of his sweatshirt.

"Grab your laptop and get out of here. I don't want whoever our visitors are to get the info on it."

"Ok, Mal."

Before Zuz could make his escape, a loud voice tore into the large underground bunker, reverberating off of the thick walls, surrounding the two men with power.

"Designate Cestus," the bass voice cut through the clouds of dirt filling the area like a warm knife through butter. "In concordance with the United States government Department of Defense, the FBI and Project: Hardwired, you are ordered to stand down and surrender to my authority and my men. Failure to do so will result in your termination with extreme prejudice."

Both men were stunned as the owner of the voice marched into the room, flanked by a pair of mercenaries wearing the dress of Project: Hardwired GMR-class soldiers.

Standing at somewhere south of five-feet seven-inches in height, the man was obviously a cyborg created by the same labs that gave Mal his bionic "improvements." The man's own enhancements seemed to consist of an irregular pattern of metal plates, mounted to every bit of exposed flesh: arms, neck, chest and face. A Project: Hardwired patch was stitched to the left arm of his black fatigues. Topping it all off was a cherub's face covered in freckles and top with thin, fiery red hair.

Mal's first impression was of a human picture-puzzle.

"Command told me to wait until Gauss arrived," continued the little man, stopping to run his hand over the mass of twisted metal left over from Mal's tantrum the night before, "but I wanted to take a shot at the Golden Boy myself. Besides, he had his chance and failed, right, buddy?"

Zuz and Weir exchanged glances, neither one completely sure what to make of the newcomer or his rather impressive entrance.

"Buddy?" quizzed Weir, positioning himself in front of Zuz to protect the man. He was worried about keeping Zuz safe while going toe-to-toe with another batch of Project: Hardwired's Frankenstein monsters.

"You remember me, don't you, Ces?" Seeing the clueless look on Weir's face, the man shook his head, smirking. "We were partners. We went on a lot of missions together: Shiraz, Isfahan, Anau, Herat, Paris…"

"Do you know this munchkin, Mal?" asked David, easing down to pick up his sledgehammer. "It kind of sounds like he has a crush on you."

"Shut up, hippie," squawked the ginger cyborg, "the grown-ups are talking."

Mal's inside voice supplied the rundown, which he relayed to the men in the room.

"He's Designate Talos, one of the heavy hitters of Project: Hardwired, and a prime unit like me and Gauss. The database calls him a...," Mal's face scrunched up at what came next. "A mechanimorph. Able to merge with metal and mechanical items, reforming them to suit his needs."

"Mechanimorph?" this time is was Zuz's turn to shake his head. "Exactly how much of the Project: Hardwired budget was set aside for inventing new words? So he's like a human erector set?"

"But shorter," quipped Mal.

"Enough!" shrieked Talos, finally having enough with the pair's insults. "GMR units Rho-Two and Rho-Three, detain Mister Zuzelo while I apprehend Designate Cestus. If the civilian resists, kill him."

"Confirmed, Designate Talos," responded the two Gomers in unison, advancing on David, MP5/40s at the ready. "David Anthony Zuzelo, you are to come with us."

"Mal?" stammered David Zuzelo, backing away from the approaching half-machine soldiers.

"Get out of the building, Z. We can meet up outside once I'm done with shorty and his friends."

In one fluid, effortless motion, Mal snatched the sledgehammer from his friend's grasp and hurled it at the oncoming cyborgs, hoping to knock one down and give Zuz time to escape. To everyone's surprise, Talos intercepted the makeshift missile, interjecting his five-foot six-inch frame into its path and allowing it to slam head-first into one of the metal plates on his forearm.

Talos's smiled widened as his eyes flashed bright yellow at the impact, which spun him almost completely around and took him down to his knees.

"Yes!" blurted Zuz, thinking the attack had taken out one of their opponents, but his celebration died out as Talos rose back to his feet, apparently unharmed and with a new weapon emerging from his body. The metallic sledgehammer had merged with the cyborg's left arm.

"Thanks for the new toy, meat," said Talos as he charged Mal, swinging his new tungsten-alloy hammer-fist.

"Run!" screamed Weir at his friend, narrowly blocking a devastating overhead strike by Designate Talos that had enough force behind it to nearly rattle his teeth out of their sockets.

From the corner of his eye, Mal saw Zuz grab his laptop from the long workbench and bolt through a side door with the pair of government cyborg grunts hot on his tail. A flurry of attacks from Talos snapped Mal's attention back to the task of defending himself. Deflecting another murderous blow from Talos that caused a rain of sparks to erupt from his forearm, Mal wished his friend a silent "good luck" and lashed out with a powerful thrust kick of his own that landed squarely in his foe's midsection, sending the diminutive man flopping down hard on his back.

Mal smiled at the small grunt of pain from Talos. He concentrated on his cybernetic arms, causing them to bulk up to nearly twice their normal size. His fingers merged into vicious blades and Mal leaped into the air in an attempt to end the battle quickly.

He was worried about Zuz's chances against two Gomers on his own. Unfortunately for both men, Talos wasn't about to let Mal go without a fight.

High above the battling pair of cyborg super-soldiers, David Zuzelo wasn't quite as concerned. After all, this was his house and no one came in and pushed him around.

They definitely didn't just come in and kill him all willy-nilly like. Zuz had a plan.

The truth of the matter was that David Zuzelo had been expecting a government-sponsored raid on his warehouse for years now and had prepared for almost every contingency. Not that Zuz thought he'd ever be fleeing for his life from a pair of cyborg assassins while another pair battled down below. That's just not something you think you'll have to plan for.

But, still, he'd been planning and building for nearly five years and was pretty sure he could escape from just about anything.

Turning down the hall where Mal had shredded the cot, Zuz made his way to a flight of metal stairs and maintenance elevator that lead from the sub-basement level to the roof nearly five stories straight up, tripping a series of switches along the walls as he went. He wasn't sure exactly how tough the "Gomers" were, but according to Mal they weren't very bright and were nowhere near as powerful as the prime units.

Hearing the steel-booted footfalls of his pursuers approaching close behind helped keep Zuz motivated. He was barely able to slide the mesh doors to the emergency lift and dive inside before the first Gomer burst around the corner and opened fire with his submachine gun. The carbon-fiber mesh of the elevator was too tight to allow the cyborg's projectiles through, but Zuz was still showered with hot sparks from the impacts.

Zuz sneaked a peek over down at the soldier, even as the lift shot up towards the roof exit at high speed. He wanted to see the man's reaction to the nasty surprise Zuz had left waiting for him four feet into the room.

He didn't have to wait long.

Rho-Three advanced into the room, unrelenting in his attack on the cage containing his prey, trying to damage its motors enough to stop its rapid ascent out of optimal firing range. The Gomer was so focused on its attack that it failed to give much attention to the freshly greased track running perpendicular to its path; failed to notice the sound of a thousand-pound tractor engine being launched along the iron rails until it was too late to dodge.

Zuz smiled as he watched the cyborg mercenary get crushed by his first line of defense. He hadn't expected it to work so well in real life after he'd gotten the idea from an old episode of 'Scooby Doo.'

With a silent 'thanks' to Freddy Jones and the whole Mystery Incorporated crew, Zuz leaned back and started to activate his second round of traps as the elevator jerked to a stop at the roof access point. The sound of Rho-Two mounting the stairway, taking three steps at a time, reminded David Zuzelo that he wasn't out of the woods yet.

In the battle against the military cyborg, Designate Talos, things had quickly gone from "going pretty well" to "getting your ass royally kicked" for Malcolm Weir.

At first the fight was incredibly one-sided, with Mal's extensive training in hand-to-hand combat coupled with the devastating melee focus of his cybernetic and nanotech arms proving to be too much for his smaller opponent.

A shuto-uchi knifehand strike to the jugular took Talos to his knees, follow up by a tetsui-uchi hammerfist that fractured his collarbone and a hiza-geri knee, shattering his nose with a satisfying crunch and spray of bright red blood. Mal's attacks flowed with a grace and power he had never before felt, thanks to Project: Hardwired's 'upgrades.'

"Is that all you've got," sputtered Talos, his mouth full of blood. "I thought you were supposed to be a tough guy, bro."

Mal's second series of attacks was even more vicious, and the small, metal-plated soldier with blazing crimson hair was unable to mount even the most basic of defenses against them.

The brawl was so brutally unequal, and Talos was taking such an unimaginable beating, Mal started to feel bad for the little soldier. Brutally unequal, that is, until the mechanimorph was hip-tossed into a forklift by Mal after a failed attempt at a rather clumsy ude-gatame straight-arm block.

For the briefest of moments, the fight looked to be over. Mal couldn't imagine someone, even a billion-dollar government-built cyborg killing-machine, walking away after an impact like that. The steel frame of the yellow and black lift truck was pushed in on itself, and even its hard metal guard cage was contorted and bent into a pale mockery of protection. So powerful was the collision of flesh and steel that any ordinary man would have died instantly.

Regrettably for Malcolm Weir, Designate Talos was no ordinary man. The cyborg's deep, resonating laugh and the sound of tearing metal announced the coming of a new world of pain to Mal.

"Wow," came the rich voice of Talos from out of the steam erupting from the obliterated construction vehicle in a cloud too thick for even Mal's enhanced senses to break through. "You really don't remember anything do you. If you did, you probably wouldn't have made that rookie mistake, eh?"

"Aw, hell," spit Mal as comprehension sucker punched him

in the figurative gut and a six-foot yellow rusted fork slashed out of the miasma of water vapor and hydraulic fluid mist and struck him in the literal one, sending the former soldier on an arc that took him twelve feet into the air and hurling twenty more across the now gloom-veiled room.

Mal hit the rear wall of the garage with a sickening thud, all the breath in his body replaced by two broken ribs and three cracked ones. As Talos's shadow, now more than twenty feet tall, pushed through the shrouding, greasy-gray fog, and headed for him at breakneck speed, one thought stuck in Mal's head: I hope Zuz is doing better than me.

Over two tons of man and machine hit Mal's prone body, taking him through the roof of Zuz's workshop and into oblivion.

CHAPTER 10

On the pitched, corrugated aluminum roof of the building, David Zuzelo stood over the smoking, still-twitching and very much dead form of Rho-Two. He smiled to himself, happy to discover that fifty-thousand volts was more than enough to kill one of the pertinacious bastards.

He was also happy that 'pertinacious' had been on his word-of-the-day calendar that morning.

Zuz dropped the rod attached to the junkyard's live power-coupling and headed over to the edge of the room as surreptitiously as he could. A quick look at his cellphone notified the bald conspiracy theorist someone was still jamming all communication functions in the area, which meant he couldn't contact the computer in Mal's head to let the reluctant cyborg know the Gomers were dead and that he was out of immediate danger.

The sight of a seven-man squad of the infantry-class GMR cyborgs setting up in a strategic position out in the heart of the junkyard made David laugh.

"As out of danger as one can be with a team of government assassins out to kill me, that is." Zuz's chuckle cut off as he spotted a rather conspicuous RV parked just outside the entrance to his hideout, covered from stem to stern in an uncountable number of silvery antennas. "There you are, my pretty."

The brains in charge of the operation must have figured the runt and his men would be more than enough to handle him and Mal. Zuz couldn't think of any reason for them to have parked their command vehicle in such an obvious spot.

Knowing his continued existence probably rested on taking

out that heavily armored 'recreational vehicle,' and with Mal tied up with the 'hard job' of battling a Talos, Zuz decided he would have to do the 'easy job' of crossing a three-acre junkyard swarming with armed and deadly half-machine soldiers bent on his death.

Scurrying down a camouflaged ladder at the rear of the building, Zuz concluded that he'd let Mal do the 'easy job' next time.

And the hard jobs.

And any other jobs they came across.

"After all," thought Zuz, leaping to the ground, "I'm a delicate flower."

Sticking to the shadows of burned out Cadillacs, rusted out Fords and out-and-out dead Chevys, David Zuzelo made a beeline for the men who wanted him dead. Zuz was so focused on his task he failed to hear Malcolm Weir's body blast through the old windows of the main garage building and crash into the back of his car, leaving a gaping hole filled with glass and blood where the hatchback door had been.

Consciousness returned to Malcolm Weir less than a second before his uninsured collision with the Nissan Cube parked just outside of the grime-encrusted garage window he had been thrown through by Designate Talos.

Mal marveled the Japanese-made mini MPV was still mostly in one piece as he disentangled himself from its ruined rear end. Watching as a two-story robot with a gooey human center broke through the front wall of the building in front of him, intent on his destruction, Mal desperately hoped his own parts came from the same manufacturing plant.

Splinters of wood and glass and aluminum showered the area in a deadly rain, coating every inch in deadly debris. Looking around for an escape route, Mal cursed Zuz's choice to make his home in a dump filled with ammunition for Talos. Why couldn't he have lived in a nice, empty open field or on a boat?

Gutted cars and refrigerators and old industrial air conditioning units flew by Mal's technologically enhanced form and were tossed carelessly out of the way, crushed flat by, or absorbed into the ever-growing form of Talos.

Mal hazarded a glimpse behind him to see the government killer topping twenty-five or thirty feet in height with no signs of slowing down. He had to figure out how to stop the monster fast or there'd be no way out.

Ducking into an ancient school bus to catch his breath and avoid being stepped on, Mal found his relief to be fleeting as he came nose to barrel with the MP5/40 submachine gun of GMR Rho-Five.

Even more disturbing for Mal was a voice from the past emerging from the robot-like solider.

"Steve? Steve Douros?"

"Halt or be terminated, Designate Cestus," echoed the voice of US Army Sergeant Steven Gus Douros coldly. Almost no trace of his Pennsylvanian accent remained in his words and Mal found no hint of recognition in his former friend's face. A face almost entirely replaced with the same gleaming metal shared by all GMR-units.

Gleaming nano-tech arms snapped up in a sign of non-aggression. Mal was dumbfounded at the sight before him, positive that Douros had died in the same helicopter crash that started him down his current road.

"What happened to you, Sarge?" said Mal, backing slowly out of the bus, arms still raised in faux-surrender.

The sound of six more military weapons chambering rounds and preparing to fire halted Mal's retreat, but no more so than staring into the glassy, uncomprehending eyes of a dead man. Mal allowed his internal computer system to inform him of the presence of seven GMR-units surrounding him, not able to rip his gaze from the sergeant.

"What did they do to him?" Mal demanded of his computer.

"Rho-Team, Unit Five, formerly known as Steven Gus Douros, retired first sergeant serving in Third Battalion, Seventy-Fifth Ranger Regiment. Classified unfit for service and discharged on an RFM approved by Lieutenant Colonel Michael Denman," rambled Mal's personal version of Wikipedia.

The man once known as Sergeant Douros signaled the rest

of his team to close in and Mal sprung into action even as his computer continued its litany of facts.

"Diagnosed in a persistent vegetative state, Rho-Five was removed to the Project: Hardwired facility in Houston, Texas on the authorization of Director Gordon Kiesling."

Mal burst into action even as a pair of the GMRs opened fire on him, launching himself to his left into a third Rho Unit and shoved his clawed metal fist through the protective Kevlar of its bulletproof vest, into its stomach and out its back. Pieces of spine dropped to the ground in a soup of human entrails and bits of tattered uniform.

In less than the time it took to sneeze, Rho-Four was dead and Mal was moving again, a trail of bullets from his would-be captors kicking up divots of asphalt all around him.

"Douros was an early test subject in the GMR Upgrade process led by Doctor Jean Ryan. Eighty percent of his brain was replaced by cybernetic implants which allowed him to be controlled by the main Abraxas command protocol."

"Is his like me? Is Steve still in there," Mal leapt over Rho-One, dragging his six-inch claws through its neck and face in a geyser of gore, splitting its helmet in half. Four of the remaining five Gomers dropped their guns, allowing the weapons to hang freely from harnesses attached to their torsos, and unsheathed electrified truncheons that glowed blue and sparked evilly in the shadows of the junkyard. An elbow strike from above drove the eleven-inch forearm spike through the head of Rho-Nine, slicing its skull neatly in half and ending its pitiful existence.

"Negative," came the computer's response, punctuated by Mal blocking an overhand strike by Rho-Seven. Mal knew from previous experience the electricity would do little harm to him as long as it only made contact with his cybernetic arms. The nanotech of Mal's left arm reformed itself into a shining, mirror-polished, three-foot long blade, a blade he used to slice Rho-Seven in half, from right shoulder to left hip. "Rho-Five's original personality construct was terminated with the surgical removal of his higher organic brain functions. Only involuntary systems remain."

"Those bastards," spit Mal, gutting two more of his robotic

attackers with ease. He was glad the Gomers weren't as tough as Gauss or Talos. "Where is Talos, anyway?" he quizzed as he faced off against the final GMR, Rho-Five, his former friend.

"Designate Talos inbound. Fifty meters and closing at a speed of twenty-two miles per hour," Mal wasn't sure, but he thought he detected just a hint of humor in the electronic voice. He was starting to hate the thing.

"Bloody great," said Mal, charging into battle against Rho-Five, desperately trying to drown out the sound of a pissed-off four-thousand pound junkyard titan bearing down on him with death in its eyes.

The decaying skeletons of long-dead luxury automobiles, the cracked and corroded frames of defunct exercise equipment, and the fast deteriorating shells of once-cutting edge televisions formed alleys of rotting plastic hope and high walls of decomposing oxidized dreams. It was deep amid of those alleys and walls that David Zuzelo had squirreled himself away.

Casting an eye around the tottering stack of balding steel-radial tires he'd selected as his lookout station, Zuz strained to hear the discussion coming out of the open side door of the Project: Hardwired operated communications rig less than ten feet away.

Zuz's approach to the vehicle, while less than the ninja-like affair he'd hoped it would be, had been completely overlooked by the occupants of the twenty-foot long, nine-foot high, box-shaped transport due to the sounds of the pitched battle going on somewhere in the middle of the scrap-yard. Of course, the giant "trash mech" Zuz saw smashing its way through his formerly organized yard helped add to the sound pollution. It took every ounce of self-control he possessed to keep from yelling "Geroni-do-run-run-roni-moooo" when Designate Talos's "Junkion" form came jogging past.

Talos had better be careful, or he'd get sued by Hasbro for his new look.

Zuz just about shat himself when one of the communications officers appeared in the open doorway of the RV from hell, an unlit cigarette half-dangling from his lips and a pair of high tech binoculars clutched chest-level in his gloved hands.

From his position on the vehicle's exit, the soldier, whose enormous chin caused Zuz to dub 'Leno,' pressed the field glasses up to his face and began talking back to an unseen partner hidden from view, "Ho-lee shit, Connors! You should this. I've never seen Talos so beefed up. He's got to be thirty, thirty-five feet now. It's nuts to see two Primes going at it for real."

The cigarette slid lower and lower on the man's lip, dropping down a bit with every sentence. Each exclamation threatened to cause the cancer stick to fall away completely, but it stayed attached as if by force of the man's will.

"Designate Cestus is a badass for sure; it's probably why they sent two of the big guns out after him," a second solider, this one with flaming-red hair, cropped short to his scalp, poked his head out from behind the first. There was no choice for Zuz but to name him 'Conan.'

That got the attention of both Zuz and Leno.

"Two?" the first soldier's head snapped back around to face his friend, causing his seemingly forgotten cigarette to flap like crazy as it held on for dear life.

Seizing the binoculars away from his teammate nonchalantly, Conan squinted out to watch the battle, "Designate Gauss is inbound. E.T.A. less than eight minutes with three squads of Gomers. We're streaming a live feed of the op to him now. Even if Cestus takes Talos down before Gauss arrives, we'll have enough data to hack his on-board systems and shut him down cold."

Leno snatched the matte-black glasses back.

"You think?" he asked, not quite as confident as his comrade-in-arms. "So far, the new biotech the lab installed in him has ignored everything we've thrown at it. If I didn't know better I'd say it was learning from every attack."

Conan headed back inside, mocking Leno, "You're an idiot, private. We'll get him, it's just a matter of time."

"Shitshitshit!" Zuz scrambled away from the men in a panic. He'd heard enough about Gauss from Mal to know the man would tear them both a new hole if they were still in the yard when he arrived. The computer-engineer turned professional conspiracy buff was positive he didn't want to see what happened when a batshit crazy cyborg with magnetic powers landed in a scrapyard filled with ferrous metals.

If they were going to survive, the pair needed to escape before reinforcements arrived. Even more immediate, Zuz knew the tech truck, and whatever it was trying to do to Mal, needed to be taken offline. They could not be allowed to shut him down.

Leaping to his feet after a fifteen foot crawl through detritus, Zuz hauled ass towards a section of the compound a short distance away that held some of his most-prized pieces: a half-destroyed 727 airliner, a pair of Korean-era army jeeps, and, the thing he was sure would be their salvation, a four-hundred and ten horsepower 1969 Caterpillar D9 bulldozer he'd purchased from a Hollywood auction house. The monster had been sitting in a production studio's warehouse for over 40 years after having 'starred' in the 1974 film, 'Killdozer!,' and had been his pet restoration project for the past nine months.

At a forty-nine ton operating weight, Zuz was confident it'd make short work of the Comm-vehicle and the men inside. Zuz climbed up onto the machine's tread and tossed open the door to the driver's compartment before climbing in, feeling like the cavalry about to ride in and save the day.

That is, until the D9 decided not to cooperate with him.

Zuz tried and failed to hot-wire the beast's ignition five times before giving up and retrieving the keys from his utility shed. Luckily, all the Gomers he'd seen running around the yard like ants earlier had found something more important to do than shoot a middle-aged, balding former computer technician.

If the sound of gunfire and explosions on the other side of the compound was any indication, then they had just run into Mal and, in the parlance of the iPad generation, 'shit just got real.'

The sound of an engine as big as a car roaring to life caused an insane grin to spill across Zuz's face. He was pretty sure sitting in the driver's seat of the 'Killdozer' was what it felt like to ride a thunder cloud.

Obliterating a line of tattered Chevys that were relics from the Great Depression, Zuz pushed the construction vehicle to 'warp 9.' The only thing more satisfying to Zuz than the feel of power rumbling beneath him was the look of Leno's face as he emerged from his vehicle a quarter second before impact.

The unlit cigarette finally dropped from the soldier's quivering lower lip as the 'Killdozer' launched itself over the dilapidated husk of a once bright blue Pacer and plowed into the mobile comm-station, pulverizing it beyond recognition.

Zuz's scream of exaltation rang out over the clamor of the D9's mammoth diesel engine, but he knew his work wasn't done yet. He had nullified the computerized threat from the men in the mangled heap before him, but the pair had no more than five minutes to make good their escape or it was all over. Gauss was coming and with him guaranteed capture.

Pulling as close to a 180 degree 'bootleg' turn as a one hundred thousand pound bulldozer can do while going twenty miles per hour, he lowered the six massive hydraulic arms attached to the U-blade, and charged straight for the mechanical giant beating the snot out of his friend.

"OK, sweetheart! Destroy!" was his battle cry.

God, Zuz loved that movie.

A steel and aluminum fist the size of a phone booth slammed into Mal's back, even as he eviscerated Rho-Five. The sheer force of the blow, and subsequent full-body pain Mal experienced from it, kept the cyborg from dwelling overly long on the death of his former compatriot.

Rolling out of the way of a follow-up strike from the gargantuan hand of Talos, Mal resolved the best way to mourn for the soldier—the friend—who had been Steven Douros, would be to take down the bastards that turned him into a mindless automaton. To take down the men responsible for what happened to both of them.

Of course, Mal's line of thinking continued, the only way to do that was to not get killed by the colossal walking pile of rust currently doing its damnedest to squash him like a grape.

A gout of flame spewing forth from the oxyacetylene

torch merged with Talos's right forearm punctuated just how unlikely survival would be. Heat from the fire lance blistered Mal's back and caused his shirt to light up. The nanotech in his bloodstream set his healing into overdrive, making Mal realize just how much he hated the itchy feeling the things gave him when they were active.

Not that the half-machine man was going to complain, though. Having an uncontrollable urge to scratch himself all over was better than dealing with the discomfort of third degree burns over forty percent of his body.

Mal tore off his flame-licked shirt and hurled it in the human face of Talos staring out from the upper chest of his patchwork iron shell. The giant reflexively protected its face with a large hand, allowing the smaller cyborg to rush between its legs.

Thirteen inch long talons sprung from once human hands and tore through the cables, girders and rods supporting the titan's legs. With the groan and screech of metal shredding like tissue paper, forty tons of man and machine folded in on itself, crashing hard enough into the ground to send a spider web of cracks radiating out from it. A fifteen foot high stack of flattened sedans was upended by the earthquake caused by the falling cyborg, dropping unceremoniously onto its head.

"That went better than I had hoped," smirked Mal, a bit too sure of himself.

Recent events being what they were, he should have known things wouldn't be quite that easy. Ignoring his better judgment, and the little alarm of warning going off from the computer in his head, Mal formed one arm into a meter-and-a-half blade of gleaming metal and vaulted onto the back of the prone Talos, planning to finish off the Project: Hardwired assassin with one stroke of the sword.

Well, "sword arm" or "arm sword" or whatever it was.

Before the forty-eight inches of indestructible top-secret titanium alloy could puncture the armored enclosure Talos's flesh and blood form was hiding in, the entire structure lurched and jerked, reforming under his feet and tossing Mal back to the cracked and crevassed pavement.

"Oooh," the air was knocked from Mal's lungs and he felt

pebbles and small rocks forced into areas he really didn't want them in.

By the time Mal kicked up to his feet again, Talos was ready for him. Somehow, the over-sized cyborg had beaten him to a standing position. Mal was stunned that something so big could move so fast.

"Gotcha!" echoed Talos's rich voice from deep within the junk titan he'd become as his left hand shot out and gripped Mal's body, pinning his arms to his sides.

Mal was trapped in a hand as big as an industrial freezer. Even worse than the fact he was probably about to be crushed to pulp was that a little shit like Talos was going to do the crushing.

Grunting as the titanic appendage tightened its vise-like hold, Mal struggled to no avail.

"You were always Kiesling's number one draft pick. Now, you ain't shit, are you?" Talos leaned his body over so he could watch as he squeezed the life out of the renegade cyborg.

"Fuck you." The words were less than a whisper. Mal tried to spit in his enemy's face as a final gesture of defiance, but the pressure on his chest and lungs was too great and the wad of phlegm just slid down his chin and onto his neck.

"I'm going to enjoy breaking you in half, Cestus."

The sound of something huge crashing through the piles of scrap metal startled both men, snapping their heads to attention. The crunching and banging was joined by the pulsating bleat of a behemoth diesel engine and the horrific off-key voice of David Zuzelo singing 'Ice, Ice, Baby' at the top of his lungs.

Hurling out from between a pair of wasted Volkswagen buses, the D9 bulldozer slammed into the side of Designate Talos with the force of a locomotive, and caused Malcolm Weir's world to go sideways.

Mal wasn't sure how long he lost consciousness, but it was at least a handful of seconds. One second, Zuz is driving a huge-ass bulldozer into Talos, and the next, at least according to Mal's rattled brain, there was a mushroom cloud of dust in the air and the entire north-facing wall of the garage was gone, collapsed in on itself.

A scream of terror and pain from within the decimated

building snapped Mal out of his near-concussive funk, sending him running towards the sound. He reached down to pull a grenade belt off the corpse of Rho-Five, blanking out the fact that it was body of his fallen friend.

Making his way head-first through the powdery-gray fog at a speed that would make an Olympic sprinter green with envy, dodging the shattered pieces of destroyed cars as he went, Mal demanded a status update from his internal computer.

"Systems operating at ninety-three percent. Minor cosmetic damage in twelve locations. Three fractures in the following bones: right tibia, right ulna and right ulna. Repairs will be complete in four minutes, three seconds. Recommended intake of one-thousand-eight-hundred calories of protein and calcium to compensate for projected loss in bone mineral density."

Mal could feel the cuts and scraps dotting his body close up and heal over.

"Good enough," thought Mal as he broke through the fog to see Zuz suspended a good ten feet in the air by what was left of Talos's exoskeleton.

Both of the giant's legs were gone, along with one arm and most of its chest. Talos himself was now nearly completely exposed, the metal cage he had been protected by was dented inward, its bars bent and broken. The bulldozer itself was destroyed, barely recognizable. Despite the extensive damage, Talos was laughing as his one good arm held Zuz upside down by one leg.

"Once I rip your buddy's legs off, I'm coming after you, Cestus," bellowed Talos, shaking his prisoner in the air, eliciting another shriek from Zuz.

Faster than either Talos or Zuz could react, Mal leapt the twenty plus foot distance between the building's ruined perimeter to his enemy's chest, howling insanely as he did. Living metal hands sank into rusted steel armor to find enough purchase to brace the living weapon Mal had been turned into. An instant later, Mal had punched a clawed fist through the stomach of Talos, bounded across to where Zuz was being clutched by massive fingers and cut the man free.

Blood gurgled from between Talos's lips as the two men dropped to the ground.

"This won't stop me, Ces!" called Talos, swinging his massive arm at the fleeing pair like a club. "My Prime Unit is stronger than yours! You'll never escape!"

"Fuck me," groaned Zuz, eyes going wide as he saw Talos freeing himself from the wreckage by drawing its mass into his body.

Mal pushed his friend behind a half-standing piece of wall for protecting and turned to face Designate Talos, a determined look etched into his face.

"Hey, Talos," Mal called back, raising his right arm and holding up his thumb and forefinger to mimic a gun. Eight metal pins hit the ground at Mal's feet, released from where they hid in his palm. A smile tugged the corners of Mal's mouth, "Bang."

Talos looked down at where Mal was pointing and noticed a Rho-Five's grenade belt sticking out of the shredded flesh of his lower torso. His human arms came free of his exoskeleton to claw furiously through the gore, trying to reach the explosives.

He was too late.

The concussive force of the multiple grenade explosions threw both Mal and Zuz clear of the building as nearly half of it was blown to hell. Mal covered Zuz's body with his own, shielding the man from the rain of fragments and wreckage that followed.

Once it had stopped, Mal helped Zuz to his feet and the men stood in silence for nearly a minute, taking in the devastation.

Gripping Mal on his shoulder, David Zuzelo finally broke the silence.

"Mal, man, we have to get out of here right now," Zuz squinted against the light and heat of the aftermath of the explosion. He could feel the flames singeing the fine hairs of his eyebrows and the fringes of his goatee. "The baddies have reinforcements inbound."

Nodding in understanding, Mal's hands motioned to his anxious friend for one more moment. "One sec, Zuz. I need to make sure shorty is down for the count. That's not a bastard I want coming back for me."

"Well, hurry up. Chatter over the wire says Gauss is en route with them, and I'm not sure either of us is ready for him to tag in."

With his enhanced senses, Mal navigated the flaming wreckage that littered the area with ease, quickly leaving Zuz far behind. Vaulting over displaced steel girders and the still-burning husks of Zuz's collected of junked vehicles, Mal raced through the area, looking for proof that Talos was a corpse.

Dropping twenty feet down into what remained of David Zuzelo's once impenetrable underground garage workspace, the silent computerized voice in Malcolm Weir's head gave him the bad news.

"Designate Talos located," came the calm, passionless voice. "Unit has initiated self-repairs and will regain system integrity in t-minus seven minutes…"

There was more, but Mal stopped listening as a cool gust of metallic wind from above cleared the area of smoke and dust, revealing a terrifying sight.

Mal's eyes went wide as he saw what was left of the human parts of what had once been the man known as Designate Talos, his skin liquefied and oozing freely over charred bones. Hair and eyes burnt to cinders. Despite the massive damage—damage that would have been a gruesome death for any normal human—Talos was still alive and his cybernetic implants were merging with the bulldozer's broken husk.

Already the involuntary systems that had been grafted onto Talos had rebuilt his spine and left arm, even as the blackened jaws of his skull opened and closed in a silent scream.

"Dear God," was all Mal could say.

From the floor above, David's voice called down, "Is he dead?"

Mal climbed back up and stood next to his friend.

"No. Somehow, he's still alive," Mal whispered, strangely moved by the plight of the man who had just tried to kill him. "Whatever those bastards did to him won't let him die. It'll keep him coming until one of us is completely destroyed."

Words left Mal as Zuz joined him, both men staring down through the oily black smoke at the decimated form twitching and spasming below them.

After a moment, Zuz's laid his hand on Mal's metal shoulder, giving it a firm tug.

"We have to go, Mal. They'll be here any minute."

"I can't leave him like this," Mal's voice was a hollow echo of itself.

Zuz rummaged around in the pockets of his cargo shorts, spilling change, keys and other unidentifiable bits to the ground as he did. After a few heartbeats, he found what he was looking for and tossed it to his distressed friend.

"Here."

Mal looked me to do with this," puzzled Mal, turning it over in his metallic palm, "call 911?"

"I've got thermite on every support beam and hundreds of pounds of C-4 planted all over the yard outside and in the walls of the garage. Even in the foundation right under Talos," Zuz turned and walked away from the conflagration. "For just in case."

Mal nodded as he turned to follow his friend after a final look below.

"With the jamming signal gone, it's not just a phone," continued Zuz. "It's a detonator."

"Let's go," Mal said, pocketing the electronic device.

The pair hurried from the building. At first, Mal wasn't sure where to go, but Zuz guided him back to where his car had been parked.

The Nissan sat in the same spot Zuz left it, surrounded by destruction.

"I hit that thing pretty hard earlier," said Mal as Zuz unlocked the car's doors with his remote key fob. "There's no way it's still going to run. Let's hop the fence and steal something on the street."

Zuz ignored his friend and hopped into the driver's seat, sliding the black-tipped key into the ignition.

"Don't be stupid, man...we'd don't have time for..."

Mal's mouth dropped in pure awe at the sound of the car starting on the first try. Not only did it start, but the engine seemed as strong as ever. Well, as strong as a one point five liter straight-four engine could be. Zuz smiled and buckled his seat. Mal hopped in, amazed.

"How is it that in all of this mess, all of this destruction, that your piece of crap Nissan is still running?" Mal asked, incredulously.

"I told you not to dis my ride, Mal…don't make me say it again."

"Fair enough," was Mal's response as the duo peeled out of Zuzelo's Junkyard and Recycling Center. Half a block later, Mal punched send on the tiny phone, sending what was left of Zuz's former life straight to hell.

Their car was out of sight as the sound of a quartet of military helicopters bearing the seal of Project: Hardwired filled the skies.

Dressed in his standard uniform of a black tank top and matching black fatigues, Designate Gauss had already shoved open the cabin door of the lead Sikorsky UH-60 Blackhawk helicopter and, without waiting for it to set down, leapt out at nearly fifty feet above the ground.

The Project: Hardwired Prime Unit cyborg super-soldier landed with such force his steel-reinforced boots splinted the concrete and asphalt just outside the location the eggheads up in tech had identified as belonging to the man who helped Designate Cestus escape from the downtown L.A. labs. Gauss was up and running a heartbeat after his feet hit Terra Firma.

"Base, can you connect me with anyone from Rho-Squad?" Gauss demanded into his radio headset. He could feel the frustration already building in his stomach. "This place is a mess and I'm getting no sign of their team."

"Negative on Rho-Unit, Designate Gauss," responded the nasally voice of the mission's comm-officer. "Rho-Unit had a jamming vehicle on site and communication was no-go during their op."

"Well, shit, Base, is there anything at all you can tell me or are you just sitting around with your head up your ass?" Gauss looked down on the normal humans he served with. After all, they were all safe-and-sound back at HQ, monitoring things remotely, while he and his men were out in the thick of things. "Where is Designate Talos?"

"Unknown," came the voice over the radio. "His vitals flatlined two minutes ago."

"What?" Gauss was more annoyed than surprised by the loss of a fellow Prime operative. "How the hell did a mechanimorph lose a fight in a junkyard? I always thought Talos was an asshole. Give me his last recorded location."

Gauss lifted up the polarized sunglasses he wore to better scan the area. Too much dust in the air had coated his favorite Oakleys and messed with the effectiveness of even his enhanced vision.

The flickering glow of flash buried deep within an ocean of smoke caught the cyborg's attention. Gauss saw the fiery remains of David Zuzelo's workshop garage building and knew his quest was over.

"Belay that," barked Gauss into his headset, "I think I found Designate Talos...or, whatever is left of him."

Extending his highly polished metallic chrome arms in front of his body, Gauss's body hummed as he activated the power of his cybernetic implants. The hum built to a moan, which built further to what felt like the bass-line at a rock concert, and finally cumulated into a reverberation more felt than heard. Gauss ripped his arms back apart at the apex of the effect, sending a cone of force out in front of him that hit the scrap like a tornado, clearing a path to the smoldering ruins fifteen feed wide by nearly sixty feet long.

"Secure the premises. Eyes open for Designate Cestus and the civilian, David Zuzelo. Consider them both armed and dangerous," ordered Gauss to the soldiers climbing out of the four choppers that had finally landed behind him. "Zeta-Unit, you're with me."

A moment later, Gauss and the ten GMRs of Zeta-Unit stood over the burning pit containing a hundred tons of collapsed building and, somewhere beneath it all, the blasted charcoal remains of Designate Talos.

"That's what they get for sending a midget to do a man's job."

Zeta-One stepped forward and spoke, "Area secured, Sir. No sign of Designate Cestus or the civilian."

A quick hand signal announced the team was finished and Gauss turned on his heel to march out of the smoke-filled remains of the building, with Zeta-Unit close behind.

"Have command get the boys from tech down here to clean-up this mess, and let them know Designate Cestus is still in the wind."

Gauss climbed back into his waiting helicopter and was in the air almost instantly. Staring down at the blistering mess below him, Gauss spat thickly into the heart of the steam and oily smoke, "Asshole."

CHAPTER 11

The rolling hills and highway billboards streaked by the boxy Nissan Cube so fast it seemed like Han had just told Chewie to jump to light speed. If he was forced to take a guess, Zuz would have said they were tearing down the freeway at a shade under a billion miles per hour. With one hand wrapped tightly around the vinyl 'oh shit' handle just over the passenger's side door and the other pressed firmly onto the dashboard, the decision to allow Mal to take the wheel was looking to be one of the worst so far.

And that included the one that led to having his junkyard blown up. Twice.

Teeth grinding together from an emotion that existed somewhere between abject horror and mind-numbing terror, Zuz decided conversation might be the best way to take his mind off his fear.

"I still can't believe. I'd have bet money I had hidden my tracks well enough over the years to avoid something like that. I'm surprised they were able to track me down so easy."

"You're surprised?" laughed Mal, jerking the steering so hard in order to avoid an old pickup loaded down with gardening supplies that two of the car's wheels left the hot afternoon asphalt. "I'm more surprised you had that place loaded with five hundred pounds of explosives, and why the hell would you have a bunch of Doctor Evil-style death traps?"

If Zuz's hands hadn't already been preoccupied with holding on for dear life, he would have 'Z' snapped at his friend and exclaimed "Oh, no you didn't!"

"I don't know, uh, to make sure a black ops team of assassins didn't waltz in and crush my nuts one day," Zuz let himself get worked up into a frenzy. "And besides, Mister Billion-Dollar Cyborg, I saved 'yo ass, didn't I?"

"Good point," conceded Mal. "Where did you get the idea? It's not like there is a "paranoid crackpot" home security catalog…is there?"

"A: I take offensive to that statement," replied Zuz, relaxing a bit finally. "B: I got the idea from that Will Smith movie."

"Hitch?"

"Hah!" Zuz shook his head. "No, the one with Gene Hackman. I can't remember the name"

Mal shrugged.

"C'mon, man. Tony Scott directed it," frustration began to bubble up in Zuz's chest. "Lisa Bonet…Jon Voight? Any of this ringing a bell?"

"Dude, I have no clue."

Zuz bit his lip, an idea popped into his head.

"Ask the computer," Zuz tapped a finger to the side of his head. "In there."

"You want me to use the military computer the government wet-wired into my brain to figure out the name of a Will Smith movie for you?" Mal gave his friend an incredulous look.

"It'll drive me crazy if you don't," pleaded Zuz, jutting his lip out in the worst pouty face Mal had seen in his life.

"Seriously?"

Zuz's head bounced up and down in enthusiastic affirmation.

"Fine. One second."

Mal split the lane between a pair of semis, nearly causing Zuz to void his bowels in shock.

"Computer," There was no need for Mal to speak out loud to his internal systems, but he knew making a big 'to do' out of it would help appease the man sitting across the car from him. "Will you please tell me the name of the motion picture which starred Will Smith and Gene Hackman?"

"Directed by Tony Scott," Zuz wagged his fingers to get Mal's attention.

Mal sighed. "And directed by Tony Scott."

Eyes lit up like a child on Christmas morning, Zuz was nearly bouncing in his seat.

"Enemy of..." started Mal, repeating the information supplied by his inner voice.

"Enemy of the State!" interrupted Zuz, his nodding growing to resemble an insane bobble-head doll. "Enemy of the State, that's it. You ever see that one?"

"No," responded Mal in the most serious tone he could muster, "I never could stomach action movies—too much excitement for me."

The pair stared at one another for a second before both erupted into uncontrollable laughter, which continued for nearly five miles and ended with Zuz wiping tears from the corners of his eyes.

They'd both been so wound up with everything that had happened that the emotion release was cathartic. Once it was done, though, neither man was sure what to say and silence filled the car as it continued down the 57 freeway.

With his home gone and the government now actively hunting for him in addition to the runaway cyborg, an uneasy realization crept over David Zuzelo.

"What are we going to do now, Mal," asked Zuz, fiddling mindlessly with the black automatic window buttons set low on the charcoal gray lining of his door.

Mal's face went serious, the familiar line burrowing its way back between his eyes in response to his brain kicking into high gear.

"I recognized one of the soldiers back there...one of the Gomers," said Mal, eyes still focused on the road ahead. "He was a sergeant. A member of my unit that went down in Iraq and I'd have sworn he was dead."

"Not to restate the obvious, but you were killed, too," quipped Zuz.

"I was able to access some of his files in my head, so I know what they did to him. I just can't figure out why...or who did it."

"Did you get anything from the sergeant before you, y'know, re-killed him?"

Mal laughed a cold, humorless laugh at his friend's comment.

"No. It seems like once they've been converted, whoever they were before is gone. They erased who he was somehow and replaced it with a living robot they control."

"So you've got no idea at all?"

"His file mentioned our old commanding officer, Lieutenant Colonel Michael Denman," Mal sped up, dodging around cars, forgetting the two were supposed to be keeping a low profile. "Maybe he can give us something. If we can find him. Do you think you can track him down in the data you pulled out of my head? Maybe he's in there somewhere that I don't have access to?"

Zuz unbuckled his seatbelt and flipped around in his chair to more easily rummage around in the back seat. After a quick search, Zuz swiveled back around clutching his laptop tightly in his arms.

"I don't know, Mal," Zuz stared intently at the computer's screen as it started up. "Until we crack the encryption, there's no way for me to figure out what I pulled down. Our best bet might be for me to hook back into that port at the base of your skull and see if I can access the info directly."

"Do it."

Zuz jumped a bit at Mal's response.

"What? Now?" choked Zuz at the thought. "While you're driving?"

"We'll be fine," retorted Mal. "I've got super reflexes, remember? I can handle anything."

Zuz was unconvinced. Wouldn't it be better if they just pulled over somewhere and tried? Somewhere they weren't doing nearly a hundred miles per hour?

The laptop was opened and wedged in the space between the top of the dashboard and the windshield of Zuz's side once he decided trying to convince Mal to stop the car somewhere was hopeless.

Zuz fished around in the backpacked resting in the floorboard between his legs for a couple of seconds before locating the object of his quest: a bright blue computer cable.

A red pocket knife appeared in Zuz's right hand and he set about to stripping the outer covering from the cable. When he was done, the knife disappeared back into his pocket and he reached over to yank out the car's cigarette lighter.

"Never thought I'd use this thing again once I quit smoking."

Mal's eyes went wide as he caught sight of what Zuz was doing in his peripheral vision. The man had inserted the stripped wires into the metal of the lighter's casing. It all looked terrible to the renegade cybernetic soldier.

"Wait...what are you going to do with that thing?"

Attaching one end of the cord to a side input of his laptop, Zuz turned to Mal and advised, "You're going to need to keep your head still for a minute while I get you hooked up. The connection isn't a standard one, so I had to improvise."

"I don't know that I want you sticking that nasty thing in my head, Zuz."

"Don't be a pussy, Mal. It's the only thing I have that will fit in your hole," said Zuz, placing his knees in the seat so he could swivel to face Mal and get better access to the opening in the back of his head.

"Do it fast," said Mal, giving in, his voice sounding uncomfortable. "And, swear you'll never say that to me again... ever."

In the heat of the exchange, neither of the men noticed a black Ford Crown Victoria Police Interceptor with the gold markings of the California Highway Patrol stamped on its white doors slide silently behind the battered Nissan.

Oblivious to what was coasting in their wake, Zuz leaned across the car's center console, wire in hand, and tried to set up the interface. Regrettably, the man slipped, slamming his friend's head down into the steering wheel. The impact caused Mal to swerve across the road, giving probable cause to the police car trailing them.

The bright lights, rotating red and blue, and the harsh blare of the police cruiser's siren startled both men, snapping them to attention.

"Civilian law enforcement vehicle approaching with a crew complement of two California Highway Patrol officers, standard armament," rang Mal's computerized conscience. "Evasive maneuvers recommended."

"You couldn't have spoken up BEFORE the cops snuck up on us, eh?" Mal lectured his internal system aloud, more for Zuz's benefit than anything else.

"Aw, hell, Mal. What are we going to do now? Out run 'em?"

"You want me to try and out run them? In this hunk of junk?" Mal gave his friend his best 'are you freakin' crazy' expression, more than a tad shocked by the suggestion. "I'm surprised it hasn't fallen apart yet."

The sirens pulsed shrilly once more, this time accompanied by one of the officer's calling out over their vehicle's loudspeaker, "Please pull your vehicle to the right, sir."

"What are we going to do?"

"The nice officer said to pull over," responded the cyborg. "We're going to pull over."

Mal's head did its best impression of an owl, turning right and left to check the surrounding traffic.

"You're not going to kill them are you, Mal?" asked Zuz, worried, the coloring draining from his face at the thought.

"Not if I can help it," was Mal's response as he reached up to pull down the Nissan's turn signal level and proceed to maneuver the car through the other automobiles to a clear stretch of roadside.

Threadbare tires nearly vibrating off their wheels as they rolled over the rumble strip and bounced to a stop on the freeway's shoulder was more than enough to kick Zuz's agitation level up to the boiling point.

"He's going to ask for your license—you don't have a license or any type of ID at all," Zuz was rubbing his head so fast Mal was convinced the man was going to start a fire. "What are you going to do when he asks for one? Are you going to stab him in the thorax?"

Chuckling at the idea, which his internal computer seemed to be in complete agreement with, Mal shook his head and put his hand on his nervous friend's shoulder, "I'm not stabbing anyone in the thorax, David. We'll just see what they want."

By the time the cop car had pulled to a complete stop behind them and the driver had climbed out of it, Zuz was nearly ricocheting around the inside of the Nissan.

The fidgeting stopped when the officer rapped on the driver's side window with the back of his leather-gloved hand, indicating Mal should roll it down.

Keeping his eyes locked on the view straight ahead of him, Zuz leaned over and whispered to Mal out of the side of his mouth, "Don't worry—I've got a plan."

The statement caused Mal more concern than the police officer did. Mal quickly lowered the glass and looked at the uniformed cop standing less than six inches away. He did his best to block out his computer's recommendation to drive one of his living metal talons through the door and disembowel the potential threat.

"Hi, Officer..." Mal read the name embossed on the man's badge, "...Tillman. I know I was going a little fast.

Officer Tillman's blond right eyebrow shot up while his left moved down.

"A 'little fast?' Sir, you were doing almost a hundred and swerving all over the road," interrupted the tall highway patrolman, sliding a clipboard that had been trapped in the crook of his armpit. The man's uniform was pressed to perfection and not a spot of lint could be found anywhere on it. His boots were spit polished and the sun glinted off his polarized Ray-Ban shades. Mal noted that even the hair on top of the public servant's head was perfectly set, giving off the impression of a Ken-doll.

Flipping up the clipboard's protector to ready a new traffic ticket, Officer Tillman finished in a clipped, precisely metered tone, "License and registration, sir."

Mal reached up and removed the automobile's registration from its hiding spot behind the sun visor folded over his head, using his right arm in hopes the officer wouldn't notice the unusual bumps and lines of its living metal armor. The last thing they needed was Officer Tillman getting jumpy and shooting into the car from his elevated position. Sure, Mal could probably survive a couple of bullets, what with his new healing factor, but the same couldn't be said for his completely human friend.

Before Mal could hand over the paperwork, Zuz leaned over

almost into his lap and spoke in a voice that had skittished itself up almost an entire octave.

"Officer, this is all my fault," announced Zuz, winking to Mal in an attempt at reassurance that failed miserably.

"Excuse me?" Officer Tillman warily leaned his face down into the window to identify who was speaking to him, resting his arm on the roof of the vehicle.

"Yeah, I was dropping 'Jager Bombs' with homies this morning," slurred Zuz in a painfully exaggerated fashion. Both the cop outside and Mal sitting next to him grimaced a little at his choice of words. Zuz was way too Caucasian to be using the word 'homies' comfortably in casual conversation. "And I got the munchies, dude…Officer Dude. Mal here volunteered to give me a ride."

The cyborg glared angrily back at Zuz as the man smacked him in the chest to accentuate the point. He decided to let it slide this time, on account of getting his friend's home blown up and all.

Officer Tillman slid back the sleeve of his left arm and glanced down at the face of his bright silver diver's watch. The dial read 11:16 A.M.

"It's only eleven in the morning, sir. Isn't it a bit early to be drinking?"

The cop stepped back and ran his gaze along the outside of Zuz's car, tilting his polarized Ray-Ban sunglasses down to the tip of his nose so he could take in all of the damage done to the car in the past twenty-four hours.

"Are those bullet holes?"

"I live in a pretty rough neighborhood, Officer," called Zuz back through the open driver's side window.

A flick of the wrist and Officer Tillman snatched the registration document out of Mal's hand.

"I'll be right back, gentlemen," said Tillman as he turned and headed back towards his fellow officer waiting parked half a car length behind them. "Wait here and please stay in your vehicle."

Mal's mouth formed a veritable smorgasbord of silent expletives directed at Zuz, who seemed far more pleased with his performance than he should have been. Once the cop was safely out of earshot, Mal launched into the tirade he had been holding back.

"That was your plan? 'Oh, hey, officer dude, I was drunk.' What goes on in your head that thinks 'drunk' is a good plan?" ranted Mal, annoyed and baffled at his friend's line of thought.

"It was better than stabbing him in the thorax," muttered Zuz, mostly to himself.

"Say 'thorax' once more and I'm going to stab you in yours. Be quiet for a second, they're calling us in now," Mal reached up to adjust the rear view mirror so he could watch Officer Tillman hand over their registration to his partner to radio back to their dispatcher. "If we're lucky, the Project: Hardwired guys don't want to involve the local sheriff's office and we'll just get a citation."

"Yeah, we've been real lucky so far, Mal."

"Damn it," swore Mal, his heightened senses allowing him to detect a spike in the second officer's heart rate from inside the police cruiser. A quick glance in the rear view mirror revealed Officer Tillman approaching the Nissan, unholstering his Smith & Wesson M&P40 pistol and sliding its safety into the 'off' position.

"What is it," started Zuz before Mal pushed his head down below the car's window line, causing him to yelp in a rather effeminate manner.

"They're on to us. Officer Tillman is on his way back with his gun out and his partner is radioing in for back-up," said Mal, unbuckling his seat belt. "Stay down until this is over."

Seeing the panic on his friend's face as he jerked the car door open and slid out, Mal joked, "And don't worry, this one's only got a little gun."

"Get down on the ground!" The barrel of Tillman's pistol jerked up to point at Mal.

Raising his hands in as non-threatening a manner as he could manage, Mal slammed the car's door with his hip and moved slowly toward the advancing officer.

"There's been a misunderstanding, Officer Tillman," said Mal in a calm voice, continuing to move forward.

"I repeat, get down on the ground or I'll be forced to shoot you!" ordered the cop, taking careful aim at Mal's bare chest, confident there was no way he'd miss at the ten foot gap between them.

Mal's body blocked the late morning sun for a moment, giving the patrolman a good look at his cybernetic limbs.

"Your arms," stuttered Tillman. "What's wrong with your arms? Stay where you are or I'll shoot!"

"I don't have time for this," growled the super-soldier, sending the living metal of his arms the command to enter melee combat mode and bulk up to nearly twice the size of their relaxed state.

Mal charged the cop, sending a spray of rocks and dirt splattering against the white paint of the parked Nissan.

To his credit, Officer Tillman was able to discharge his weapon twice before Malcolm Weir was on him, the first of which went wide and shattered the driver's side window of the Cube. The second pinged harmlessly off of the titanium alloy of Mal's shoulder and spiraled off into the thick brush lining the freeway's edge.

Tillman's finger was starting to squeeze off a third shot as Mal reached him and a nanotech powered bionic backhand smashed into his jaw, shattering it and rendering the man mercifully unconscious.

Mal caught the fallen cop's crumpled form and dropped him safely to the ground a few feet from the solid yellow line marking off the beginning of the freeway's slow lane.

It wouldn't do to have the unfortunate public servant become the victim of vehicular manslaughter after Mal had worked so hard to not kill him.

"Ten double zero!" a voice from nearby grabbed Mal's attention even as the computerized hitchhiker in his head reminded him the patrolman's partner still needed to be dealt with.

The remaining officer was almost halfway out of the patrol car, screaming into his radio, by the time Mal turned his attention to the man.

"Officer! Officer down! Send back-up!"

Mal braced himself with a hand on the car's roof and used the car's trashed rear end to springboard himself across the fifteen foot gap to Tillman's vehicle, drive his unyielding fist through its windshield, and clip the surprised cop in the side of his head, rendering him unconscious.

Mal stood still for a moment, staring at his fist as it came free of the hole he'd punched in the windshield, amazed at what had just happened. In less than five seconds he'd taken down two armed members of the highway patrol without breaking a sweat.

Emotion overwhelmed him for a moment and his still-human knees nearly gave out as he realized he'd never get his old life back.

In the blink of an eye, his fear and despair turned to rage, and something inside of Mal snapped. A primal scream exploded from the cybernetic warrior. Before the scream ended, Mal slammed his fist into the patrol vehicle's hood. The force of the strike punched through the cover and split the engine block nearly in half, sending steam and shattered metal shards flying.

A grim mask covered Mal's face as he turned back to Zuz waiting for him in the Nissan. Mal wondered if there was anything at all left of Malcolm Weir or if only Designate Cestus remained?

Reaching his getaway vehicle, Mal tossed open the passenger's door and ordered Zuz to drive. The determination setting the cyborg's jaw was more than enough to keep Zuz from arguing.

"Always let the wookie win," Zuz thought to himself as he jammed his foot down onto the accelerator and the car peeled out into traffic.

"Here," said Zuz, holding up a scrap of paper with a telephone number scrawled on it.

"What's this," asked Mal, taking the paper in his hand.

"I found Lieutenant Colonel Michael Denman while you were playing with the 'Ponch' and 'John' back there."

Mal's eyes lit up at the news.

"Yeah? Where?"

"He's right here in Southern California, stationed at Fort

Irwin out in San Bernardino County," said Zuz. "We can be there in an hour."

"Fort Irwin? What's the old man doing out here?"

"I don't know, but that's his number," Zuz zigged in and out of traffic as he spoke. "Should we give him a call and find out?"

"No," said Mal grimly. "I don't want any surprises waiting for us when we get there."

CHAPTER 12

A quartet of boxy black Cadillac Escalades, detailed to a gleaming finish an hour earlier and massive V8 engines idling quietly in unison, sat waiting outside the entrance to the US Bank Tower. The four sunglassed drivers, each nearly as bulky and massive as the vehicles they were operating and dressed in matching black suits blatantly announcing them as covert government operatives, seemed completely oblivious to both the red-painted 'no parking zones' they were parked next to and the miles of bright yellow 'crime scene' tape covering the area.

The normally crowded downtown Los Angeles sidewalk in front of the active business center had been a virtual ghost town since the automobiles had arrived ten minutes earlier. As if warned off by the collective unconscious or by ten thousand years of dealing with self-important government thugs, the foot traffic normally ever present along the northeast side of West Fifth Street had moved across the road.

Behind the dark polarized lenses of their glasses, the eyes of all four men darted back and forth, tracking and taking note of every person or vehicle moving past their location. Each man kept one hand up to the radio wires trailing down from their left ears and the other hand clamped tightly around the MP5s slung over his shoulder.

"Veeps in motion, people," barked the driver standing near the third armor-plated SUV in line, signaling his fellows through his headset.

Driver three moved away from his still running luxury sports utility vehicle, striding across the glass covered, bloodstained courtyard Cestus had fallen into less than twenty-four hours earlier, only to halt halfway between the street and the grand entrance to the US Bank Tower. After a quick visual sweep of the immediate vicinity convinced him the single janitor in charge of clean-up was non-hostile, the security guard signaled to the building with a wave of his hand.

The malfunction of Designate Cestus and explosion at Project: Hardwired's hub had put everyone from the highest echelons of command to the lowest interns on edge. Because the boys in tech still had no idea what exactly went wrong or who was behind the disaster, the powers-that-be had declared the protection of Director Kiesling to be the top priority.

The security detail accompanying Kiesling as he exited the fractured high-impact glass of the cavernous lobby surrounded both him and Ms. Roslan in a wall of flesh and bone and high-caliber weapons. Almost twenty men escorted the pair to the cars waiting to spirit them away to a meeting with the US Secretary of Defense.

Sliding into the rear of the Escalade along its polished leather seats, Gordon Kiesling had to admit that, in spite of the trouble it was causing, he did enjoy the increased security and attention the escape of Designate Cestus had caused. The extra guards, bulletproof cars and openly displayed automatic weaponry made him feel incredibly presidential.

It was a feeling Kiesling very much wanted to experience for real in the future.

Ms. Roslan interrupted Kiesling's White House daydreams as she eased into the SUV next to him, smoothing down the deep blue material of her short skirt to keep it from revealing too many of her executive assets.

Noting the way her perfectly sculpted eyebrows stitched a harsh line just above her nose, Kiesling asked, "You look unusually flustered today, Ms. Roslan. Who pissed in your porridge?"

Director Kiesling's right-hand woman stared sharply at the driver, waiting until he had closed the large, faux wood-paneled door and hopped into the front seat out of ear shot.

Once the convoy was in motion, Ms. Roslan finally answered.

"It's Congressman Fountain, sir."

"Fountain?" Kiesling was surprised. "I thought we had our favorite politician on lockdown at one of the off-site suites. How much trouble can he cause us without outside contact?"

"We've got his cell blocked and no landline or Internet access going in to his rooms. He should be completely cutoff." Ms. Roslan's voice trailed off as her face became a mask of frustration.

"Should be...but isn't?" finished her superior.

"I've been fielding calls about the Congressman all morning. Somehow he's spent the last twelve hours doing his best to throw as many monkey wrenches as he can at us. We just can't figure out how. If we're not careful, he's going to get us shut down."

"Don't be foolish, my dear," scoffed Kiesling, dismissing the idea with a wave of his tanned hand. "If he gets in our way, we'll get rid of him just like the others."

"I'm afraid we may find Congressman Fountain to be quite a bit more trouble than the last two government liaisons, Director," countered Roslan in the closest impression of a grumble Kiesling had ever heard cross her lips. "He has some pretty heavy-duty connections on Capitol Hill."

Kiesling laughed loudly at the idea but found his own retort cut off by a call coming through to Ms. Roslan's phone. She smiled apologetically and stuck her index finger into the air in the universal sign for 'one moment' as she answered.

"Yes?" Roslan said into the tiny phone that was a weapon as fearsome as the semi-automatic pistol she kept concealed on her lithe form at all times.

Kiesling could hear the raspy, weak-chinned voice of one of Project: Hardwired's technicians filter out from the phone, but couldn't tell which. Not that it made much of a different to the Director. One nerd was much the same as any other.

Leaning back, Kiesling half-tuned out his assistant's one-sided conversation as the parade of vehicles turned off of West Fifth onto the Harbor Freeway on-ramp. They accelerated to seventy miles-per-hour and were well on their way to their meeting location when Roslan called for his attention.

"Mr. Anderson says they've got a hit on Zuzelo's car," she said, muting her phone for privacy. "A California Highway Patrol unit in Orange County called in a traffic violation attached to the vehicle's registered license plate. CHP dispatch lost contact with the officers involved."

"Two lone cops against one of our Prime Units? They didn't stand a snowball's chance in hell," said Kiesling, punctuating the statement with a derisive snort. "I can't imagine Cestus leaving the officers in any sort of an identifiable state."

"The two officers are in critical but stable condition. Local law-enforcement has APBs out for the car and occupants," Roslan continued her recap of the information she'd been passed by Anderson. "Do we let them run our fugitives down for us or pull them off the trail?"

Kiesling blew out a long, hard breath. He liked the idea of someone else's budget taking the beating of trying to take down the rogue operative. On the flip side, he hated the thought of word getting out that he'd lost control of the situation. He saw no way to avoid the heat he'd get for having the locals back-off, but there was no way around it.

"This situation has gotten far enough out of hand without bringing in the state police. Get me the CHP commissioner on the line."

"What about Designate Cestus? All indications show he and Zuzelo are heading out towards San Bernardino County," Roslan asked.

"Why there? Another hideout of this David Zuzelo like the junkyard?"

Ms. Roslan braced her phone between her shoulder and the crook of her neck, keeping Mr. Anderson on mute, and pulled a tablet PC out of the dark brown leather satchel at her side.

"Best guess is that he's going to see this man," she showed the Project: Hardwired Director a montage of images containing Malcolm Weir and an older gentleman in the uniform of a United States Army officer. "Lieutenant Colonel Michael Denman, former commanding officer of Malcolm Weir's Ranger unit in Iraq."

Rubbing his chin, Gordon Kiesling tried to put it all together in his head before issuing his next round of orders. What did Weir's old CO have to do with this—who else was involved? Nothing was adding up.

"Send a unit to follow them," responded Kiesling. "I want to know exactly what Designate Cestus and this Zuzelo fellow are up to. Who they're talking to. We need to find out who broke Mister Weir's programming and how they did it."

Ms. Roslan nodded and quickly relayed her boss's orders to the man on the other side of the cellular connection.

Pausing to listen to a question, she looked up and asked, "Do you want Designate Gauss in pursuit?"

Kiesling's handsome face scrunched up in thought as he considered the question. The director's face answered her with a frown.

"No," responded the overseer of Project: Hardwired, shaking his head. "Gauss had his chance to bring Weir down. Twice. He's on the bench for now."

Well-manicured hands reached out and snatched away the tablet computer Ms. Roslan had resting on her lap. The pair sat in silence as Kiesling moved slowly through a mountain of computer data, hunting. He smiled as he found the subject of his search.

"We should give someone else a chance, especially now that Designate Talos is gone," he said as he held the thin silver and white computer screen up for his assistant to see.

Kiesling enjoyed the look of surprise on Ms. Roslan's face.

"Him? Are you sure?" asked the beautiful woman. "His last mission was...messy."

"I've been trying to keep things clean up until now," said Kiesling, icy blue eyes growing dark. "But I think it's time to get a bit messy."

Roslan nodded and moved her tiny smartphone back up to her mouth.

"Mr. Anderson," she said, "Have the May brothers reactivate Designate Pyroclast. We've got a job that requires his...unique set of talents."

CHAPTER 13

The single piece of wisdom David Zuzelo would always remember from his time on the run with Malcolm Weir was this: arriving at an active military facility in a bullet-ridden vehicle, wearing burned and battered clothing and asking to see the man in charge of the base will only result in having a large number of fully automatic weapons pointed out you.

That was precisely what occurred when Zuz and Mal rolled up to the front gates of Fort Irwin and announced their desire to meet with Lieutenant Colonel Michael Denman. The sentries, dressed in standard-issue gray and black urban pattern ACUPAT uniforms, took one look at the pair, pointed their M16A4 riles menacingly at the men and promptly called for back-up. Which, according the Mal's internal computer system, resulted in a grand total of sixteen guns being aimed at them.

Zuz was pretty sure the computer had miscalculated the number of arms with a bead on them. By his own count, there were closer to a billion guns about to shoot them.

Give or take, that is.

"Please exit your vehicle and keep your hands above your heads," shouted one of the soldiers. "Move it!"

"I'm starting to sense a pattern here, Mal," Zuz said flatly as he started to open his door as slowly and non-threateningly as possible. "I feel like people have been pointing guns at me all day."

"Same here—and it's beginning to piss me off," growled Mal, the plates and cables of his living metal arms bulking up substantially in reaction to the potential threat posed by the cadre of soldiers focused on them.

Seeing his friend's nanotech transforming into a more aggressive attack profile, Zuz began to hyperventilate.

"Mal," he wheezed, "I don't want to get shot—don't get me shot, Mal."

The only response Zuzelo received was a not entirely reassuring half-smile from his friend as the cyborg exited the car, palms held high and facing out to show he was unarmed. The staccato drumbeat of nearly every gun snapping focus onto Mal echoed across the open grounds surrounding the public entrance to Fort Irwin and the National Training Center, causing Zuz to unconsciously smile. At least they were no longer pointing in his direction, thought the terrified man.

Paying no heed to the potential storm of small caliber fire from the near dozen-and-a-half MPs training their ordnance in his direction, Mal targeted the soldier nearest to him and marched forward slowly towards the man.

"Sir, stand down or we will be forced to open fire on you," ordered the solider, a pretty-faced private with the name ADORNO emblazoned over the left pocket of his uniform.

Mal stopped less than six feet away from the private and caught the young man with his eyes.

"My name is Captain Malcolm Weir, Third Battalion, Seventy-Fifth Ranger Regiment, Private Adorno," Mal said, shooting a withering stare down the barrel of the machine gun pointed at him by the youth. "I'm a grunt, just like you."

Adorno licked his lips, caught as he was in Mal's gaze and unable to look away. Sweat ran down the back of his neck and for one brief moment Zuz was afraid the beleaguered youth was going to start shooting.

"What can I do for you, Captain Weir," said Adorno, finally lowering his weapon and signaling for his comrades-in-arms to do the same. Zuz could feel the tension drain away from everyone in the area as guns were slung, pistols were holstered and the soldiers returned to their stations.

"Thank you, Private Adorno," smiled Mal, warmly. "If you'd be so kind as to get Colonel Denman on the horn for me. Let him know Malcolm Weir is here for the poker game. He's expecting us."

"Yes, sir," answered the youth, visibly relaxed.

Mal watched the private disappear back into the small guard booth positioned to the left of the hydraulic gate arm barrier Zuz's car had stopped in front of. The cyborg's enhanced senses picked up Adorno calling Denman's office on the hard wired land line phone mounted in the tiny shack. The man quickly repeated Mal's request to see the Colonel.

A moment later, Adorno had hung up the phone, raised the yellow and black barrier, and pointed Zuz towards the large, five-story building housing the offices for Lieutenant Colonel Denman.

"See?" chirped Mal as the Nissan puttered and spat its way through the gate and down the road surrounded by mothballed military vehicles to their destination. "No one got shot. You're fine."

"You may be fine, but I need a new pair of underwear," responded Zuz, easing his car into a visitor's spot and sliding the gear shift into 'park.'

Waiting for them just outside the entrance to the National Training Center's main administration building was Denman's assistant, Corporal MacAnders, a short but stocky man whose height pushed five feet six only with a lot of imagination, and close-cropped hair so red in color it made his scalp look sunburned. The most interesting thing about the man was the beat-up dark hard leather holster and antique six-shooter strapped to his right hip and looking rather out of place on a twenty-first century soldier.

"Is that an M1917?" Zuz asked the man, nearly hopping in excitement. Mal was completely confused by the change in his friend's demeanor. As far as he knew, Zuz wasn't a big fan of firearms. "It looks like an early Colt model."

"Good eye, Mr. Zuzelo," smiled the man as he took them through the double glass doors that lead to the administration building's air-conditioned interior. "It was my great-grandfather's sidearm in the First World War, and my grandfather's in the Second and Korea."

A ridiculous smile split Zuz's face, and he pointed at MacAnders' holster as the trio mounted a large flight of stairs leading from the lobby to the offices on the second floor, further confounding Mal.

Comprehension finally slammed into Mal's brain when Zuz mouthed the words 'Indiana Jones' while pointing at the sidearm. They were escorted down a tiled hallway and passed a row of office doors by the Corporal before finally stopping in front of a heavy wooden door flanked on one side by an American flag and wall of pictures, and by a tidy steel desk on the other.

Gesturing for the visitors to wait, Corporal MacAnders leaned over his desk and pressed a button on his phone, activating its intercom.

Waiting for the beep, MacAnders spoke clearly into the machine, "Colonel Denman, sir?"

"Yes, Tommy," came the slightly static-y voice of an older man over the intercom's tiny speakers.

"Captain Malcolm Weir and Mr. David Zuzelo have arrived."

Half a tick later the door swung in and powerfully-built man in his mid-fifties, dressed in the same digital-camo patterned uniform that seemed to be standard attire at Fort Irwin, stomped out of the office, a look of disbelief shone out of the two granite-gray eyes set deep in his face.

The man, whose height topped out a good inch or two above Mal's own, stared down at the cyborg, thick black brows bunching into a single, furry caterpillar above eyes, for a full thirty seconds before the salt-and-pepper whiskers of his mustache parted to reveal the yellowed teeth of a lifelong coffee addict in an expression Zuz could only assume was a smile.

"Hol-ee shit!" bellowed Colonel Denman, clapping Mal roughly across the shoulders. "If it ain't my favorite ground pounder!"

"It's good to see a friendly face, Colonel," Mal grinned, shaking the man's hand. "Even one as ugly as yours."

"Time was, a soldier could be court-martialed for saying that."

"I'm not a soldier anymore, Colonel," countered Mal, deadly serious. "Tell the truth, I'm not sure what I am anymore."

Denman nodded grimly, understanding that something had happened to his former soldier.

Casting an askew glance towards the Zuz, who was busy trying to look as inconspicuous as possible, Denman quizzed, "So, who's your girlfriend?"

To Zuz's annoyance, Mal chuckled, his mood lightening up at the good-natured ribbing from his once-commander.

"I'd like you to meet David Zuzelo, my best friend—only friend in the world right now."

"Nice to meet you, Mr. Zuzelo," Denman reached out with one of his giant, calloused hands and gripped Zuz's tight.

"You too, Colonel Denman," responded Zuz, politely trying to extricate his fingers before the big man crushed them.

Corporal MacAnders pretended to sort papers as he watched the exchange from the vantage point behind his desk.

"What brings you back to my corner of the world, son?" asked Denman.

"I need to know what happened in Dahuk, Colonel," answered Mal. "What happened to me—to my men."

The Colonel's face darkened at Mal's request.

"Let's go inside my office and talk, Captain" said Denman, cutting off Mal's line of thought and pushing the two visitors through the door. Denman called back to Corporal MacAnders that they were not to be disturbed and Mal thought he caught a flash of paranoia in his former CO's face as he allowed himself to be led into the office.

The door slammed hard behind the group and the Colonel loomed over them, eyes blazing in barely restrained fury.

"You've got ten seconds to prove to me that you're Captain Malcolm Weir before I have you arrested," growled Denman, hand tightening around the textured grip of the Glock-22 holstered at his waist. "If I don't shoot you myself first."

Both Mal and Zuz were stunned by Denman's sudden reversal in attitude.

"I don't understand, Colonel."

"Son, I was sure as Christ you were dead," the Lieutenant Colonel responded, pure amazement coloring his tone. "How in God's name are you up walking around—even a year later? It's impossible. No one comes back from what you went through. Not as a whole man."

"No one said I came back whole, sir."

Mal slowly removed the jacket he'd been wearing and showed his former commanding officer the full price of his miraculous recovery.

"Dear God," was all Denman could say as he took in the sight of Mal's nanotech arms, watching as they changed shape, grew spikes and turned into living weapons. "What did they do to you, Weir?"

Allowing his arms to return to vaguely human shape and size, Mal responded, "That's what I was hoping you could tell me, Colonel. I woke up yesterday in a secret government lab with a hole in my memory. Tell me what happened in Dahuk."

"How much do you remember?"

Mal laughed, "I'm CRS, sir. Can't remember shit after our chopper was hit."

Denman told the men to take the two padded wooded chairs facing his desk and the large bank of windows behind it. The old soldier sat on the sole clean spot on the ancient oak desktop, rubbing his chin slowly, eyes narrowly slits as he decided where best to start his tale.

Grunting, the Colonel looked up into Mal's face as the words began spilling from between his lips.

"Our regiment had been stationed at FOB Sykes for less than a week when rumors of unrest in the outskirts of Dahuk came over the horn. I ordered your unit out to scout the area and get back with a sit-rep. A trio of black hawks carrying your men lifted off at nineteen-hundred hours on April 3rd of last year.

"Your birds must have been coming in too low to the ground when they were hit by enemy-fired rocket-propelled grenades and crashed just inside the Dahuk city limits, well outside our area of control. Most of your men were killed on impact. As far as the boys in intel could determine, only yourself and the two sergeants—Douros and Jay—walked away from the crash.

"We were able to set up a CASEVAC point at an abandoned hotel about a mile from where you went down, but communications broke down and we lost track of you boys. I can only guess that you were ambushed on your way to the dust-off location.

"Regardless of whatever happened after the crash, by the time the black hawks arrived to pull you boys out, the extraction point was a hot mess. All three of you were torn to shit. Word was Sergeant Douros was already down with a bullet through his ACH. Staff Sergeant Jay was wounded, spitting blood and barely able to stand.

"From what the medics told me, you should have been dead, Weir. You'd already lost an arm, and your torso was shredded—one lung was collapse and most of your spleen and one kidney were blown to hell. You'd taken an insane amount of shrapnel to your chest, neck and face from an IED.

"The evac team said it was a free-fire zone when they arrived and that you were still kicking, surrounded by dead hostiles. You'd propped yourself up in front of your men, with your M16 set to rock-and-roll, still trying to fight when they pulled your team out.

"Once the docs had you and your men stabilized, you were all packed up on a C-17, pretty as you please, flown to Edwards Air Force Base and taken to the hospital there.

"They did their best to patch you up, but you were messed up—worse than dead, really. Paralyzed and stuck in bed, eating through tubes and kept going on life support—conscious, but that was it."

"What about the other two men from my unit—Douros and Jay?" asked Mal after digesting the information he'd been given.

Colonel Denman exhaled a slow, deep breath of sadness and responded.

"Sergeant Steven Douros was a vegetable. Unresponsive, no brain activity," Denman dropped his eyes as his continued, voice cracking. "Staff Sergeant James Jay died on the table in surgery a day or two after you were brought stateside."

Reaching down onto his desk, Denman picked up a pale folder filled to the bursting point and bound with a red rubber band. Tossing the documents to Mal, he added, "It's all here in the reports."

Mal passed the thickly packed folder to Zuz without looking at it and nodded for Denman to continue.

"One day, about two weeks after you boys got back in the

world, I had a had a couple of the boys fly me out to the air base—told 'em it was a training mission.

"That's where it all got weird.

"You see, when we got to the hospital, you were gone. All three of you. And the medical staff couldn't tell me how, where or why. Just that you'd been removed on orders from somewhere up the food chain. Somewhere over their pay grade.

"Official word was handed down to me when we got back to base. You were all classified 'removed for medical reasons' and being pulled from the Rangers...all three of you. Including Staff Sergeant Jay. And that's the bit that struck me all sorts of queer. I had always thought dead was dead and there was no reason to set up an RFM for a dead man."

Denman slammed his fist down, still upset by what happened and his inability to find out why.

"Any idea what they did with me? Where they took me?" Mal asked, his own frustration echoing Denman's.

"No idea at all, son. All I could figure out was that you were gone and it was on the order of some asshole from Washington named Kiesling.

"When I tried to investigate I was shut down—with extreme prejudice.

"Hell, that's how I got stuck out here," snorted the Colonel. "Supervising training and as far out of the way as possible. Someone wanted to make sure no one was looking too closely at your case. After banging my head against a wall of red tape, I had to give up and leave it alone. I was told it was that or my career."

"Hey, Colonel," interrupted Zuz. "This report mentions a fourth man wounded in the operation and classified as RFM along with the others. It says he disappeared from the hospital at about the same time as Mal and the two men from his unit."

Denman thought for a moment before his face lit up in remembrance.

"Yeah," the old soldier said, sitting back down at the chair behind his desk. "He was a member of the evac team sent in to pull Mal's unit out of the hot zone. The man was wounded during the escape. Near as I could find, he died...the same as you, Mal."

"Do you remember the man's name," asked Zuz, flipping through the thick manila records folder, searching for more information.

Zuz held up a familiar photo for Mal to see as Denman finally answered.

"Captain Marc Morrell."

"Captain Morrell isn't any more dead than I am, Colonel," spat Mal through his teeth. "Morrell is still alive."

"What?"

"He's alive, got a house out in the burbs, a two-car garage," confusion and anger fought for dominance in Mal's head. "The best part is: he's married to my ex-fiancée."

"When you get yourself into shit, you make sure it's deep, don't you, Captain?"

"I'm in it over my head this time, sir."

"You need to get your girl out of there. Get her somewhere safe and hunker down for a bit. We'll see if we can figure it out together, son," Denman reached down and punched his thick finger hard into the white intercom button on his phone. "Get your ass in here, Corporal, we've got trouble."

"This means a lot, Colonel Denman," stammered Mal, grateful. "I didn't know who to trust."

Mal lost the Colonel's response as his internal computer screamed out in alarm, alerting the super-soldier of an impending attack.

Before the cyborg could react to the warning, the soft pop of a bullet punching a hole through glass filled his ears, and he watched as Colonel Denman's head exploded into a fine red mist.

CHAPTER 14

Gore covered nearly every inch of space in front of Colonel Denman's desk, sent there by a high caliber sniper's bullet blasting its way through the soldier's head. Realizing what happened, a shriek tore itself from Zuz's throat as he looked down to find himself covered in blood and brains and tiny fragments of skull.

Mal held up his metal hands, now coated crimson in the cooling plasma of his friend. The cyborg's computerized brain continued its alarm, notifying Mal a split second before Denman's assistant burst through the door.

Taking in the sight before him, Corporal MacAnders saw the headless corpse of his boss and snapped, assuming the two unexpected visitors were Colonel Denman's killers, caught in the act.

Snatching up a radio from one side of his belt and the Colt M1917 six-shooter with the other, MacAnders screamed, "The Colonel's been murdered!"

Mal's superhuman reflexes flipped him over the back of his chair, allowing him to dodge the first shot squeezed off by the frantic Corporal. His body landed low in a fighting stance, his arms elongating into knives even as they bulked up in size.

Bracing himself to leap across the room and disarm the little ginger-haired member of the United States Army, Mal is brought up short by Zuz beating him to the punch, literally, with a haymaker to the man's jaw.

"Nice punch, Z," said Mal, impressed with his friend's out of character display of force.

"I think I broke my hand, Mal."

"We've got to get out of here," said Mal, urging Zuz to head for the still open office door. "Someone's set us up."

Staring down at the unconscious form of Corporal MacAnders, Zuz ignored Mal's urging and bent down to pick up the man's discarded pistol.

"Now this is what I'm talkin' about," said Zuz through a cartoonish smirk, performing a ridiculous 'action hero' pose with the weapon.

Mal shook his head and pushed his friend towards the exit. "Keep moving, Doctor Jones."

The pair made it less than two feet before all hell broke loose behind them. A chopper, cheerfully identified as a Boeing AH-64D Apache attack helicopter, dropped down suddenly from the sky overhead to the wide space between the training facility's buildings, and filled the wall of windows behind them.

The cyborg didn't need his computer to tell him the two pilots pointing at him from the vehicle's cockpit were there for less than friendly reasons.

"Get down!" barked Mal, tackling his friend, shielding Zuz's body from the torrent of high explosive rounds spitting out at a rate of 625 rounds per minute from the M230E1 chain gun mounted on the undercarriage of the Apache.

A hail of 30mm gun fire blasted into the room for a full thirty seconds, punching holes through walls, blowing apart furniture, sending papers, foot-long splinters of wood and shattered glass into the air, which quickly grew thick and unbreathable with dust and debris.

"Aw, hell," came Zuz's voice from beneath his half-human guardian. "I think you bruised my spleen."

Yanking his friend up forcibly by the arm, Mal ushered him toward the exit. He knew the Apache's chain gun would need to cycle down, and they'd have about two minutes before it could fire again.

"This thing felt a lot more impressive before they start shooting at us with the canon," said Zuz, tossing the century-old revolver across the room and stumbling along on unsteady feet.

Mal swore as he sensed the helicopter releasing its payload

of two AGM-114 Hellfire missiles, enhanced ears registering the sound of their solid-fuel rockets igniting and propelling the deadly air-to-surface projectiles rushing forward, guidance systems locking on with deadly accuracy.

With less than a heartbeat to react, Mal reached out, grabbing Zuz and the unconscious MacAnders around their waists and tossed the men from the room to the safety of the hall.

"This is going to hurt," was the cyborg's final thought before the twin missiles slammed into the side of the building in excess of nine-hundred miles per hour, exploding in a brilliant white flash, vaporizing everything in the room and a good chuck of the floor above it.

For the first time since he woke up on the cold steel operating table the day before, Mal was glad for the enhanced range of senses he'd been given. Although his eyes were completely blind and his ears were deaf from the burst, the computer center of Mal's cyborg brain still allowed him a certain amount of awareness of the surrounding room. He could still 'see' through pressure and heat variations felt in the nanotech 'skin' of his living metal arms, which allowed him to take advantage of the cover of smoke packing the room from blazing floor to shattered ceiling.

A status report sounded off in his head even as he made his way to where he had hurled Zuz and the unconscious soldier to safety. The computer was reporting just under 7% of his body had suffered 3rd degree burns and that self-repair had already begun. The idea that microscopic machines were coursing through his veins was still mildly disturbing to the former Army Ranger, but he was quickly adjusting to it.

"At least I'll never have to worry about wearing sunscreen ever again," he thought, jerking the scorched office door open and allowing a flood of smoke to billow out into the hallway beyond.

Mal's eyes were returning to normal as he located his friend kneeling on the ground. A half-hearted attempt at a smile looked back at the cyborg, reassuring Mal that Zuz had escaped from the blast with little more than a couple of bruises.

"Get out of the building any way you can, Z. They're after

me and should leave you alone," ordered Mal, relived his friend
was alive and mostly unharmed.

"What are you going to do, Mal?" asked Zuz, winding his
way through rubble in what was his best guess at the exit.

"Something very stupid," replied Mal, waving his friend off.

Taking three deep breaths, Mal gripped the edges of the
broken door frame and rocked back on his heels like a sprinter
preparing to do the forty yard dash.

Locking the attack copter outside the second story window
in his sights, Mal exhaled, "This is a bad idea…"

Mal propelled himself forward, legs pumping as he charged
across the ruined, still burning wreckage of what was left of
Lieutenant Colonel Denman's office. Just beyond the bullet-
riddled glass of the room's floor-to-ceiling windows, the Apache
was angling itself, guns forward, to begin another barrage of
high caliber automatic gunfire. The cyborg threw his shoulder
forward and doubled his speed as the multi-barrel of the Gatling
gun took aim and spun in preparation for renewed assault.

The half-man, half-machine super-soldier coiled his muscled
legs when his leading foot hit the last sliver of floor and fired
himself out into the yawning, smoke-filled gulf of space past the
flaming walls. Nearly a hundred steel-bodied rounds spat out
from the AH-64D's chain gun in the time it took Mal to cross the
distance. The arc of his trajectory was enough to keep him clear
of the searing stream of death.

The look of surprise on the faces of the pilots as they
attempted to move their chopper out of the path of Mal's leap
warmed his heart, but they were too late. His vault carried
him nearly thirty feet to slam into the front of the helicopter,
his clawed arms gripping its nose as the impact shook the craft,
spinning it along its axis.

Before the pilot could straighten the Apache out, the cyborg's
fist dropped onto the bulletproofed safety glass shielding the
cockpit, sending a spider-web of tiny cracks through it. The
glass held and Mal's computer informed him it would take
him another ten seconds to penetrate it using blunt force and,
reforming the fist into a yard-long spike, suggested an alternate
approach.

The tempered glass of the windscreen offered little resistance to the thrust of brutal blade, which punctured both protective barrier and the body of the soldier beneath. The Apache's co-pilot was killed instantly as Mal's nanotech-forged armor pierced his heart.

Mal tore his hand from the soldier's chest, coating the helicopter's interior with arterial spray. The second soldier, a more wily veteran than his companion, drew his sidearm from the holster on his thigh and shoved it through the hole created by Mal's attack, emptying its magazine into the bionic-warrior at point blank range.

Hot knives punched through Mal's torso, his internal diagnostic announcing four bullets had struck him, perforating his kidneys, spleen and stomach. The now all too familiar itch of nanobots invading his non-robotic flesh spread over Mal as his cybernetic systems rushed to heal his wounds. A back hand from his free arm knocked the pistol from the remaining pilot's hand, sending it free-falling to the pavement below.

"Omega class threat detected," chimed the inhuman voice sharing Mal's brain. "Project: Hardwired Prime Unit Designate Pyroclast fifty meters and closing."

Mal looked up in time to see a half-track armored troop carrier slow to a stop and a half-human figure jump off the back.

"Recommended strategy: evasion," finished Mal's electronic conscience.

"Oh great, another one," thought Mal as the newly-arrived government cyborg raised his arms and let loose with an uncontrolled burst of burning plasma.

Using his arms to brace himself, Mal kicked off from the spinning helicopter, diving out of the way as the burning wreckage of the Apache crashed into the ground, its explosion covering a twenty meter radius with burning debris.

Staring through the helicopter's flaming ruin, Mal caught his first good look at Designate Pyroclast, even as he opened up once more with the twin-barreled plasma rail-gun mounted where a human's left arm had once been. The man's flesh, what little of it still remained, was burned and scarred beyond recognition—it almost seemed to run molten in some places where tubes and rods merged with meat. The body of the creature—and Mal was unable to process the cyborg as anything else—appeared to be held together by a series of metallic and carbon fiber-reinforced material, unable to remain whole on its own. A series of irregularly shaped venting pipes emerged at odd-angles from Pyroclast's arms, legs and shoulders.

"What the hell is that thing?" Mal asked himself.

Failing to recognize the question as rhetorical, the computer continued its summation.

"Designate Pyroclast's main form of attack, the burst emitted by his rail-gun, is generated by the dense plasma focus machine mounted to his torso. The generator makes up 28% of his body mass."

Six heavily armed GMRs joined the flaming newcomer, in groups of three on each of his flanks, firing at the wreckage in concentrated bursts with their MP5/40 submachine guns. The group seemed to operate on a wordless level as the subordinate units alternated firing to keep a consistent barrage of bullets blasting away at Mal's location, keeping him pinned down.

"Enemy has been classified with a series of extreme mental instabilities, caused by extended exposure to the intense radiation emitted by his modifications. He was placed in stasis by Project: Hardwired lead scientist, Doctor Jean Ryan, until sufficient advances could be made on radiation shielding."

As if on command, Pyroclast stepped forward, almost like a quarterback moving into a pocket to throw a football, and let another cone of plasma lance out from the weapon merged and melted onto his body. The super-heated material engulfed nearly a third of the maimed and mangled helicopter, turning it almost instantly into a mass of molten slag.

"Great. So he's a nutjob with a nuke strapped to his back," mumbled Mal. "You got any other bad news for me?"

"Three M113 armored personnel carriers approaching at high-speed from the northwest. Crew contingent approximately thirty-nine soldiers," came the response Mal was dreading. A quick look over his shoulder confirmed the men were heading right for him, cutting off Mal's most direct avenue of escape, and trapping him in a pincer between two very hostile groups of enemies.

"Any suggestions?" Mal asked himself without too much hope in an answer that wouldn't involve getting killed.

"Engage non-enhanced troops."

The response didn't make Mal happy—the last thing he wanted to do was kill a bunch of innocent grunts just for getting in his way. Watching the vehicles growing closer with each passing second, Mal realized he was running out of time.

"Pull up a satellite image of the training grounds—there has to be another way out of this place."

With his attention focused on the photograph being displayed in his mind's eye, Mal failed to notice a pair of GMRs approaching from the opposite side of his rapidly vanishing cover behind the flame-consumed chopper. A stream of bullets stitching up his right arm spurred the cyborg into action and made his decision.

Mal charged the GMRs, deflecting another cycle of weapon's fire with arms morphing into yard-long blades, and decapitated both men with a flick of his wrists. By the time the headless bodies hit the ground, their heads bouncing off down the blackened road, Mal had covered the nearly twenty yards of asphalt that lead to the entrance of the area of the training center containing the fake Middle-Eastern village called Medina Wasl.

From the information in his databases, Mal knew there were enough twists and blind alleys that would interfere with his hunters' ability to target him, and that the buildings would be tough enough to slow Pyroclast down long enough for the super-soldier to make his escape into the desert beyond.

Mal leapt up at the corrugated metal entry gate and flipped himself over. Tracer fire from the government robot-men punched holes through it behind him as he went.

A strange buzzing in Mal's head caused him to pause, ducking down an alley between the outer wall and first row of empty homes made of baked brick and concrete. He didn't have time to wonder what it was as Zuz's voice filled his ears.

"Mal? Are you there?"

"Zuz?!

"I took a chance and called your old cell number—the one that sent me the text," replied Zuz, his voice full of self-congratulation. "I made it out to the car. Can you get to me?"

Leaning out to peak through one of the holes, Mal evaluated the situation. Pyroclast and the GMRs, along with the vehicles they had arrived in, had moved towards the enclosed training area Mal had escaped in to, but were cut off by the three thirteen-ton APCs. Soldiers in the forward turrets of each vehicle trained their twin-mounted M2HB .50 caliber Browning machine guns at the phalanx of government cyborgs.

The men of Fort Irwin didn't look happy.

"I'm working on it, Z. I'll be there as soon as I can," replied Mal. "Stay safe."

Mentally disconnecting the 'call' with Zuz, Mal watched as a solider approached the Project: Hardwired command group, made up of five men in what could best be described as 'techie chic' uniforms: short-sleeved blue button-up shirts, khaki slacks and loafers. Three of the five wore thick glasses, and all carried black equipment cases of varying sizes, which the men were looking for a location to set up.

Straining his enhanced senses, Mal lingered in his hiding spot, trying to pick up the men's conversation.

"What in blazes are you men doing here and what is that thing?" demanded the army lieutenant, keeping a wide distance from Pyroclast. The cyborg was giving off enough heat from his radioactive core to have everyone in the area sweating profusely.

There wasn't a dry armpit in the house.

Jason May stepped forward and flashed a badge he'd pulled from one of the many pouches around his waist.

"Agent May, Project: Hardwired," said the technician in his most authoritative voice. "We're here on orders of the Dee-Oh-Dee, pursuing the terrorist cell responsible for the attack in Los Angeles yesterday."

The head of Project: Hardwired's weapons division passed the lieutenant, a red-faced man with a bowl-cut in his mid-thirties by the name of Hughes, a print-out containing a blown-up photograph of Mal.

"This man, ex-United States Army Ranger Malcolm Weir,

made his way on to Fort Irwin early this afternoon to kill his former commanding officer. Your Colonel Denman," continued May as Hughes looked over the photo. "We were too late to stop him."

"Colonel Denman is dead?"

Lieutenant Hughes was stunned but was still able to offer the assistance of his men of his detachment.

"We've got the terrorist pinned down in that training area," stated May.

"Keep your men out of my way, Lieutenant Hughes," interrupted Pyroclast's hissing, inhuman voice before turning to the GMRs under his command. "Gamma-One, have your squad secure the perimeter around the village. Lock down all exits and wait for further orders. Designate Cestus is mine."

The unstable cyborg headed for the entrance to Medina Wasl, venting hot vapor from his pipes and powering up his rail-gun for another barrage.

"'Clast," the Project: Hardwired weapons tech yelled after the radioactive killer, causing him to pause. "Remember, Doctor Ryan's team needs Cestus intact. He's got all of their data stored in his head, so they need it unmelted. Got it?"

"Did command say Designate Cestus needed to be delivered to Ryan alive?" countered the radioactive cyborg, causing the asphalt to melt under each slow step he took towards the training area Mal had fled to.

"No, sir," responded Pyroclast's handler, grinning.

From his vantage point, Mal grimaced at what he inferred from the conversation: the bad guys needed the computer they stuck into his head in one piece, but the rest of him was fair game for the creepy flaming cyborg to burn to cinders.

Excellent, he thought sarcastically. At least Mal didn't have to worry about Pyroclast incinerating the entire area and him with it. With his orders in place, the maniac would have to fight Mal on a more personal level—and hand-to-hand is something he had always been very good at.

"Let him come," said Mal, diving for the cover of the shadows deeper into the counterfeit village as a concentrated burst of superheated plasma turned its wall into a pile of kindling.

Mal didn't have to wait long.

Twin gouts of flame belched through the razed gates and were followed closely by the slow moving figure of their creator. Stalking inside, Mal's foe twisted his body in a wide arc, coating everything in radioactive flame, turning everything it touched into an uncontrolled conflagration.

"Come out, Mr. Weir," blustered Pyroclast. "I'll burn this place to the ground and you with it!"

Leaping out from behind his cover to avoid a ten-foot section of wall liquefying into glowing orange magma, Mal regretted his decision to hide in an enclosed area with the madman. Realizing his best chance at survival was to pit his speed and agility against the slower, more powerful cyborg, Mal closed the distance between them, angling himself in what he hoped was Pyroclast's blind spot.

Faster than a thing his size should have been able to move, Pyroclast met the attack with the searing hot barrels of his main weapon, the rusted-looking surface of it sizzling and popping everywhere it touched Mal's bare skin.

"I may be an older model, but I've got the same sensor suite you do," laughed the harsh, raspy voice of Mal's horrendously disfigured assailant, following up with a pulverizing blow from his scarred left fist.

The jolt of Pyroclast's rock hard fist pounding into Mal's side sent him sliding across the uneven, rocky ground of the training compound, the hero losing an outer layer of skin in the process. The hiss of steam venting from the series of pipes climbing Pyroclast's spine was all the warning Mal had before another shaft of plasma surged towards him, causing the ex-Ranger to twist out of the way, groaning as his back and neck were charred.

Staggering to his feet, Mal blocked a clubbing overhead blow from Pyroclast that nearly knocked him back down. He should have been fast enough to take his opponent out, but the heat and radiation were too much for him. Just standing within arm's reach of the bastard was killing him.

Mal wondered how much longer he could hold out.

Much to his chagrin, Mal's internal diagnostics answered

him: while his cybernetic implants and the nanites they contained would continue to operate at near-peak efficiency for another five minutes, the organic portions of his body would begin to fail in less than sixty-seconds of exposure to the extreme radiation seeping out of his attacker. Failure to evacuate the area would result in permanent damage and death.

Luckily, with the way Pyroclast was beating the living daylights out of him, Mal was pretty sure he wouldn't last another minute. The super-solider was a goner if he didn't think of something fast.

"Give me a run down on Designate Pyroclast." Mal ordered his cybernetic brain to scan the data encrypted in it, hoping he could get the thing to find what he was looking for.

"Accessing," it replied and was silent for a moment.

The information torrid that came an instant later was almost enough to knock Mal off-balance.

Detailed plans, blueprints and specifications scrolled through Mal's brain—most of which went right over his head, but enough sunk in for the germ of a plan to begin forming. Mal confirmed the scheme with his computer before stopping in his tracks and turning to face his fiery foe, arms nearly doubling in size and hands reforming into a ten pack of knives that would have made the people at Ginsu green with envy.

Mal charged his enemy, leaping over one searing plasma burst and deflecting another off his heavily-armored forearm so he could close the distance between them.

The last few feet Mal covered in a leap, hammering into Pyroclast's deformed jaw with a raised knee that staggered the beast. He followed up with a series of battering blows from his fists and an elbow strike as he looked for a way to finish things off.

Outclassed by the larger cyborg in terms of size, strength and power, Mal had to rely on his own augmented speed and the lethal power of his own implants to avoid being crushed by a vicious counter-attack from Pyroclast's flame-covered fist.

The peppering of blows across his body and face drove the scarred half-man into a psychotic rage, finally giving Mal the opening he needed. Pyroclast put every iota of his godlike strength into a haymaker, launching it with abandon in an attempt to utterly destroy the gnat that had been badgering him, an attempt that left the cyborg over-extended, off-balance and vulnerable. Mal ducked under the attack and propelled himself up under the crazed cyborg's defenses, slashing out with the elongated blades of his fingers to cut deeply into its blackened, grotesque flesh down to the plates of carbon-fiber reinforced nickel that made up its chest.

Latching onto the covering to the dense plasma focus machine melded into Pyroclast's chest, Mal planted his feet and strained with all his might. Realizing what the smaller man was attempting to do, Pyroclast clamped the mangled, disfigured fingers of his right hand around Mal's neck in an attempt to dislodge him.

Too late.

Ignoring the pain from the giant's hand wrapped around his throat and fighting back unconsciousness, Mal planted his legs beneath him and hauled back, ripping free the covers to the generator at Pyroclast's core, along with half of the cyborg's chest. Both men were showered in muscle and meat and whatever cruel liquid now accounted for Pyroclast's lifeblood, and raw nuclear power blazed forth, scorching everything it touched with the unrestrained power of a sun.

The effect on Mal was almost instantaneous as the flesh of Mal's exposed torso and face began to burn and blister at the inferno of Pyroclast's torn open chest. A white hot light, unbearable to look upon, shone from where the insane cyborg's heart should have been.

Teeth clenched together with enough force to shatter stone, Mal knew what he had to do.

Pyroclast let loose with an inhuman howl of pain and rage as Mal plunged both hands into the nuclear furnace housed in between the carbon-fiber ribcage that held it in place. A second scream joined in, surprising Mal as he realized it was his own.

He could feel the radiation leaching his life away one heartbeat at a time. Mal prayed he had the strength to finish the job.

The radioactive cyborg beat down at Mal's head and

shoulders, to no avail. Hair and clothing and skin bursting into flames from the furnace, Mal pushed one final time, his arms tearing through Pyroclast's back and rupturing the dense plasma core that powered him.

Mal's living metal arms glowed white as he jerked them free from the spasming Pyroclast. He was forced to duck out of the way as a fountain of deuterium oxide coolant erupted from the dying man's chest.

Both cybernetic men dropped to their knees and Mal watched as his enemy fell bonelessly to the ground in death, sighing in relief.

The relief was short-lived.

"The ruptured core of Designate Pyroclast will reach critical mass in twenty-nine point nine seconds. Immediate withdrawal from the area is advised."

"For Pete's sake!"

Leaping to his feet, Mal forced every ounce of energy he could into the muscles of his legs and ran full speed across the flame-enshrouded grounds of the fake village he'd been trapped in. The eighteen-foot high outer wall offering little obstacle, Mal's legs cleared the structure in a superhuman vault that surprised the pair of Gamma-Unit GMRs assigned to guard the area's perimeter. The cyborg slammed into them, knocking the government drones to the ground, and tumbling back to his feet in a run before the GMRs knew what hit them.

All the while, the computer counted down, each second seeming to come faster than the last. Before the final instant ticked away, the computer droned, "Initiating EMP counter-measures." With that, a strange electrical surge ran down the length of Mal's spine, along his nanotech arms, and out to the tips of his fingers.

The man renamed Cestus by the government didn't have time to wonder what precisely his systems were doing, or if they'd work, as the forward concussion wave from Pyroclast's detonation picked up his muscular body and tossed it fifteen feet into the air like a rag doll.

Mal realized he must have blacked out because he found himself lying stretched out on cracked pavement, surrounded by the overturned husks of old tan-colored tanks and armored-personnel carriers. Even his metallic arms hurt. Sitting up, Mal's chest burned as he was wracked with a fit of coughing that filled his mouth with the coppery taste of blood.

Sore, tired, covered in burns and nothing else, Mal made his way slowly to where Zuz waited for him at the edge of the explosion's blast radius.

The bald conspiracy-buff was looking daggers at his friend as Mal stumbled slowly over to the car and struggled to force the dented, nearly concave passenger's side door open. Zuz's angry eyes continued as the cyborg slumped down into the seat next to him and pulled the tiny level that allowed him to sit back, resting.

"You owe me a radio, Mal," spat the man as he started the car up and pulled away from the devastation behind them. "A good one."

Mal lifted the forearm he'd decided to shade his face from the sun with and squinted at Zuz, puzzled.

"Forgive me if I'm a bit dense from the nuclear explosion and all, but what on God's green Earth are you talking about?"

"You owe me a new radio," repeated Zuz.

Seeing that Mal needed more of an explanation, he pushed the power button for the device set into the car's dashboard. Nothing happened.

"I was listening to the news—keeping my ear to the ground for intel—when everything blew up and the radio died. Hence, you owe me a radio," said Zuz.

Mal was dumbfounded.

"So you're saying it's my fault that your radio shorted out from the explosion? And that I have to buy you a new one?"

Zuz nodded enthusiastically.

Grinding the warm metal of his palm into his right eye socket, Mal sighed.

"Please, Zuz, for both our sake's, shut up and drive," said Mal, stretching out as much as he could in the tiny car and closing his eyes. "We need to find Kristin."

"Sure thing," responded Zuz who remained silent for almost thirty full seconds before speaking up once more. "Hey, Mal…"

The sound of his friend's voice grated along the ends of every nerve in the cyborg's exhausted body.

"What...Is...It...Zuz?" asked Mal, exasperated. As if on cue, the computerized portion of his brain began listing the nearly one hundred ways the driver could be killed from Mal's current seated position.

"Why aren't you wearing any pants?"

CHAPTER 15

There was very little in life Gordon Kiesling hated more than having to report to his so-called superiors. Sure, some of them were nice enough, and a few were downright pleasant in some circumstances, but the idea that he, the head of one of the most powerful black-ops organizations in the world, should have to answer to pencil-pushers from D.C. flat out pissed him off.

There were days Kiesling wished he could just have every politician in the country taken out and shot.

Sitting there in a tiny, windowless waiting room on an incredibly tacky pleather sofa, face-to-face with the man most identified on organization charts as his 'boss,' Kiesling was experiencing one of those days.

The only saving grace in Kiesling's eyes was that the only people in the room were the Secretary of Defense, Ms. Roslan, and Kiesling himself. At least there were no witnesses to his prostration.

"Director Kiesling," came the voice of the United States Secretary of Defense from just across the small reception area. Dressed in a dark gray suit with what both Kiesling and Roslan had decided was a horrid canary yellow tie and thinning hair more white than anything else, the politician was seated on a large faux black leather couch with his legs crossed and arms spread along its back. "I had been under the assumption the entire point of a top secret and covert governmental organization was to remain top secret and covert. Perhaps you can clarify the past twenty-four hours for me so that I can properly explain it to the president."

A slight scowl turned up the corner of Kiesling's mouth in complete defiance of his usual self-control. Normally the Secretary and Kiesling were on positive terms that bordered on friendly interaction. That ended as the man directed the attention of Project: Hardwired's man-in-charge to the television monitor positioned at the rear of the room they lounged in.

Looking back at Kiesling and Ms. Roslan, seated next to him, was a bird's-eye view of the National Training Facility at Fort Irwin. Flames ran rampant through the military base almost uncontrolled and, even almost two hours later, a small mushroom cloud cast the area into a dirty twilight of billowing browns, reds and yellows.

"Is it wrong to assume that was one of yours?"

Before answering, Kiesling leaned down to confer with his assistant who had been on the phone with Mr. Anderson and the other Project: Hardwired heads constantly since they had left the offices two hours earlier. She quietly informed him that surviving operatives on the ground at Fort Irwin confirmed the explosion had been as a direct result of Designate Pyroclast's dense plasma focus core rupturing during his skirmish with Cestus at the army base. The eggheads back at the lab had estimated the explosion from the unstable nuclear generator had been the equivalent of nearly fifty tons of TNT. Radioactive fallout would cover nearly ten square miles around the detonation site and clean-up would take years, if not decades. Jason May and most of his team in the weapon's lab were MIA and presumed dead.

Worst of all, both Designate Cestus and his civilian cohort had been identified as having fled the scene mere seconds before the blast.

Malcolm Weir was still alive and running free.

Kiesling took a deep breath and proceed to do his best to answer the question without actually admitting to it.

"Intelligence on the ground at Fort Irwin has been spotty at best. A small-scale nuclear blast has apparently gone off at or near the facility and an electro-magnetic pulse has knocked out all electronics within twenty miles of the base. Every attempt to determine the cause of the blast have been, as of yet, inconclusive."

"I don't have time for your 'Texas Two-Step,' Gordon," snapped the Secretary. "Tell me straight-up: did a renegade Project: Hardwired agent set off a nuclear device in the middle of a God-damned military training facility here in California? Yes or no?"

"Yes, Mr. Secretary," admitted Kiesling after as long a pause as he dared. "The nuclear generator housed within the frame of Designate Pyroclast was rendered unstable through an attack by the rebel cyborg formerly known as Malcolm Weir."

"So that's two of your billion-dollar Frankensteins the rogue operative has taken out. Along with God-only-knows how many of the Gee-Em-Ar sub-units. How do you explain this, Gordon?" demanded the head of the Department of Defense, perplexed.

"With the Abraxas system down, none of the Prime Units have been operating at peak capacity, Mr. Secretary."

"Well, except for this Weir fellow," harrumphed the Secretary. "He seems to be operating just fine without it."

Kiesling agreed with the man through clenched teeth.

The older politician couldn't resist throwing in an extra jab at the usually cocky younger man.

"Perhaps we should have hired him to run your department, eh, Director Kiesling?"

The two men locked eyes in a battle over who exactly was the 'Alpha Male' in the room. It was a dangerous game for Kiesling to be playing, one that could end his career, but he'd been pushed too far since Weir's short circuit and defection. Luckily for the powerfully-built head of Project: Hardwired, he had an ace up his sleeve in the form of his exceedingly capable assistant.

A rapid set of fake coughs took the focus of both men from one another to Ms. Roslan, successfully breaking the stalemate without either man having to lose face.

The white-haired older man shook his head, tired of the game his subordinate was playing. He leaned forward and jerked his liver-spotted hand at the video of Fort Irwin burning to the ground playing silently on the wall to their side.

"What are you going to do to fix this little mess of yours?"

Nodding at the politician, Kiesling replied the Abraxas configuration would be back on-line in less than a day and that they'd be able to track Weir anywhere on the planet—his cybernetics gave off a very specific form of radioactive signal the Hardwired system could locate from space. Once the network was back at full operation, Dr. Ryan's boys should even have the ability to do a complete shut down on the traitorous cyborg.

He was as good as caught.

The man across from Kiesling wasn't as confident with the abilities of the sentient computer network.

"You've got forty-eight hours to bring Mr. Weir under control," stated the Secretary of Defense, shooing the pair out of his sight. "Forty-eight hours and we'd better not have any more of these incidents. Are we clear, Director Kiesling?"

"As glass." The words came out just this side of a growl and the Secretary noticed. "Sir," added Kiesling after a pregnant pause.

The head of Project: Hardwired and his assistant must have hesitated too long for the elderly head of state's liking because he tossed a stack of papers at the pair and bellowed, demanding to know why they still stood around.

Hands clenched into tight fists with knuckles blanching bone white from the pressure he was putting on them, Gordon Kiesling took half a step towards the man who currently held control over his career. Half a step ahead of him and keyed in to the emotional state of her boss, Ms. Roslan intercepted the man and directed him towards the exit, saying "We're on it, Mr. Secretary."

"Keep it quiet or you're all going to be looking for new jobs," called the man as Ms. Roslan shut the door behind them.

Based on the heavy silence hanging in the air during the short walk back to the elevator bank leading to the governmental building's parking garage, Ms. Roslan knew her boss's temper was about to boil over.

The ride down six levels to the underground level was no better and Ms. Roslan was relieved to see their Escalade waiting at the ready when they stepped out of the lift and into the green-tinged flickering fluorescent lights of the cold concrete garage labeled as 'P-2.' The driver held the vehicle's door open for the pair, motioning for them to climb aboard.

Director Kiesling didn't move, seemingly lost in thought, completely ignoring everything around him. The pale blue orbs set deep in his face flickered to and fro were all that revealed something was at work in the man's brain.

A quick wave from Roslan's delicately shaped hand dismissed the driver back to his side of the waiting automobile. The best way to deal with one of the Director's black moods was to leave him be, but time was ticking away and Ms. Roslan needed the man to snap out of it.

"Sir?"

Ms. Roslan was shocked by the venom in Kiesling's eyes as her employer finally looked up at the sound of her voice. Yup, she thought, this is going to be bad.

"Give me the secure line, Ms. Roslan," came the Director's cold voice, ignoring the open car door waiting for him to enter.

Removing the high-tech device from the easy-to-access compartment in her handbag she kept it in at all times, the concerned woman handed over the satellite phone to her boss. The unit worked with a special encryption, shielding it against anyone trying to listen in, and only the Director of Project: Hardwired knew its access codes. In their four years working together, Kiesling's executive assistant had only seen the man use it twice.

Kiesling's immaculately trimmed nails punched in a nine-digit telephone number, with a bit more force than normal. Holding the phone up to his ear, he stared through the woman at his side and muttered, mostly to himself.

"I'm going to take care of that little bastard once and for all."

Over the tiny handset a series of tiny rings echoed, waiting to connect to the unknown party. Ms. Roslan knew better than to inquire into the recipient's identity, following her boss into the large back seat of the big car and allowing the door to seal behind them.

The faint sound of a woman's voice answering caused the first hint of relief in Kiesling's shoulder's.

"Hello?" asked the unknown female.

In response, one word spilled from the lips of Gordon Kiesling, audible only to the person on the other end of the connection.

'Galatea' was all he said before disconnecting the call. Gordon Kiesling smiled for the first time in hours and sat back to enjoy the ride.

CHAPTER 16

The two-hour drive from Fort Irwin to the Westwood Mall in Century City had been nearly unbearable for Mal. He'd been calling his ex-fiancée almost constantly since they'd left the ruins of Fort Irwin, to no avail.

Mal knew the woman always kept her phone within arm's reach and was almost obsessive about never missing a call. Something had to be wrong if she wasn't answering and would bet dollars to donuts it had something to do with her new husband.

"Are you sure this is a good idea, Mal?" Asked Zuz as the pair watched the entrance to the upscale 'pan-Asian' restaurant Mal's computer had tracked Kristin's cell phone to. "At what point is this considered stalking?"

"You heard what Denman said," Mal responded, impatiently. "Morrell was part of the accident in Iraq. He was there at the hospital at the same time. Just like Steve was...and the government agents. I know he's tied up in this mess—it's just too much of a coincidence."

"Maybe you don't like him because he's banging your woman?" countered Zuz matter-of-factly as he 'air humped' the back of a bench.

Glaring, Mal reminded the man that he'd already killed twenty or so people today and that one more wouldn't make much of a difference in the grand scheme of things.

"Do you have a plan, Kemosabe?"

"Yeah," said Mal, heading with purpose for the double glass doors to the restaurant. "Save Kristin. Kick her husband's ass... hopefully in a way that doesn't make her mad at me."

"Great plan," moaned Zuz, following his friend inside.

The restaurant's interior was an odd mix of a number of Asian cultures, all thrown together in what seemed to be an attempt to meet some sort of Hollywood checklist of the most gaudy, and most stereotypical decor from all of them. Dodging four-foot long golden dragon statues, Koi ponds, and waitresses dressed as geisha, Mal didn't know what the official Webster's definition of 'pan-Asian' was but he was pretty sure one of its synonyms was 'Hollywood douchebag.' Affliction brand shirts, skinny jeans with white belts, and glowing Bluetooth headsets filled the place.

It was the kind of place—the kind of people—Kristin had hated while they dated, an emotion Mal fully empathized with.

Catching a glimpse of Kristin's blond hair, partially tied back into a topknot that let it cascade down onto the middle of her back, Mal pushed past the rather hyperactive maître d' dressed in a black suit and made a beeline for her table. She was seated with her back to the exit, with seven large men spaced out around her.

Seeing the cyborg approaching the table with fire in his eyes, one of the men leaned over and said something to the man next to Kristin in a voice too quiet for Mal's superhuman hearing to pick up.

Mal got a good look at Marc Morrell as the second man turned and revealed his identity to the newly arrived pair. Standing, Morrell met Mal's fierce gaze without blinking, jaw set firmly, and said, "Nice of you to join us, Captain Weir."

Spinning around in her chair, stunned by the pair's arrival, Kristin demanded, "Mal?! What the hell are you doing here?" She tossed the dark red napkin, snatched from its position on her lap, down onto the empty plate in front her and jumped up to her feet in a huff. "I thought I told you to stay away from me this morning."

Stepping between Kristin and her new husband protectively, Mal kept every sense targeted on Morrell as he answered, "You have to come with me, Kris. Your husband isn't who he says he is."

"Are you insane?"

Clutching Kristin's arm, Mal pulled her away from the table, pushing her towards Zuz, who was fidgeting from foot to foot as he grew increasingly anxious at the situation.

"I don't have time to explain, Kris," said Mal firmly, finally looking away from Morrell. "Go with Zuz and we'll tell you everything outside."

"There's no need for that, Captain Weir," interrupted Morrell, stepping towards the arguing couple.

Like lightning, Mal's free hand shot up, the first two fingers of it elongated into burnished blades seven inches in length and gouged two shallow strips of flesh from the man's chest. "Stay back!"

"Malcolm stop!" screamed Kristin. Every head in the room snapped around to watch the unfolding drama.

An invisible communication must have flashed between the men, signaling that the time for subtlety was at an end, causing the remaining five to stand in eerie unison. Morrell stepped forward, clamping down on Mal's forearm with an outstretched fist. Amazingly, Mal could feel the man's inhuman strength through the neural connections in his cybernetic limb. The power in Morrell's grip would have shattered Mal's wrist if he had been a normal human.

Preparing himself for the inevitable violence that was about to occur, Mal hoped this one didn't shoot flames like the last one did.

"Designate Cestus," said Morrell, the modulation of his voice mimicking the now all too familiar robotic nature of a Project: Hardwired GMR unit. "You are hereby ordered to submit to my authority as a duly appointed representative of Project: Hardwired."

Without warning, Mal cold-cocked Kristin's soon-to-be ex-husband with a left-cross to his jaw, sending the man sprawling across the floor.

"Run!" screamed the cyborg super-soldier, springing into action.

Flipping the table up in the air with his hands, Mal roundhouse kicked it into Morrell and his team of government-sent assassins, sending them all crashing to the black tiled floor in a heap of tangled limbs. An instant later he had Kristin and Zuz running through the restaurant towards the exit.

Compact MP5K machine guns sprang into four of the downed men's hands and opened fire, spraying the front of the restaurant with an angry hornet's nest of steel-jacketed rounds. Mal intercepted dozens of the rounds, deflecting them with his armored prosthetics, but dozens more raced passed him, shattering the fake golden statues lining the entrance and obliterating the double glass doors a split second after the fleeing pair made their way through.

"David, why are my husband and his friends shooting at us?" asked Kristin, allowing herself to be led away from the gunfire.

Angling the perturbed woman towards a nearby escalator leading down to the outdoor mall's underground parking lot, Zuz responded that people had been shooting at him for two days now and he still wasn't completely sure why.

Now that he didn't have to worry about the safety of Kristin or Zuz, Mal went on the offensive, his arms expanding and lengthening to gorilla-like proportions, hands transforming and merging into three-fingered machetes. These men were all that stood between him and reuniting with his beloved, and nothing would stop him.

The first of the GMRs to rise, a tall, thin man with chestnut brown hair and thick sideburns, tried to bring his gun to bear but was cut short as Mal's bladed right hand took him in the mouth, spearing through the back of his head. Mal ripped his hand free, bringing with it the top of the man's head and most of the soft tissue of his throat.

Using the GMR's body as a shield, Mal charged as a second GMR let loose a blistering torrent of bullets from his shortened MP5K, tackling the agent and taking him to the ground. The man spit blood as eighteen-inch blades pushed through the corpse pinning him down and into his chest.

Mal blocked an attack by his third would-be assailant, a bear of a man standing more than six-and-a-half feet in height, who tried to club him from behind with a stun-baton. Mal caught the man with the back-swing from his arm as it pulled away from his comrade dying on the ground, cleaving him in half.

Seeing a river of blood and body parts falling to the ground, what few onlookers remained broke for the doors, screaming in terror. There was only so much even a jaded Los Angeles crowd could take and the fight had moved well beyond that.

An explosion of pain erupted in Mal's side as Morrell took advantage of the distraction, moving in with a series of powerful blows to the cyborg's torso. The area was still tender from the earlier battles despite the rapid healing abilities given him by the nanobots running freely through his veins.

There was something different about Morrell, thought Mal. The man wasn't a standard GMR unit—he was stronger, faster, and seemed to act on his own initiative. But he didn't seem to be as powerful as a Prime like Gauss or the others. Whatever the good Captain Morrell was it certainly wasn't human.

The two men exchanged a series of blows, each in turn attacking and blocking to test one another's strengths and weaknesses. If he had been uninjured from nearly twenty four hours of fighting Mal knew he would have had the upper hand—his reflexes were faster and his cybernetics gave him far more power when it came to melee combat. But the newcomer was fresher and had back-up from the remaining three Gomers. Whenever Mal would focus attention on one in an attempt to take it out, the others would move in and tag him. Although their blows weren't much on their own, in unison they were wearing Mal down little by little.

Realizing he had to do something fast, Mal caught a punch from Morrell and catapulted the man across the room in an Aikido throw. With the mightiest of the Project: Hardwired agents out of the fight it was an easy matter for Mal to evade the others and bolt for the shattered glass doors to outside.

Mal refused to look back even as the sounds of fresh magazines being loaded into compact machine guns hounded he from behind, bolting for the railing at the edge of the mall's open air walkway, praying to God the ground wasn't as far down as he remembered.

Deep beneath the mall itself, Zuz opened the Cube's back door and told Kristin to get in as he started the vehicle. Once she was settled, he pulled the car into the massive line of cars trying to exit the parking garage in an attempt to get away from the chaos Mal and his Project: Hardwired playmates were causing in the Mall levels above. Hundreds of vehicles, with horns blaring and drivers shouting obscenities at one another, jockeyed for escape.

While they waited their turn to leave, Zuz did his best to fill Kristin in on what had happened—as much as he figured Mal would be okay with. He told her about finding Mal the day before and being on the run for most of the day. For her part, Kristin sat back and tried to take it all in.

When the woman asked about her husband and what the real story behind him was, Zuz sputtered and rolled his window down, using the distraction of having to pay ten dollars for thirty minutes of parking as an excuse not to answer her question. The bald man decided that Mal would have to take care of that can of worms himself.

When the lot attendant raised the tiny exit gate, revealing freedom beyond, Zuz began the turn onto Santa Monica Boulevard, wondering where Mal had gotten himself to and if the man was okay. Before he could complete the maneuver, the pair was startled by a downpour of glass and stone debris from overhead. They were even more surprised when Mal shot out into the empty air space above them, followed by the sound of enough automatic gunfire to make it sound like the 4th of July.

"Mal!" shrieked Kristin in shock and worry as gravity reasserted itself on Mal's body, dragging him down with enough force to crash through the top of a city bus unfortunate enough to be driving by at precisely the wrong time.

Zuz commented that it was okay, Mal seemed to be jumping out of things a lot lately, but was cut off when a trio of the Project: Hardwired GMR units Kristin had been dining with a few minutes earlier jumped off the mall's second level overhang in an attempt to pursue their target. None of the government agents had the power or velocity of Mal's Olympic-beating leap with all three crashing to the road directly in front of Zuz's escaping Nissan.

Smiling to himself and in the mood for some payback, Zuz

slammed his foot down onto the gas pedal, bowling throw all three men with a satisfying thud and shudder of his car.

"Did you just run over those men?!"

"Yeah," grinned Zuz, pleased with himself. "It was pretty cool, huh?" Noticing the look of concern on Kristin's face out of the corner of his eye, Zuz reassured her they weren't normal 'men' and would survive the hit-and-run with his car—if anything. Heck, they probably did more damage to it than it did to them.

But it sure did feel good was his only thought as the car zoomed away at high speed, disappearing quickly into the distance.

Recovering from his less-than-stellar landing on—and then through—the 'out of service' Beverly Hills bound bus, Mal climbed to his feet, proud of himself. All of the GMRs were either dead or disabled, and their boss was too far away to harass the cyborg during his getaway. Yup, thought Mal, heading for the front of the bus to get off, things were finally going his way.

That is until the elderly Hispanic bus driver yelled something about 'oh, no, we're going to die' in his native tongue—Mal had gotten a 'C-minus' in Spanish back in high school, so he wasn't positive about his translation—banged open the vehicle's folding doors and hurled himself away from the bus. Although his mastery of the Spanish language was iffy at best, the driver's action were universal in nature, causing Mal to rush forward to gaze out the bus's large front window and see a fiery plume of super-heated exhaust gases illuminate Morrell, thirty feet above street-level, as the government operative fired a FIM-92 shoulder-mounted Stinger at him through a gap in Westwood Mall's second floor security railing.

Arms and legs pumping furiously, Mal had nearly reached the rear of the empty bus when the miniature missile crashed into its front, detonating on impact and sending flames rocketing back after him. He was followed through the rear window by huge tendrils of fire and smoke as he drove himself headfirst through it and out onto the black asphalt road behind. An instant later he was forced to pitch himself to the side in order to avoid being crushed as the force of the rocket-powered projectile exploding flipped the bus end-over-end to land upside down, collapsing under its own weight.

Mal used the flames and subsequent second explosion from the bus's gas tank to escape from the wreck unseen by his foe, contacting Zuz's cellphone with the wireless connection provided by his internal computer system to arrange a meeting spot a few blocks away.

Zuz and Kristin were already waiting when Mal arrived thirty seconds later and climbed into his usual spot on the passenger's side. The car was in motion, zipping through traffic, before the cyborg could get the door closed. With everyone safe, Mal could tell Zuz wanted to get the hell out of dodge before anyone else jumped out to try and kill them...again.

Mal leaned around his seat and smiled warmly at Kristin, trying to reassure her with a pat on her leg.

"It's all going to be okay, Kris. We'll get you somewhere safe. They're after me, not you or Zuz. You two can lie low until I get it all sorted out."

The car cut through the late afternoon traffic, aimless, just trying to get as far away from the government agency so desperate to capture Mal they'd risk shooting up a crowded public place like the restaurant and mall. Hundreds of civilians had seen the attack that time. It was insane.

After a few minutes of driving, Zuz finally asked Mal where they were going.

"Take Coldwater Canyon over Mulholland Drive. The hills should help throw off anything they might have to track us with. When we get over to the Valley side, I'll see if my sensors can find any bugs or tracers they might have on any of us." Looking back at Kristin, Mal said, "I'm sure that bastard Morrell must have planted something on you, Kris, just in case we got away."

The woman in the back seat nodded her head weakly. Mal and Zuz exchanged glances—they could tell it was quickly becoming too much for her. They needed to get her out of sight and protected, fast.

As Zuz turned the Nissan onto the long, winding street lined by trees and houses built precariously up on steep hills,

Mal told Kristin to get some rest. It would all be OK once she woke up.

Kristin laid her head back, struggling to keep her tears from falling. She wasn't sure if she should be furious with Mal or glad he was there, and no matter how hard she tried she couldn't make sense of what had happened to Marc. What was he? Was their marriage even real?

Her eyes closed as she ran the day's events through her head, exhaling deeply in a sigh. She listened as the car sped over miles and through the mini mountain range that bordered Beverly Hills, heading towards the San Fernando Valley and the 'somewhere safe' Mal promised.

Somewhere away from the husband who tried to kill her.

"Oh, Marc," she whispered, this time unable to hold back the tears.

A buzzing almost soft enough to escape notice caught Kristin's attention, sending the exhausted, confused woman rummaging through the handbag she'd kept clutched tightly in her grip during their escape.

The shootout at the restaurant had to already be all over the news, she thought. It was probably just her mom or her best friend, Lynda, calling to make sure she was okay.

Kristin's caller ID revealed a number she'd never seen before but something about it clicked somewhere in the back of her mind, causing her to push 'answer' and hold the bright green phone up to her ear.

"Hello?"

The well cultured bass voice on the other end of the call spoke one word before breaking the connection. "Galatea."

The phone fell lifelessly from Kristin's hand and the orbs of her eyes glazed over as she reached into the side pocket of the Kate Spade purse, extracting the dull black Smith & Wesson SW99 pistol hidden within. Silently, Mal's ex-fiancée raised the weapon and fired pointblank into the driver's side seat at an unsuspecting David Zuzelo, sending two .45 caliber rounds into the center of his back and a third at his head.

CHAPTER 17

The first two shots took everyone in the car by surprise, blasting gaping holes through the padding in the Nissan's seat and taking Zuz square in his back. His left lung had collapsed by the first bullet, and half of his right kidney burst with the second. Mal had recovered in the quarter second it took Kristin to readjust her aim to base of the bald man's skull and was able to deflect the third out through the top of the car.

The car's horn bleated miserably, pressed solidly by Zuz's head slamming down onto it as he blacked out from pain. Pandemonium reigned inside the vehicle, with Mal having to split his attention between fighting Kristin as the suddenly insane woman tried to unload the rest of her clip into Zuz, and trying to keep the still moving car from rolling over into oncoming traffic.

"Kristin?! What did you do?" shouted Mal while Kristin fought against him like a trapped lioness, kicking and striking as if a tornado had been released in the backseat of the car. Her attacks were so vicious she was able to force the car off the side of the road, causing it to hop the curb onto the sidewalk, and run headfirst into a light pole. The car spun uncontrollable for a minute, sideswiping a number of parked vehicles before coming to a complete stop just inside the parking lot for a large pharmacy and grocery store.

At the last instant before impact, Mal tossed his body across Zuz's, protecting the man as much as possible from additional blunt force trauma. The choice caused the cyborg to lose hold of his ex-fiancée, who used the commotion to make her move. Before he could stop her, Kristin dove out of the backseat and avoided Mal's attempt at subdual. Three steps later, she spun on her heel, firing three more rounds into the nearly junked car, blowing out the tires on its passenger's side.

"Zuz, I've got to get you out of here," said Mal, worried about the vast amounts of blood oozing from his friend's midsection. Faster than the blink of an eye, Mal kicked open the bashed in, unresponsive door at his side, slid over the hood of the car and pulled Zuz from the vehicle, cradling the man in his arms. "Hang on, Zuz…I'll get you to a hospital."

Mal's eyes darted around the area, taking in every piece of information he could, trying to figure out how to save the dying man's life. A bullet shattered what had to be the Cube's last remaining piece of unbroken glass, forcing Mal to keep his head down. Nearby, the sound of the automatic doors of a large local pharmacy opening and closing caught Mal's attention. Immediately, the man was in motion, with Zuz held tight against his body, heading across the large open parking lot and into the awaiting air-conditioning of the store.

Five bullets chased his mad dash across the charcoal-colored asphalt, gouging chunks out of its surface in a tight line behind the fleeing super-soldier.

"Unit Galatea reporting," said Kristin into her phone as she ejected the spent magazine from her pistol and replaced it with a loaded one. "Target David Anthony Zuzelo has been injured and his vehicle incapacitated. Designate Cestus is attempting to flee the scene on foot. Back-up required near the corner of Van Nuys Boulevard and Cedros Avenue in Sherman Oaks."

"Confirmed, Unit Galatea. Designate Gauss in route. Keep eyes on target and standby for backup to arrive," responded an emotionless female voice over the cellphone's speaker.

"Affirmative."

Sprinting across the parking lot, high heels flying off in her wake, Kristin headed for the threshold of the shop only to be blocked by a mob of people, terrified and screaming, rushing out directly into her path and slowing her down.

Mal's own entry into the large, brightly lit emporium had been as loud and violent as he could make it, in hopes of using the turmoil to get some time to stop Zuz's bleeding. He scoured the wide, quickly emptying aisles, looking for bandages. Mal knew the only chance Zuz had was at a hospital, but he also realized there was little hope the man would make it to an emergency room without a field dressing to staunch the flow of blood from his wounds.

The urgency of the search was reinforced by a series of gunshots from the front of the building announcing Kristin's arrival, and continued general mind-controlled attitude, inside the commercial establishment. The screams and commotion had gone quiet, with only the store's security alarms blaring filling the otherwise vacated building.

The quest for gauze and sterile pads led Mal on a mad rampage up and down what seemed like countless aisles containing foodstuffs, make-up, office supplies, and a million other things that were of no use to Mal. A trail of Zuz's life's blood spread out in a crimson river as they went.

Near the east corner of the store, next to the pharmacist's window, the cyborg found what he was looking for, stacked neatly on a half-sized block of shelving-units. Mal made quick work of tearing through a box of gauze and surgical tape, going to work on stemming the tide of gore leaking freely from Zuz, all the while keeping an ear open for the ever approaching footfalls of his pursuer.

Before he could complete his work, a cold sweat broke out on Mal, rolling down the back of his neck and following the curve of his spine, as Kristin's voice, monotone and emotionless, rang out, reverberating throughout the store and filling the cyborg with heartbreak.

"Designate Cestus," called the voice, sounding more like an unfeeling recording than the woman Mal had loved so dearly. "You are hereby ordered to power-down and await the Project: Hardwired sanctioned retrieval team."

Licking his lips, Mal finished his makeshift battle dress and darted down a back hall heading for the loading dock, trying to get as far away from the cruel voice as much as from the mind-controlled woman hunting him.

The voice followed him.

"Failure to submit will result in immediate termination for you and Citizen Zuzelo."

A living metal arm punched through a wall-mounted fuse box, showering the cyborg in a torrent of sparks and killing all power within the drugstore. Aware of Zuz's rapidly degenerating condition due to constant updates on the man's blood pressure and heart rate from his cybernetic senses, Mal stopped with his hand inches from the back door and freedom. He had to save his friend—the man who had saved his life more than once since he escaped from the lab—but what about Kristin? She needed him, too.

He wouldn't just leave her. If he could incapacitate her, they could put her somewhere safe while Zuz got medical attention, and Mal could figure out how to break whatever conditioning she'd been put through. Pushing open the door to a darkened back room lined with broken-down boxes stacked chest high in some places, Mal made up his mind, deposing the unconscious body of his friend, blood already seeping through the make-shift bandages wrapped tightly about his abdomen and chest.

A minute, he thought. Maybe less. That was how much time he had to take Kristin down and get the three of them back on the road and to a hospital. Any longer and Zuz was as good as dead—there's no way he could hang on beyond that.

"If Hardwired took control of Kristin, her files should be in my head somewhere," thought Mal as he stalked out of the near total darkness of the 'employee's only' area of the shop. Kristin was trying her best to operate in stealth mode but she was still human and no competition for Mal's cybernetically-enhanced senses. As Mal turned from hunted to hunter, he ordered his computer to pull up all information on his ex-fiancée. He wanted every bit of information Project: Hardwired had on her.

"Records for Kristin Julia Meyer, now Meyer-Morrell, located. Access denied," responded the computer embedded into Mal's cerebellum.

"'Access denied?'" came Mal's nonplussed reaction. "How can the files in my head be 'access denied?'"

"Records sealed by Project: Hardwired Director, Gordon Kiesling. Executive order Alpha-nine-one-seven-two-beta-five."

"'Sealed?!' What kind of super computer are you? Can't you just open the damn things—hack them or whatever it is you and Zuz do?"

"Negative. Encryption encoded with a 512bit key. Only Project: Hardwired Director, Gordon Kiesling, possesses the key."

Mal shook his head, annoyed, and ducked down to remain out of Kristin's line of sight as she hunted the darkened store for any sign of him.

"So, I'll have to make him give me the key," thought the cyborg grimly, edging his way closer to the woman, deadly silent.

Mal's internal systems chose that rather inopportune moment to deliver news that brought the amount of crap the cyborg was in to a whole new level.

"Four Apache AH-64D helicopters inbound to present location, heading north-northwest at approximately one-hundred sixty-five miles per hour. ETA thirty seconds."

There was no way he could take Kristin down and still get away safely with Zuz before the cavalry arrived. Mal swore to himself, more loudly than he had intended. A pair of bullets struck uncomfortably close to where he knelt in the shadows. The cyborg was forced to tear through an eight-foot high steel shelving unit filled with assorted bread products, all labeled as 'fresh baked,' to avoid taking three more bullets to his chest from Kristin who barreled around the corner gun blazing in response to his poorly-timed exclamation.

Turning to see where his ex-lover had gone, Mal took a thrust kick to his stomach, toppling him over amongst the damaged baked goods. He barely recovered in time to avoid another series of shots to the flesh portions of his body, swinging his living metal arm up to deflect the bullets. A quick leg sweep sent Kristin flopping on to her back, but the woman was able to hold on to her gun and fired again, nearly taking Mal in the temple.

The two squared off, Mal dropping into a low defensive stance to protect himself, with Kristin thrusting her gun nearly into his face.

They were at a stand-off that ended as quickly as it began.

Mal cursed again as the sound of approaching helicopters was now audible to his human senses. They were close—too close—and the cyborg knew his time was up. He had to do something fast, or they'd all be captured and Zuz would die.

Evading a pair of shots that emptied Kristin's clip of rounds, Mal flipped himself over the woman, knocking the gun out of her hand along the way, and landing on his feet in a full run. Lurching around the corner, Mal stared down a row of frozen goods, smiling as he trotted to the opposite end and waited.

Kristin appeared, hot on his tail, completely ignoring the fact she was unarmed and ordering Mal to surrender.

As Kristin charged down the cold aisle toward him, Mal gripped the freezer unit to his left with both hands and pulled, straining every muscle in his body. The woman leapt at him with a flying kick, too late, as the entire structure gave way to the irresistible force of his cybernetic strength and capsized onto her, pinning Kristin to the ice-chilled floor.

Praying to God that Kristin would be all right, Mal turned and headed back to where he had hidden Zuz to collect the man, who had grown deathly white in the cyborg's absence. At first Mal was afraid he was too late but his computer sensors picked up a heartbeat, faint and nearly imperceptible even to his superhuman senses.

He still had time!

With Zuz in his arms, Mal crashed through the heavy wooden loading dock door and moved into the late afternoon sun shining down on the worker's parking lot behind the building. The roar and whine of landing helicopters masked the sound of a shattered window as Mal found a car to 'appropriate.' Mal had the vehicle hot-wired and in motion mere seconds after placing Zuz delicately into the backseat, peeling out and punching down hard on the gas in a race against the clock.

Thick-soled combat boots ground the broken glass littering the pharmacy's tiled floor into a fine powder beneath them as a veritable army of battle-ready Project: Hardwired soldiers swarmed into the building. The men, machine guns at the ready, swept through every inch of the building, securing entrances, exits, and everything else in between. A moment later they were joined by a tall muscular man with shimmering metal arms and a silver cybernetic eye.

Gauss surveyed the situation for a moment, analyzing the information being fed to him by his ocular enhancement. Nearly every inch of the store's interior was destroyed—the whole place virtually reeked of Cestus's handiwork. He'd been on enough missions with the rogue cyborg to recognize the sort of mess the man tended to leave behind.

"I need a sit-rep?" demanded Gauss of a group of GMRs working their way through the clutter. "Where is he?"

"No sign of Designate Cestus, but we have two squads canvassing the immediate vicinity now, sir," answered the top ranking GMR present, his name-tag read 'Lambda-One.'

"Ran away again, Cestus? This is getting redundant," muttered Gauss to himself, then demanded to know where the girl was.

"Unit Galatea is trapped beneath one of the freezer units near the center of the store," responded Lambda-One. "Tau-Unit is bringing in equipment to free her now."

"Don't bother." Gauss stormed past the lower level Project: Hardwired grunt. The lack of initiative programmed in the Gomers was a real pain sometimes, thought the cyborg, stomping his way to the area where Kristin's struggling form was still pinned beneath two tons or more of heavy machinery and rapidly defrosting boxed dinners. "Fall back and secure the front of the building—I've got this," he ordered the ten or so GMRs of Lambda-Unit loitering around the mess of broken metal and spilled milk.

Reaching out with his mastery of magnetic fields once the area cleared out, Gauss slid one hand underneath the fallen refrigerator and flipped it across the room as if it's almost five-thousand pound weight was nothing. Splitting in half, the ten-foot long icebox crashed through aisle after aisle, sending shelves toppling and smashing into one another before hammering into the rear wall.

Gauss stared down at the unconscious figure splayed out

on the ground in front of him. A small groan escaped from her lips, causing the cyborg to grin, revealing his perfect white teeth. Mirror-finished titanium fingers slid through Kristin's long golden hair, reflecting back the tight smile carving itself into Gauss's face.

"But now that he knows we have you, Cestus won't be running for long."

Mal watched the emergency room staff so intently as they wheeled Zuz's nearly lifeless body down the ammonia-scented halls of the Encino Hospital Medical Center that he completely missed the fact one of the nurses had stayed behind and was attempting to get more information out of him. It took her no fewer than nine 'ahems' and four more 'excuse mes' before she was at last able to grab his attention.

Referred to as a 'fireball' by her co-workers, Heidi Jensen was small, compact, and full of a seemingly endless amount of energy and attitude. Unfortunately for Mal, he was the target for both.

"I said, we're going to need you to fill out an incident report and wait here for the police," the tiny woman had gotten so worked up from being ignored that her dirty-blond ponytail was snapping back and forth faster than a whip. "What exactly did you say happened to Mr. Zuzelo?"

Looking down quizzically, Mal answered as if on auto-pilot, "Carjacking. They tried to take his car."

Unconvinced, Nurse Jensen gave Mal the once over again for the eighth or ninth time since his arrival at her emergency room: he was tall and good looking in that sort of way that you'd regret the next morning, dressed in jeans and an old, threadbare Christmas sweater with tiny reindeer and snowmen on it—something Mal had scrounged up in the back of the Volkswagen he'd stolen from the pharmacy's employee parking lot. All of that in and of itself was enough to set off the nurse's finely-tuned trouble alert, but when combined with the burns and copious amounts of blood covering nearly every inch of his body, Jensen's alarms were blaring away at full volume.

"What about you? That looks like a lot of blood—it looks

like you were in a fight yourself," she asked, doing the little hop and stretch short people do when trying to see over a crowd as she attempt to locate one of the on duty police officers that frequented the hospital. "We should have one of the doctors check you out, too."

"I'm fine...the nanites have me back to 98% operating capacity," responded Mal still lost in his thoughts.

"Excuse me?" Jensen said, finally able to catch the attention of the slightly rotund Officer North from his usual spot flirting in front of the nurses' station. She waved him over frantically.

Mal snapped back to reality and looked around, seeing the cop heading towards him with resolve in his eye and donut on his chin.

"I have to go."

Protesting, the nurse tried to get her hands around Mal's arm only to stop, horrified at the inhuman way it felt beneath the wool material of the sweater's long sleeves. The cyborg pushed his way down the hall and was outside before the huffing Officer North reached Nurse Jensen, asking if everything was okay.

Staring after the vanished man, Jensen nodded. She just hoped he stayed vanished.

Unsure if anyone was still pursuing him, Mal rushed across the busy car lot outside the hospital's front doors, dodging vehicles and people with uncanny agility. Along the way to the purloined vehicle waiting for him with its doors still open from the hasty exit he'd made to get his friend inside, Mal had made his decision.

He was done.

"It's time to stop running," thought Mal, determined. He was tired of having to watch his back every second of the day, and tired of having his friends threatened—having them hurt. It was time to take the fight back to where it all began: Project: Hardwired.

CHAPTER 18

For the first time since the September 11th terrorist attacks, the US Bank Tower building was closed to the public.

At precisely one hour before the normal close of business at the tower, an announcement blared over the public address speakers requesting the immediate shutdown of all businesses operating at the location. A few minutes later, all residents were escorted from the premises by heavily-armed US government troops and informed that the facility would re-open the next morning.

When pressed on reasons for the abrupt evacuation and shut down of one of the largest business centers on the west coast, the soldiers, uniformed in a manner unrecognizable by even the most experienced of military veterans working at the facility, would only say it was a precaution against terrorist threat. More than one overly vocal tower resident were escorted off-site at gun point when they refused to vacate the area.

None of the civilians knew precisely what was going on at their place of business, but deep down they knew it was something far beyond what the Kevlar enshrouded men were telling them.

Tension was thick in the air and grew thicker as the minutes ticked away after the evacuation. As one hour passed and then two, everyone on duty grew anxious. They knew an attack was coming, but not when or how. The cadre of men stationed around the building were fully aware of who was coming and what he was able to do, and the tension quickly spread.

The attack came just as the sun began to kiss the horizon. Men on the periphery began disappearing, their radios hissing static and then nothing, their vital signs flat-lining on the monitors high up on the seventy-sixth floor in command and control.

"Target has breached the perimeter!" The GMR overseer's voice screamed out across the radio waves. From his position seated behind a bank of computer screens, monitors were flashing more and more red as the lives of his charges were snuffed out. "Weapons free, deadly force authorized!"

In spite of the nearly impenetrable contingent of seventy Project: Hardwired soldiers, human and cybernetically-enhanced GMR alike, the living weapon known as Cestus had found a way to breach their defenses: the sewage tunnels lining the area were child's play for him to enter a few blocks away. As the number of disappearing men hit ten, the cyborg took advantage of the resulting chaos and popped up in the midst of a group of the black-clad mercenaries. Two were decapitated, and a third bifurcated from collarbone to groin before the men realized death had landed amongst their group.

With enemies surrounding him on all sides, Cestus gave his mind completely over to the programming that had been forced into his brain and the world turned red with blood and rage. He punched through the first unit of urban warriors like they were single-ply toilet paper in a shoddy gas station bathroom. Within seconds, men were dismembered and left lying in bloody pools covering the ground in his wake. The unyielding claws of his nanotech-driven arms showed no mercy to anything they touched.

Responding to the screams of the dying, a second and third battalion of Hardwired GMRs crashed down onto Cestus from every direction, guns blazing. Humanity repressed, the cyborg dove headfirst into the wave of men attempting to bar him from gaining access to the building and exacting his vengeance. His claws scythed out like the blades of a metal and flesh grim reaper, snuffing out life with each touch.

When it was over, the flesh and bone barrier made up of six dozen men lasted fewer than ninety seconds against the berserker fury of the super-soldier.

Covered in blood and cordite residue, and dripping with

perspiration, Cestus was barely winded. Seventy men had been killed in the time it took to heat a convenience store burrito and it meant nothing to the government-spawned killing machine he'd become. It did nothing more than whet his appetite for death.

Pulling up a tactical update from his internal sensors, Cestus saw that nothing lived within a one hundred meter radius of the carnage surrounding the building. A blank spot in his readouts, corresponding with the building's immense entrance, caught the super-soldier's attention, drawing his gaze magnetically toward it.

The almost colorless blue eyes of the cyborg narrowed to razor slits, fighting against the darkness staring back at him from the shadowed skyscraper's interior, struggling to pull clues from the twilight within. The computer augmented eyes of Cestus quickly deciphered the subtle movement of cloth and steel, identifying the next obstacle the head of Project: Hardwired had placed in the cyborg's path.

Cestus smiled coldly as his eyes finally revealed to him the identity of the man standing across the battlefield from him: Fortified at the center-point of the lobby with an M246 SAW machine gun at the ready and flanked by thirty armed-to-the-teeth GMR warriors was Captain Marc Morrell, the sight of whom filled Cestus with a particularly intense need to kill. Reacting of its own accord, the cyborg's body bulked up even further, thick armor plates formed across his chest and back, and his arms grew, lengthening to gorilla-like proportions, growing serrated flanges, blades along the forearms. Wicked knives extended out twenty inches from his hands and twitched in anticipation.

As the transformation completed, Cestus launched himself forward at the mass of enemies waiting for him inside.

"FIRE!" ordered Morrell at the top of his lungs, his SAW echoing his voice with a scream of more than 200 rounds per minute, perforating the ground around Cestus with a hail of hot lead.

The cyborg danced through the withering storm of high caliber rounds, ignoring the odd shot that glanced off the thick armor of his prosthetics. Bursting into a run directly toward the heart of the gunfire, Cestus leaned low, reached out with the gnarled talons of his hands to catch the thick nylon straps lining the back of a fallen GMR, and pulled the corpse up from its final resting place to act as an unliving shield for his advance. With the limp body flopping over one shoulder protecting the cyborg's torso from incoming attacks, Cestus' left hand reached up and tore the MGL-140 free of its restraining harness on the dead soldier's side, and aimed into the center of the rapidly disintegrating plate glass lobby wall. Titanium-alloy fingers tightened on the trigger and let loose with a volley of 40mm tear gas shells, covering the front of the besieged building in a dense fog.

"Maintain fire!" Morrell screamed in response.

Thousands of rounds lanced holes of light through the gray cloud of smoke rolling into the lobby, trying to catch a lucky break and take down the advancing Cestus.

Tear gas mixed with gunpowder clouds and steam from red hot weapon barrels, transforming the once gleaming marble lobby into a hellish cavern lit only by flashes of gunfire and the fading light from outside. For more than a minute, the Project: Hardwired response team poured bullets into the growing fog bank blindly, having lost sight of Cestus seconds after their barrage had begun.

Eyes squinting against the burning chemical gas, Morrell finally removed his right hand from the trigger of his smoking weapon and held it upright, signaling his men to cease fire wordlessly. As one the robot-like GMRs stopped firing.

Ten long seconds passed in complete silence as the men waited to see if they'd stopped the rogue cyborg. Ten seconds that seemed to drag on for a week to Morrell. With the silence a thunderous drumbeat in his ears, the officer ordered a squad of five members of GMR Unit Upsilon forward with weapons at the ready.

Before the automaton soldiers disappeared into the foul-smelling gas cloud, Upsilon-Six called out "Something's movi—" before his arms and most of his face were torn from his body by a shining silver flash from deep within. A microsecond later, Cestus burst forth from the densely packed gray mist, arms slashing out in front of him. Three GMRs dropped, the top halves of their skulls sliced cleanly from their heads.

Like puppets on a string, the remaining GMRs let their machine guns swing back on their side harnesses and drew electro-batons in near perfect unison. They charged Cestus as one and somewhere seventy-five floors up the controllers prayed it would be enough.

It wasn't.

Cestus moved like a whirlwind through the attacking men, carving flesh and ignoring blows from the electrified weapons the May brothers had guaranteed Director Kiesling would nullify his threat. Men fell before him in droves, dead or dying, as he pushed his way towards the man responsible for taking Kristin from him.

Swearing aloud, Morrell decided it was every man for himself and swung his SAW around, aiming into the mass of his own men surrounding the crazed cyborg. Taking Cestus down once and for all was worth the cost of a few GMR lives—besides, Morrell knew the boys in the tech department could patch a GMR back to fighting capacity as long as its brain case was mostly intact. The soldier opened fire, shredding everything in front of him.

Dodging beneath the stream of armor-piercing rounds, Cestus dropped to his knees, snatched an MP5 from one of his fallen foes, and in one fluid motion let loose with a burst of shells that took Morrell in the right side of his chest, disabling his arm and causing the man to lose grip on his weapon with a shriek.

The empty space between them took Cestus three long strides to cross and backhand the wounded Morrell, knocking the giant machine gun away from him. Losing blood rapidly, Morrell attempted to gain some distance from the rampaging cyborg with a snap kick to the chest that caught Cestus by surprise and spun him around on his heels. Morrell used the distraction to back away from his reeling foe. He jerked the 9mm Beretta 92FS from the holster on his thigh, thumbed it to semi-automatic and begin firing as fast as he could.

Dancing around the wounded man's attack, Cestus stepped behind Morrell, shoved the serrated blades of his hand claws into the soldier's back and ripped away seven inches of spinal column with a wet slurping sound.

Morrell flopped onto his back bonelessly, his mouth continuing to scream soundlessly as the final few breaths fled from between crimson-stained teeth.

"There will be more upstairs," Cestus thought to himself as he watched Morrell's vital signs fade away with his computerized senses, confirming the man's death.. There would be more GMRs and at least one Prime Unit waiting, ready and eager to kill him. But it didn't matter to the battle-hungry cyborg. He knew the lesser units were only a challenge in large groups, and even then all they could do was slow him down. As for the Primes like Gauss and the others, their enhanced abilities were no match for his own melee-specific capabilities in the tight confines of the skyscraper's upper floors.

Outside or there in the lobby's large open space—places where the Project: Hardwired pawns could act freely and without constrictions—had been their only real shot at stopping him.

Heading for the high-speed access to the top floors of the building, Cestus couldn't believe they'd made it so easy for him.

The melodious ping of an elevator arriving on the floor and a voice announcing 'round two' over the building's PA system cut Cestus's internal celebration short, his instincts dropping him automatically into a defensive stance at the sounds.

The cyborg was prepared for anything except for what emerged from between the parted lift doors.

"Oh, my God."

CHAPTER 19

Kristin Meyer, once the love of Malcolm Weir's life, strode out of the harsh fluorescent lighting of the open elevator, and paused to smile at the dumbfounded super-soldier.

"Kristin?!"

If the situation had been one iota less serious or deadly Mal's mouth would have dropped to the floor at the outfit his former lover was decked out in. As it was, it nearly knocked him off his feet.

With thigh-high stiletto-heeled black leather boots, a military-grade Kevlar corset, and covered in straps hung with weapons, Kristin's outfit could only be described as high-tech mercenary by way of Victoria's Secret, or Nazi stripper from Hell. Mal knew it was all done to gain a psychological advantage against him—the only thing worse would have been to dress her up as a slutty Catholic schoolgirl.

In contrast to her inviting appearance, the weapons in her hands, a Brugger & Thomet MP9 machine pistol in her left and a glowing steel katana with, according to his sensor readings, nearly forty-thousand volts crackling along its blade, gave off some of the worst mixed-signals the cyborg had ever gotten from a date.

Living metal arms twitched and bulged, elongated spines flexing and mismatched plates rotating, as Mal forced his arms to relax into something more closely approximating 'normal,' hoping it would keep Kristin calm. The woman's six-inch-high heels created a staccato drumbeat as she strode mindfully across the lobby's marble and stone floor, weapons held tightly in each hand but, to Mal's relief, kept low in a less-aggressive profile.

If he could keep her at ease, Mal was convinced he'd be able to work through whatever brainwashing Project: Hardwired had put her through. He was sure he could bring her back.

"Honey," said Mal, moving forward to meet the woman in the lobby's center. "Are you okay? Did they hurt you?"

Kristin's head cocked to one side, her golden hair falling in a stream over her shoulder, the weapons dipped lower into an almost casual position. Mal stepped forward and reached his hand out to brush her chin lightly.

The merest hint of a smile started to form on her pretty face. Mal knew he could reach her.

"It's okay, Kristin. I'm here now...we can go home."

The smile grew and the lovely girl leaned in, nuzzling her lips on Mal's neck, the fresh scent of the strawberry shampoo she favored filled his nostrils and sent goose bumps bubbling up across his skin. He could feel her warm breath and her mouth moved up to brush his hear.

Then she spoke.

"Is that right, Mr. Weir?" said Kristin in a deep, masculine voice not her own. "Come to save your pretty little girlfriend?"

There were no words for the amount of revulsion Mal felt at hearing the voice of Gordon Kiesling coming from the red-glossed lips of Kristin—lips he'd kissed countless times.

Off-balance, the possessed woman's attack took Mal completely by surprise. Kristin's energy-enhanced sword whipped out at chest height, burying itself deep in the thick scar tissue of Mal's side where human flesh merged unevenly with the inhuman material of his cybernetic replacements. So fast was the attack that the blade lodged between a bone rib and Mal's metal reinforced spine before the fluctuating electrical current kicked in, sending the cyborg's body to his knees in painful spasms.

Mal's computer system seemed unable to counteract the relentless flow of electricity flowing from the katana wedged in his body. Its modulation seemed designed to disrupt his circuitry.

On the verge of blacking out, Mal felt the woman tear her weapon free in a graceful pirouette that turned into a cruel

roundhouse kick, the dagger-like steel heels of her shoes
drawing a bloody line across his face from ear to chin. Mal was
quick enough to use the force behind the attack to roll out of
the way a nanosecond before a second kick shattered the highly
polished marble slab he'd been crouched on.

A scream of pain tore itself from Mal's throat as the woman
reversed her grip on the sword and sliced his back open,
spraying the floor and the pale white skin of her exposed flesh
with blood.

The shock from Kristin's katana surging through his
nervous system turned Mal's muscles into unresponsive jelly,
ignoring his every command to get up and defend himself. All
he could manage as the woman stood over him laughing in a
rich baritone was to half crawl, half slide away from her at a
snail's pace.

Mal flopped over onto his back, planting his right hand
flat on the ground to raise himself into a seated position. A
disappointed 'tsk' echoed above him as his computer initiated
his healing factor, far slower than he would have liked.

"I'm disappointed, Malcolm…may I call you 'Malcolm?' 'Mr.
Weir' seems so formal between friends," said Kiesling's voice.
"I expected more of a fight from our most advanced unit. You're
not going to let yourself get beat by a girl, are you?"

The warm feeling of nanites sealing wounds and rebuilding
damaged tissue filled Mal, his head clearing even as his injuries
vanished.

"Kristin, I know you're still in there. Fight it." Mal's voice
was weak and unsteady from the strange sequence of events.

Sword twirling in lazy circles in one hand, Kristin brought
up her machine pistol with the other and took aim at the prone
man half-sprawled out on the ground.

"I'm afraid Kristin doesn't live here anymore," answered
the man's voice.

Bullets belched out at high speed from the gun at the squeeze
of Kristin's finger, but Mal was ready for it and deflected the
assault, smacking the armor-piercing rounds off course with
his nearly indestructible living metal arms and uncanny speed.

Needing more time to come up with a plan, Mal kept talking

as he danced through the rain of gunfire spitting at him from the MP9.

"Why are you doing this to us?" asked Mal, maneuvering through the deadly hail in an effort to get close enough to Kristin to disarm the woman. "What do you want from me?"

The woman chuckled, ejecting the empty magazine from the bottom of her fully automatic pistol. Mal used the pause to lunge in under her sword and slice into the nylon belt containing her spare cartridges, sending it scuttling across the ground out of the woman's reach.

"Why I want 'you,' of course."

Whoever had control of Kristin's body gave up on the gun, dropping it. Grasping the katana's hilt in both hands, she lashed out at Mal, who reflexively caught it in his hand. The glowing blue lightning field that danced along the sword's length jumped into the cybernetic components of Mal's nanotech prosthetic, rendering it numb and inoperable from the elbow down. The weapon seemed to have been created with Mal's specific 'improvements' in mind and left them malfunctioning and unreliable with the tiniest of contact.

"Project: Hardwired has too much time, too many resources, and far too much of the taxpayers' hard-earned money invested in your development to let you just walk out. We own you, soldier!" With that, Kristin's body, controlled remotely from a floor hundreds of feet above, hurled herself at Mal, luminous blade slashing furiously.

At first, Mal was taken aback by the wanton disregard Kristin had for her own protection. She continually over-extended swings and thrusts, leaving her vital areas exposed. When the cyborg dodged a particularly violent backhanded chop and instinctively retaliated with a crippling open-hand strike to her chest, knocking Kristin flat onto her back, realization hit him.

The man controlling her had no need for defense. No need to dodge or defend against Mal's attacks. The entire point of the exercise was to wear him down mentally as much as physically. So what if he killed the girl?

Kristin flipped off her backside and back up to her feet in a move that would have done Jackie Chan proud. Seeing the look of concern on the cyborg's face, Kristin's voice took on a reassuring tone even as she renewed her attempts to split Mal in half.

"This isn't going to end well for you, Designate Cestus. Give up. Come back to the fold. Everything will be okay," she said. "We can even give your girl back her life."

Ducking out of the way of a diagonal cleave of Kristin's sword that turned out to be a clever feint, Mal moved directly into a powerful elbow blow from the woman. Only his superior reaction time saved him from the back stroke of the sword that would have taken the top of his skull off.

"I'd be a bit more inclined to believe that if you weren't trying to cut my head off and scoop out the insides," Mal fired back, bounding over a horizontal slice intended to sever his spine just above the naval.

"You've got our intellectual property locked in there and it's coming out...one way or the other." The voice snapped and Mal realized whoever was behind the attack was getting frustrated. If he was lucky frustration would lead to carelessness and to a mistake Mal could take advantage of.

It was then Mal noticed the interface port melded into the skin at the base of Kristin's skull.

"That's how they're controlling her," he thought to himself. That would be the way he broke their control.

Mal asked his computer if it could hack into whatever was controlling Kristin. Disrupt its signal? Cut the puppet's strings.

"Negative," the computer responded dispassionately.

Another sword stroke narrowly missed dissecting Mal through his midsection. Whatever they did to Kristin, she wasn't any faster than a normal human. Now that Mal had rebounded from the initial shock of her attacks, he could dodge her forever. But that did nothing to solve his problem—it just gave Kiesling time to send more reinforcements to stop Mal. And fighting Kristin was out of the question. He needed to find a way to shut her down without permanently harming or killing her.

"Can communication with their command programming be disrupted through the physical access port?"

"Affirmative."

The computer's confirmation spurred Mal into a flurry of action. In one fluid motion, Mal used a scooping block to parry Kristin's sword arm, and twisted his body to last out with a fearsome sidekick to her midsection, causing the woman to double over in pain. An open hand chop to her wrist sent the katana spinning across the room. Still out of breath from having the wind knock out of her lungs, Kristin fought feebly, kicking and cursing, as Mal snaked a hand around her neck, forcing her head to remain in place while the living metal of his other fist altered its shape, thinning out and elongating into a grim-looking six-inch spike lined with tiny connectors.

Kristin gasped out loud as Mal plunged the spike into the hardwired port at the top of her spine, his computer taking control over her mind upon contact.

The connection was instantaneous. Mal could feel the information data flowing from the computer implanted deep within his ex-fiancée's brain, through the living circuits of his arm, and into his own mind. Direct access to Kristin's brain allowed Mal to almost visualize the wireless connection controlling her—he could see its blazing trail streaming straight up into the building above their heads. Reaching out, Mal was able to touch the heart of the Abraxas-Array, burning its location into his mind. The face of Director Gordon Kiesling stared back at him through the data stream, grinning, before Project: Hardwired computer technicians closed it down, blocking the cyborg from the system.

Turning back to the woman in his arms, Mal probed deep, trying to locate and bring back Kristin's base personality construct.

"Oh, no," he stammered in disbelief.

Mal was horrified by what his direct link to Kristin's mind revealed: the woman he knew was gone. Her mind completely wiped, reprogrammed one-hundred percent by the Abraxas-Array as it transformed her from a beautiful, kind woman into one of Project: Hardwired's mindless GMRs.

For all intents and purposes, Kristin Meyer was dead. In her place, all that remained was an empty shell controlled by Kiesling and his group.

Tears welled up in Mal's eyes, running freely down his face and onto his chest as he released Kristin's still body and dislodged the connection his cybernetics had made with the interface to her brain, allowing her to finally fall to the ground. Mal backed away from the prone figure, heart threatening to burst out of his chest.

For a full thirty seconds, Mal was lost. The woman had been his world before everything had happened. She had been his life and his reason for going on. Now she was gone forever.

No! He'd find the men responsible and make them bring her back. They'd taken his mind, and he was able to return. They could do the same for her.

And if they refused, he'd kill them all.

A quiet laughter snapped Mal out of his murderous thoughts.

"Oh, sweetie." The evil, laughing voice of Kiesling taunted through playfully parted crimson lips. The woman twisted her body just enough for the cyborg to see a tiny pin fall free from the grenade in her hand and its safety 'spoon' spring loose. "Say goodnight."

"No!"

Mal sprung for the explosive charge in the woman's hand, crossing the distance in the blink of an eye. But even his preternatural speed wasn't fast enough to stop fate and Gordon Kiesling's revenge.

The computer enhanced brain of Malcolm Weir allowed him to watch her death in slow motion—an image that would replay itself over and over in his mind for the rest of his life. It started with a tiny pulse of red flame in her palms and expanded outward at high speed, throwing shrapnel in 360 degrees, rendering flesh and bone into a thick red paste, unidentifiable as having been a living woman. Kristin's life was extinguished before the concussive blast and metal fragments punched into Mal, sending him tumbling uncontrollably across the room, bleeding from countless wounds.

Coming to a few seconds later, all Mal knew was pain. Pain from the explosion. Pain from fighting for his existence for twenty-four hours straight. And, worst of all, pain from seeing the woman he loved blasted into red vapor and chunks of lifeless meat at the whim of a gutless, power-hungry man. A man whose face and voice were now familiar to Malcolm Weir. A man who was, even now, hiding behind an army of soldiers and killers. A man who had taken everything from him. A man who wanted Designate Cestus at all costs.

He smiled. If they wanted Cestus, then that's what they'd get. Malcolm Weir breathed his last breath, eyes closing.

Something else opened them back up.

Cestus started to climb to his feet but was stopped by a sound from the street beyond the building's destroyed walls and a figure, silhouetted by the harsh outdoor lighting of the battle-ravaged courtyard.

"Hey, Cestus," called a voice from outside, a voice Cestus immediate recognized as belonging to his least favorite member of the Project: Hardwired cyborg varsity squad, Gauss. "You forgot your car."

The sight of Zuz's crappy white car crashing through the reinforced glass front wall of the US Bank Tower's main lobby forced an expletive to be summoned up from the pit of Cestus's diaphragm, along with a healthy dose of dread. Those four letters and bringing up his arms to shield the human portion of his body were all Cestus could manage before the two ton magnetically-propelled cannonball slammed into him at just under sixty miles-per-hour, driving the cyborg against the back wall of the cavernous room with a thunderclap.

Struggling to get free of the twisted steel straight jacket and fallen masonry, Cestus watched hopelessly as Gauss stalked across the debris-strewn lobby floor towards him. The Project: Hardwired cyborg looked smug as he approached.

"You better not be dead in there." Mirror-surfaced metal arms held out at shoulder height, their evenly spaced solenoid bands vibrating fiercely as Gauss reached out and grabbed the magnetic field around him with his power. Iron rebar torn from their place in concrete core joined what was left of the Nissan's frame to entwine Cestus's limbs, immobilizing him.

Gauss jerked his arms apart and the steel mesh cage lurched free of the fragmented remains of the collapsed ceiling and back wall it had once been a foundation for. The mass screeched across the floor to where the cyborg stood triumphantly. Steel girders parted like a cloth curtain as Gauss reached in to lock an unyielding grip around Cestus's neck, forcing the half-conscious man's eyes up to his own.

"I wanted to make sure you looked into the face of the man who beat you."

To the surprise of both men, Cestus smiled at the newcomer.

"Nice scar, G." Cestus's voice was ragged, with no weight behind it. But it was enough.

Rubbing the still healing wound from their earlier battle, Gauss sneered. "You're dead, Cestus...you're just too stupid to realize it."

The cyborg's ferrous fist pistoned forward, knocking Cestus into oblivion.

CHAPTER 20

Cestus woke to an intensely uncomfortable sense of *Déjà vu*, opening his eyes to the unfiltered glare of a trio of lights mounted a few feet above his horizontal position on something ice cold and unforgivingly hard. The cyborg tried to move his head to get a better look at where he had been taken and found it held fast. Attempts to sit up and to move his arms from their positions at his side gave him the same results.

He was trapped, unable to raise even a finger.

Even more disconcerting for the super-soldier, the computer systems he had slowly come to accept failed to respond to his mental call.

For better or worse, Cestus was completely on his own.

"He's awake, Director Kiesling," said a female voice from somewhere to the prisoner's left, followed by the slow, measured steps of a large man approaching the cyborg's position.

Cestus felt the presence of his captor a split second before a shadow leaned in, shading him from the blinding lights above. Unaided by his cybernetic enhancements, it took Cestus's irises a moment to adjust to the change in light. Blinking a few times to clear his vision, the cybernetic warrior stared into the eyes of the architect of his misfortune.

The cyborg recognized him immediately from the images he'd drawn through his connection to the Abraxas computers during his fight with Kristin downstairs. The man's pale blue eyes were unforgettable, burning into Cestus like ice.

Gordon Kiesling, executive director of Project: Hardwired smiled warmly down at Cestus from his position. The man's hair was still perfectly groomed, and the top three buttons of his custom-tailored linen shirt were open, exposing a rather impressive amount of thick blond chest hair. Cestus noticed a woman standing just behind the man holding the folded blue material of his missing jacket.

Somehow, the hatred Cestus held toward the man doubled when he finally spoke.

"Well, I must say it is an honor to finally meet the man behind Designate Cestus, Malcolm. I've been a fan of your work since you joined us here at Project: Hardwired," said Kiesling, smacking the thick manila folder in his hand.

"Malcolm Weir is dead," spat Cestus. "You killed him a year ago. Just like you killed Kristin." Cestus's eyes bored a hole into Kiesling. "Just like I'm going to kill you."

Looking around the brightly lit surgical suite—a pale colored room almost identical to the one Cestus had regained consciousness in the prior afternoon—Kiesling chuckled, gesturing at the dozen heavily-armed GMRs surrounding the stainless-steel operating table the cyborg had been strapped down to.

"Come now, Malcolm. There's no escape for you this time." The thick gold and diamond class ring on Kiesling's pinky-finger reflected the stark white light shining down from the fixture above the men as he motioned towards a mousy blond in thick black glasses and green surgical scrubs half covered by an overly starched cotton lab coat. "Dr. Ryan here knows more about what you are—what you can do—than you do. She's responsible for creating all the Abraxas Prime Units. She also designed the negation-restraints that are keeping your cybernetics powered down."

"How did this all happen?" asked Cestus, continuing to test his cybernetics to gauge the extent of their inoperable state.

"Excellent question, Malcolm. Excellent question, indeed!" cheered Kiesling. He half turned to the aforementioned Dr. Ryan. "Now, Dr. Ryan, in the simplest words possible, please explain to myself and Malcolm here what exactly went wrong."

"As you are aware from my briefing, the nanites we used in his upgrade were experimental—we'd never done anything like it before," said the woman, stepping further into Cestus's field of vision. "We assume their AI kicked in and took over, grabbing every piece of information in our networks before wiping out the Abraxas servers completely. Really, it's truly amazing. His tech has continually performed above and beyond our initial estimations."

Kiesling clapped in a manner that, remarkably, carried more than a little sarcasm with it. From his position flat on an operating table, waiting to have his head removed, Mal appreciated the man's ability.

"That's fantastic to hear, Dr. Ryan. Now, how do we fix it?"

Clearing her throat, Ryan gave her appraisal of the situation and her solution.

"We'll have to run a scrubbing program to recover all the lost information from the trillions of nanocomputers making up the unit's limbs, brain and nervous system," she paused and looked down at Cestus with the merest hint of sadness in her eyes. "The process will destroy his programming and his mind. It'll be a clean slate and need to be reinstalled."

Smiling, Kiesling asked, "And the original personality construct of Malcolm Weir? Will it be recoverable?"

"Oh no, Director Kiesling," replied the doctor, "The organic portion of his brain will be completely burned out. He'll be a vegetable and ready for a new artificial intelligence to be installed."

"Excellent!" Kiesling was now beaming with excitement. Things could go back to the way they were supposed to be, and he'd be able to rid himself of the politicians for a while. He reached down and patted Cestus on his head. "We'll get our favorite assassin back."

"Why me?" asked Cestus.

"'Why' you?" repeated Kiesling, finally understanding. "You really don't have a clue, do you?" The director turned towards the woman who had engineered Malcolm Weir's transformation. "Is it possible, Dr. Ryan?"

The woman thought for a moment and then nodded.

"The massive download of information from the Abraxas mainframe into the nanobots of Designate Cestus must have caused a feedback loop that shorted out his memory. Essentially, his brain was rebooted and everything since his recruitment was lost." Ryan leaned in close, shining a silver-plated penlight into the captured cyborg's eyes, testing his reaction. "My guess is he doesn't remember anything after the trauma of the accident in Iraq a year ago."

"This whole situation has got to be a real mind-fuck for you, doesn't it? Not knowing what you've missed this past year?" asked Kiesling, crossing his arms in consideration of his prisoner's plight.

"Let me up and I'll show you how much it pisses me off." The veins in Cestus's neck and bare torso bulged, his muscles testing what strength they still had against the computer-controlled restraints holding them at bay. They held fast.

"Tut-tut, Malcolm. There's no need for any of that. If you've got a couple of minutes to spare, I'd be happy to fill in the blanks for you," teased Kiesling. Tilting his head toward Ms. Roslan, he asked, "Do we have time for a story before we report in to the Secretary of Defense?"

"We've got a few minutes before we have to leave, sir."

Kiesling reach out and took a large folder from his assistant and flipped through it for a moment before looking back to where Cestus was laying. The man took a theatrical breath before beginning.

"You were all supposed to die in the crash, Malcolm," Kiesling gave a half-hearted chuckle at the idea. "Trust a group of Rangers to do everything they're ordered to do except die."

"What?!" Cestus couldn't believe what he was hearing. "What did you say?"

The cyborg was stunned at what his captor told him next.

"We'd gone as far as we could with the GMRs and beta units. Working from the corpses of organ donors or soldiers killed overseas and sent home weeks before they were finally sent to Dr. Ryan's crew. We needed better subjects for the final phase of the project. Elite soldiers, pre-selected, who would survive the conversion process.

"The only thing standing in our way was the current bleeding-heart liberal administration. They wouldn't give us the go-ahead to recruit healthy soldiers—so we elected to make our own candidates.

"The Abraxas-Array chose the subjects itself, based on extensive medical and psychological evaluations. It picked from SWAT members and military men—sifting through SEAL teams, CIA operatives, Marines..." Kiesling paused and gestured overly dramatically at Cestus. "Army Rangers.

"You were all the best of the best. All we needed was for you to be removed from active duty.

"You, Captain Malcolm Weir, were the last man selected by Abraxas. From there it was easy enough to get you stationed out in an active war zone and in position for one of our international partners to shoot down your chopper.

"It was supposed to be an easy operation. A 'crash and grab' as it were. All you had to do was stay at the crash site. Instead, you got up and walked away. Even worse, you called for help and survived long enough for the army to rescue you."

"Everything that happened—to me...to my men—it was all your doing," stated Mal flatly.

Kiesling eased up one with one leg to half-sit on the table Cestus was confined to. It was a gesture of familiarity the cyborg didn't appreciate.

"We had a heck of a time trying to catch up to you after that," sighed the man, disregarding the interruption. "It took us weeks to have you and the remaining men of your unit brought stateside and relocated to Edwards Air Force Base."

"My men and Captain Morrell?"

"Yes. And the good Captain Morrell," nodded Kiesling. "He was a lot easier to bring into the fold than you were, despite your injuries. Good man...he knows how to follow orders. You, on the other hand, took quite a bit more persuading."

"But why involve Kristin? What did she have to do with any of this?" Cestus demanded, straining against the harnesses holding his body inert.

"It was your fault, really," started Kiesling, shrugging his shoulders in an overly exaggerated fashion. The man was putting on a performance, as much for his own benefit as for the captive cyborg's. "We had to threaten your girl to get you to finally agree to submit to the project as a Hardwired Prime applicant. Even then, I didn't completely trust you to stay with the program, so I had her converted into a sleeper agent...just in case."

A tiny voice sounding in a particularly dark corner of Cestus's mind nearly caused a smile to crack the otherwise stoic mask he'd forced onto his face.

"System reboot in progress," it said.

Oblivious to what was happening less than a foot from where he was sitting, Kiesling continued his tale.

"Once we got you under control and the lovely Dr. Ryan here patched you up, you were a perfect soldier."

"Until the incident in Kabul," added Ms. Roslan.

"YES, Ms. Roslan...Until the incident in Kabul. Thank you for the interruption." Kiesling rolled his eyes at Cestus, feigning embarrassment at the disturbance. "Women!"

"What happened in Kabul?" asked Cestus in a calm voice that hid the frenzy he had building just under the surface.

"I'm afraid that's going to have to be a tale for another time, my friend...not that you'll be around to hear it." Looking down at his five thousand dollar Breitling watch, Kiesling stood up from his seat next to Cestus and stretched lazily. "Dr. Ryan, the patient is all yours. Let's go, Ms. Roslan. You know how the Secretary hates to be kept waiting—it could mess up our whole day."

A gravel-filled voice halted Kiesling's exit in its tracks. "Kiesling...your day is about to get a whole lot worse." Inside, Cestus heard the words he'd been waiting for. "System reboot complete."

"I've had enough of your stalling," said Kiesling, annoyed, waving for Dr. Ryan and her crew to get to work. "Any final words before we burn out your brain, Captain Weir?"

Cestus smiled up from beneath furrowed brows, a smile filled with death. An audible 'click' filled the room as the glowing indicators on the cyborg's restraints shut off all at once.

"I just unlocked my cuffs."

CHAPTER 21

It could be argued that since childhood Gordon Kiesling had worn an impenetrable armor of absolute self-control and confidence. It had allowed him to achieve many great things in his life: captain of the soccer team in junior high school, quarterback and prom king in high school, youngest partner at the most influential law firm in Washington D.C., all the way up to becoming the executive director of one of the most powerful top secret organizations in the entire world. He was known—had always been known—as someone who could stare down trouble, to conquer fear itself, and always come out on top.

Not a few of the many opponents who had tried to crack Kiesling's armor had joked that the only way through it was with a pound of Kryptonite and a lot of divine intervention. No one had ever questioned that Gordon Kiesling was invincible.

No one, that is, until Cestus broke free.

Every bit of that unbreakable armor, unwavering self-confidence and absolute control failed him completely at the ringing thud of high-tech restraints and titanium-alloyed manacles dropping to laboratory floor, and at the sight of Designate Cestus—a man Kiesling himself had ordered transformed into one of the deadliest killers ever to walk the face of the Earth—leaping for him with nanotech-forged living metal talons aimed for his throat, hungry to end his life.

A small, less than manly scream and incoherent babbling—meant to have been an exclamation demanding to know how the cyborg super-soldier escaped, but came out more like a frightened one-year-old trying to make words for the first time—was all the man could manage as he backpedaled away from the attack, flailing recklessly. In fact, the only thing that saved him from becoming the late-Gordon Kiesling was his less than dignified reaction and abject terror—that and tripping over the ever-present Ms. Roslan standing behind him and falling to the floor.

As it was, the stiletto claws of Cestus tore Kiesling's shirt open and sliced a quartet of inch-deep grooves into the man's chiseled chest and stomach. A hand's breadth closer and the former Army Ranger would have gutted the man like a fish, from navel to neck, ending his career and his life.

A second attack from Cestus was thwarted by a short burst of four shots from somewhere behind the collapsed man, gunfire that glanced off his arms and shoulders, forcing the cyborg to pull his armored prosthetics in close to protect his body from damage.

"RUN!" screamed Roslan's voice as she pulled Kiesling to his feet and continued to squeeze the trigger of her Glock, pushing it to expel tiny gouts of flame and gunpowder clouds in an effort to distract the enraged cyborg from his target. The determination in the woman's eyes as she faced off against a billion dollar cybernetic assassin reminded the Project: Hardwired chief executive that he still owed his assistant a raise…a very, very large raise.

Kiesling allowed himself to be jerked off the ground and ushered to the operating suite's exit, surrounded by a quartet of GMR units. The remaining eight computer-guided automatons rushed to surround Cestus in a delaying tactic to allow their boss to escape, hopefully lasting long enough for reinforcements to arrive and take care of the rogue unit.

"They'd better hurry," thought Kiesling, trying to hold his shirt together and do something to halt the flow of blood from the wounds decorating his torso. "Weir is going to make short work of the Gomers and then come after me."

"Where are the other Primes?" Kiesling demanded loudly, following quickly behind Ms. Roslan on the way to the nearest elevator bank.

"I'm here," said Designate Gauss as the steel elevator doors parted, allowing him to exit. The cyborg was ready for battle, wearing a sleeveless, reinforced body armor over his torso that still allowed his own cybernetically enhanced arms to work free from confinement. To Ms. Roslan, he said, "There is a chopper waiting for you all on the roof. It's prepped and ready to remove you to a safe location off-site. Where is Weir now?"

Ms. Roslan started to answer, pointing back in the direction they'd come from, "He's insi—" but was cut off before she could finish.

"Kill him, Gauss!" shouted Kiesling, nearly foaming at the mouth with rage. "Kill Weir and I'll cut your leash."

"What about the missing data files?" asked the chrome-plated cyborg, smiling at the idea of becoming a free agent.

"Fuck the files! I want Malcolm Weir dead!"

"It's about time." Gauss grinned evilly. His shining cybernetic eye flared like the sun for a moment, causing the electricity on three floors of the building to flicker and dim as he charged up. The magnetic field around Gauss increased to the point where all the metal within thirty feet began twitching and leaning in the cyborg's direction. "Get going...I don't know how much longer the power is going to hold out with me amping up."

So eager to watch the cause of his troubles taken care of once and for all, it took Ms. Roslan and three GMRs to move Kiesling into the elevator. He was still yelling out for Gauss to "Kill Him!" as the doors slid closed and the lift lurched into motion, heading for the top of the building, twenty plus floors up.

The sounds of fighting and gunfire and men dying spilled beneath the door to the surgical bay, filling Gauss with excitement as he waited for the elevator car to get far enough away from his magnetic ability's sphere of influence to be safe, counting down from one hundred as he did.

When the count reached 'zero,' Gauss slammed his hands together with enough force that the resulting shockwave shattered every piece of glass on the level and shook the building's structure down to its foundation.

Gauss screamed, wrapped himself in a nigh-invulnerable magnetic bubble, and charged through the wall separating him from his quarry, obliterating the barrier with less effort than it would take a normal man to swat a fly.

At last, Weir's ass belonged to him!

The room inside was silent, except for the breathing of the man at its center and the drip, drip, drip of spilled blood.

Every inch of Cestus glistened crimson with slaughter and he stood on a carpet of death, surrounded by the dismembered remains of eight men whose bodies had been corrupted by the same science that had perfected their killer. His eyes reflected only the light of unbridled violence. Cestus had accepted his role as a killer and embraced it fully. The fruits of his labor were spread out before him like a horrible banquet of annihilation and carnage.

A twitch of his wrist snapped the neck of the GMR he held out before him, suspended four inches above the ground in a grip of unbending steel. The man died with a gurgle that caught in his throat.

"Now for Kiesling," said Cestus to no one in particular.

The tiny digitized voice in the back of Cestus's mind decided to throw a monkey-wrench into his plans of mayhem by announcing it had detected a large fluctuation in the localized magnetic field of the building and that Designate Gauss was inbound.

"Is there anything you can do about that asshole, Computer?" Cestus asked the computer in his head.

"Initiating countermeasures. Negation field active," it answered as an electrical charged flowed through the nanobots invading every cell of his body.

Cestus barely noticed the floor nearly buckling beneath him as Gauss blasted the wall before him to dust.

"How long will the negation field last?"

"Sixty seconds," responded the computer.

"That's all I need." Cestus dropped the bloody carcass of the slain GMR he'd been holding to the floor and braced himself for Gauss's onslaught.

So primed with power, each running footstep Gauss planted on the ground caused the heavily-reinforced floor to fracture and crack. The walls themselves seemed to flex outward in reaction to his presence.

"Kiesling sent me here to kill you, Weir!"

The two half-machine titans met in the middle of the room with a quick series of strikes and blocks, each cyborg feeling out the other. The first time they had met in battle, a freshly-awakened Cestus had been outclassed and overpowered by the sheer explosive power and vehemence of the other man's attack; this time it was different.

Fresh and in full access of his abilities, Cestus found himself to be more than a match for Gauss: his speed was greater by a factor of two or more and allowed the super-soldier to easily dodge attacks from the magnetically-enhanced cyborg that might otherwise have blasted his bones to dust.

With each missed attack, Gauss became more and more angry, and his offense grew wilder as he realized defeating Cestus wouldn't be the walk-in-the-park he'd thought it would be.

"The only chance you had to kill me was when I first woke up," taunted Cestus, easily dodging the increasingly uncontrolled attacks from his enemy. "Now I have full access to my programming."

"So what?" snapped Gauss, a missed overhand strike that fractured the floor beneath their feet punctuated his disdain for Cestus and his programming. "Your little 'Edward Scissorhands' act doesn't impress me. You're nothing!"

"Wrong," replied Cestus, shredding his opponent's face with a backhanded strike that enraged the berserk cyborg even more. "They built me to take the other Prime Units down if any of you got out of control. I was made to kill you, Gauss...and Kiesling sent you here to die."

Cestus dropped into a defensive stance and waited for the attack he knew would follow his enemy's rage.

"LIAR!" roared Gauss, putting every iota of his power and energy into a haymaker that left him wide open and vulnerable when Cestus ducked under it.

Crossing his arms in front of his body, Cestus sliced upward with arms morphed into meter-long blades of titanium-carbon alloy, catching the overextended right arm of Gauss in their crux and tore it from his body.

Stunned, Gauss watched the amputated limb bounce across

the floor, taking with it his capacity for magnetic-control. Cestus's hand, morphed into a cruel fist of blades and spikes, tore into the shocked cybernetic-man's stomach with enough force to splinter his spine.

The voices of both men lashed out in a duet of violence, pain, and fury.

"Take a look, Gauss," said Cestus, rage fully on display across his face as he twisted the razor-blades of his fingers hard into the man's gut. "Take a good long look into the eyes of the man who killed you."

Any response Gauss had ended, dying in a crimson tinged froth upon his lips and a haggard cough. With a jerk and sickening suction sound, the living metal claw of Cestus came free, spraying blood and letting Gauss's innards flop wetly to the floor in a hot cascade.

Gauss fell in mute horror to his knees staring at the ropey pile of his intestines on the floor before looking up to his conqueror one last time. The light from the cyborg's eyes was already fading as Cestus leapt over his cooling corpse in pursuit of his true prey, Gordon Kiesling.

Entering the stairwell at full speed, Cestus took the last twenty flights to the roof four steps in a bound, taking less time that it would for a man to walk into the kitchen for a snack. He knew he had to hurry if he was going to catch Kiesling before the coward slunk away to hide somewhere out of the cyborg's reach.

Reaching the last landing and the exit leading out to the building's summit and heliport, Cestus leaned down and bowled through the metal reinforced door blocking his path without even slowing down. The super-soldier was ready for the automatic gunfire waiting for him on the fifty-foot flat expanse of roof, running in a mad-dash toward the dull black helicopter waiting to take off atop a raised platform in its center.

Four GMRs let loose with every bit of ammo they had in their MP5s as Kiesling made his way up five tiny steps towards the chopper. The two men locked eyes and knew they were in a race that meant death for one of them.

Cestus met the first GMR with a leap and dropped him with

a pair of knees to the man's chest, crushing his throat, shattering his collarbone, and collapsing his ribcage. The cyborg was dead by the time his body flopped to the ground. Spring up to his feet, Cestus decapitated the second GMR as the automaton opened fire and sprayed bullets in a mad dance of twitching death. Cestus grabbed the headless man's body and spun it around, taking the last two roadblocks in their faces, killing them instantly.

"Kiesling!" screamed Cestus as he watched the director of Project: Hardwired climbing into the vehicle with his assistant close behind.

Swearing out loud, Kiesling turned just inside the helicopter's tiny cabin and looked back and forth between the Cestus barreling in his direction and Ms. Roslan trying to climb on board. Making up his mind, Kiesling shouted for the pilot to go ahead and take off. He leaned down low towards the woman below and shoved her away from the aircraft, dropping her squarely on her backside.

"Gordon?!" she said, stunned by his sudden action.

"Get us off the ground NOW!" Kiesling yelled to the pilot. Catching Ms. Roslan's attention, he ordered, "You only need to slow him down for a minute, Melissa..."

The woman's eyes went cold as the vehicle with her boss— and her own rescue—began to lift off of the platform and move away from her position. Regaining her feet, Roslan turned towards the blood and gore soaked Cestus nearly upon her, gripping her gun tightly.

Cestus closed the distance to within feet, legs a blur beneath him, clawed arms wide apart ready for attack.

Ms. Roslan stepped meekly out of the way, arms raised in non-aggression, and allowed Cestus to bolt passed her unmolested. Momentum carrying his body towards the edge of the platform, Cestus watched as the helicopter slowly rotated away from the building, hovering ten feet up and twenty feet away from the roof and out in the yawning chasm of empty air that extended out over the Los Angeles skyline beyond. Without hesitation the cyborg launched himself into mid-air after the retreating aircraft, extending his arms to their full length. The cybernetic prosthetics groaned and stretched to over six fix, grasping out for the landing skids of the copter.

A scream tore itself from Cestus as time seemed to freeze with him hanging in air, unsure of whether or not he'd make it.

Miraculously, one clawed hand was able to hold on to the bouncing, rotating helicopter, while the other slapped the side and slid loose. Cestus dangled precariously by one hand, the ground screaming up at him from more than a thousand feet below. The chopper spun and dipped from the weight of the cyborg landing on its bottom-most structure, jerking out of the pilot's control, nearly sending Gordon Kiesling bouncing out its still-open side hatch.

"He's grabbed on! We have to shake him off!" Cestus heard Kiesling scream from somewhere right about his head.

"We're off-balance and need to land, sir," came the pilot's reply, picked up over the sound of the helicopter's diesel engine and its rotors.

The chopper tilted and started to descend, still jerking back and forth as Cestus swung freely underneath, threatening to send the man plummeting to his death on the earth below.

As the helicopter swung precariously close to the building as it dropped, Cestus made his decision to end it all right there, high up over the streets of L.A. before they landed. The cyborg grabbed the strut with both hands and used the bottom of the vehicle to kick himself into an arc, flipping into the belly of the chopper.

Kiesling was dumbstruck by the turn of events.

Seeing the murderous cyborg bent on taking his life suddenly appear less than a foot away from where he was standing sent Gordon Kiesling into a panic. He opened his mouth to beg for mercy—to offer Malcolm Weir whatever he wanted to let him go—when Cestus cut him short. The cyborg's arm morphed into a lustrous blade of silver, which shot forward, running Gordon Kiesling through at the center of his chest. The sword continued into the back of the pilot's chair, through the startled pilot struggling to regain control of the flight stick, and into the instrument panel. A shower of sparks sprayed the cockpit as Cestus yanked his arm free.

"That was for Kristin," whispered Cestus into Kiesling's ear before turning and moving for the exit of the helicopter, now spinning completely out of control and headed straight for the seventy-fifth floor of the US Bank Tower.

Cestus stared at the drop-off below him and leaped out into space, chuckling as he remembered this was the second time he'd jumped off of this particular building. He was in mid-fall when the Project: Hardwired helicopter smashed into the side of the world's tenth tallest building, rotor blades shattering and shearing off as they struck its outer skin. A heartbeat filled with breaking glass and warping steel passed before the chopper's gas tanks exploded into a fireball, destroying the four floors surrounding it in the resulting inferno. Flames eradicated all traces of the master Abraxas-Array computer and the core of Project: Hardwired.

The nightmare was over for the man known as Designate Cestus.

Nose-diving for the ground, Malcolm Weir smiled to himself and hoped the landing wouldn't hurt quite as much this time around.

CHAPTER 22

The blistering Southern Californian sun was already heading below the horizon before Mal made it back to the Encino Hospital Medical Center to check on Zuz. His internal computer system had already supplied him with the good news on his friend's prognosis—the surgery had gone fine and, aside from a few broken bones, a transfusion to restore two pints of blood loss, and a whole lot of sutures, Zuz was well on the road to recovery. A quick scan of the attending physician's charts revealed the wounded man could be out of the hospital in as little as a week.

If he behaved himself, that is.

Getting more than a few strange looks at his unusual dress: he had liberated a bulky jacket and pair of latex gloves from an ambulance parked in the rear lot of the facility while its owners grabbed dinner inside—Mal strode right up to the front desk and asked to see David Zuzelo, admitting he was the patient's younger, better looking brother when interrogated by the receptionist as to his reason for the visit.

Mal was glad when, after an intercom exchange with the nurse's station inside, he was allowed back to see his friend. In spite of how easy it would be for him to break into Zuz's room without being seen, Mal preferred the lower stress level of being invited in through the front door. A lot less risk of police being called and a brand new mess starting up.

He had just finished cleaning up the last mess, after all. Well, his version of 'cleaning' it up, that is.

Surrounded by the smell of ammonia and powerful chemical cleaners, Mal pushed open the pale green and off-white door leading to Zuz's bedside.

Striding over to his prone friend, Mal marveled to himself over the incredible efficiency, and near paranoia, of his computer systems. In the matter of seconds, he was given a full run down on defensible areas of the room, diagrams of the wiring in its walls, the number of patients and their guests in the connecting room (there were only three, all with vital signs operating in the approved 'safe' range), and even two possible escape routes. The first floor window facing the hospital's large, off-street parking lot was the one designated as best for both solo or two-man egress should Zuz need quick evacuation.

Mal paused for a moment to take a good look at Zuz. The last time he'd seen his friend, when Mal left the man in the emergency room, David had been in dire shape and was losing a lot of blood.

What a difference twenty-four hours had made, even if Zuz still looked like he'd been chewed up and shat out again.

Bandages covered Zuz everywhere not hidden by the thin hospital blankets, tightly tucked under the mattress he was laying on. A cast covered the man's right forearm and, beneath the covers, two more covered each of his shins. Miles of pale wires and fluid-filled tubes ran out of Zuz in a number of fairly uncomfortable places, including a catheter Mal wished his electronic know-it-all hadn't so readily identified.

First thing tomorrow, thought the cyborg super-soldier, I'm going to teach my computer when to shut up.

The most interesting thing for Mal was that Zuz's eyes were clamped shut, and he was snoring at just over ninety decibels, just shy of a jackhammer pounding away. Mal was impressed by the sheer volume of the noise coming out of the single untaped nostril on Zuz's face, and even more impressed by the fact that it was all an act and his friend, injured as he really was, was putting on a show for his benefit.

Zuz's attempted deception was betrayed by two things: first, the passenger in the back of Mal's brain informed him Zuz's vital signs were normal but in an elevated state most often attributed to excitement; and, second, by the nineteen-inch television mounted on the wall opposite to the bed and showing off a live feed from the aftermath of the carnage at the US Bank Building.

"I know you're awake, Dave," chastised Mal, hiding his growing smile behind his disguised hand.

Lids sliding slowly over eyes more than slightly hazy from painkillers, Zuz oozed, "Oh, hey, Mal...didn't know you were here."

"I had to bring your car back," Mal replied. "I got it detailed and had the valets park it for me."

"Really?!"

"No, that piece of shit is toast," Mal tried his best to summon a look of sincere sadness to his face, but failed miserable. "Gauss threw it at me."

"What!!"

"I know! I was surprised there was enough metal in there for him to grab!" the faux sadness was replaced by an equally poor attempt at shock. "It was flatter than your sister's chest the last time I saw it."

"You're such a dick. Do you have any idea what that will do to my insurance rates?" grumbled Zuz. "You know, if I paid them."

A pregnant pause filled the room as the two friends stared at one another, both unsure of what to say next. So much had happened between them in less than seventy-two hours.

Zuz broke the silence, "You going to tell me what happened up there?"

"What do you think of my work?" Mal answered by tipping his head towards the crappy Vizio TV just past Zuz's feet.

"It's nuts! The government puppets in broadcast news are claiming it was the second terrorist attack on the US Bank Building this month. They're showing the clean-up now," Zuz's eyes went wide at the sight of a smashed chunk of fiberglass being removed from the lobby of the building on screen. "No mention of you or Project: Hardwired. Hey, look! There's my car!"

The two men sat and watched the wretched remains of Zuz's old Nissan, pieces dropping off the entire time a crane carried it from the ruined front of the site of the car's final demise.

The passenger's side door and front tire plummeting to the

scorched pavement below caused Mal to wince, but Zuz gave a more thoughtful look.

"I'm pretty sure I can buff that right out," said Zuz from under the stark white bandages wrapped around more than a third of his skull. "Once I put in a new door, four new tires, some body work, a new paint job," he paused, considering. "New windshield, transmission and headlights...we'll be back to running away from mind-controlled robot assassins in no time!"

A dark cloud filtered over Mal's face, halting his friend's ribbing.

"Kristin is dead, Zuz. They killed her."

"She's dead? How? Why?"

Dropping down to his haunches, head resting on arms laying crossed on the bed at Zuz's feet, everything came rushing out of Mal all at once. Everything that had happened to him since Zuz's injury the day before. It all spilled out, emptying the cyborg's heart and soul, leaving him drained.

Over the course of three days he'd lost a year of his life, the woman he loved and his humanity. He was on the run from the United States government, who wanted nothing less than to remove his head and take back the secrets it held. Needless to say, he was an exhausted wreck.

All David Zuzelo could manage to say to comfort and reassure his friend was, "Wow. Rough day, huh?"

"You have an amazing way with words, my friend. I'm not sure Shakespeare himself could have said it better."

"I did minor in English Lit for one semester at college, remember?" grinned Zuz, proud of himself.

Mal dragged the hard wood-framed chair beside the hydraulic recovery bed Zuz rested on and plopped down heavily into it.

"With Project: Hardwired and Gordon Kiesling down for the count, what are you going to do now that the government isn't out looking for Designate Cestus anymore?" Zuz asked after a few seconds.

A thin line formed between Mal's eyes as he pondered the question for a long time.

"As long as they leave me alone, I'll just keep a low profile, maybe travel the country and see what I've missed in the past year."

"You could always hit the professional arm-wrestling circuit," mused Zuz.

"That's a bit too 'over the top' for me," Mal quipped back, enjoying the badinage. It was nice not to have to worry about swarms of bionic executioners bursting into the room, armed to the teeth and with a hard on to murder him in the most excruciating of fashions.

Events of the past few days replayed themselves through Mal's head, sobering him up.

"And if they don't, I've got enough running around up here," Mal tapped his forehead, "to find whoever 'they' are and make them regret it."

Fingers, morphed into razor-sharped talons and, faster than a human eye could register, lashed out to shred a saline bag hanging unused from the back of Zuz's IV stand.

"I'll show those bastards exactly what sort of killing-machine they created."

Zuz's eyes bulged at his friend's matter-of-fact statement and actions, "Mal, man, you need to switch to decaf ay-sap. If you don't, they're going to have to replace your head when it explodes."

"Like the dude from 'Scanners?' Mal smiled, trying to lighten things back up.

"Precisely!" Zuz's enthusiastic declaration was loud enough to cause the duty nurse to peek her head in to make sure everything was OK in his room.

"Is everything OK in here, Mister Zuzelo," Nurse Jensen asked, giving Mal the once over at least twice.

"He's fine, just a bit over-stimulated at the moment," Mal gave her his most charming smile. To no one's surprise, it had little effect on the rather up-tight member of the nighttime hospital staff.

Glaring at Mal for another few seconds just so he knew she was watching him, Nurse Jensen's head disappeared back through the door.

Continuing as if there had been no interruption, Zuz philosophized with the utmost of sincerity, "You know, I've always thought the 'Scanners' series was highly underrated."

Shaking his head and settling back in the less-than-comfortable gray-corduroy padded hospital chair, Mal smirked, "Well, except for that 'Scanner Cop' crap. Those movies sucked balls."

Zuz sat straight up in his bed, nearly tearing loose the numerous wires and tubes attached to his injured body, a huge grin splitting his face.

"You know, I've never loved another man as much as I love you right now, Mal."

"I'm hard not to love," Mal chuckled.

Leaning forward, Zuz reached out to touch the top of Mal's metal arm, reassuringly, and whispered in a conspiratorial manner, "In the back of my head, I've always thought 'Scanners,' 'Firestarter,' and 'Dreamscape' were all connected. There are numerous connections between the writers of those movies and the Stargate Project. The films were all used to help desensitize the American populace."

"Desensitize? To what?" asked Mal, goading Zuz into a frenzy and amazed at the level to which the man seemed to speak with his hands.

"To the existence of a psychic division of the FBI. One with the federally mandated mission of keeping tabs on the thoughts and minds of US citizens," Zuz finished with a robust, "Duh."

"Hey, what about 'Carrie?' Mal yanked a pillow out from beneath the patient's bed, jamming it down behind his head. With full knowledge of what would come next, Mal then tossed out a seemingly innocent comment, "They were both written by Stephen King and both about girls who discovered they had psychic abilities they couldn't control?"

"Oh Em Gee!" a shriek more suited to a teen-aged 'Twilight' fangirl meeting Robert Pattinson than a grown man in his forties sprang from somewhere deep inside David Zuzelo. "You're like Criss Angel, Mal...you just freaked my mind! That totally matches up with my research. Get me a laptop, I need to blog!"

Mal stretched out as much as he could in his seat and let his best friend, his only friend, ramble on long into the night. Tomorrow he'd have to deal with the consequences of his actions and whatever future he had. Tonight, though…tonight was about friendship.

When Nurse Jensen woke Zuz in the morning to take blood and change his bedpan, Mal had vanished.

"Where did he go?" Zuz asked groggily, rolling over onto his side to allow Jensen to do her job.

"Who? Your strange friend?"

Zuz nodded, wincing a little as his catheter moved in a way that wasn't agreeable to his more delicate parts.

"He left about an hour ago. Said he had to get ready for work," her face scrunched up in distaste. "No offense, Mister Zuzelo, but that guy creeped me out. Seemed on edge, like he was hiding from something."

Locking gazes with the medical worker, Zuz said, "He's had a tough time. His fiancée just passed away."

"This woman has the bedside manner of Doctor Doom," Zuz thought to himself.

The nurse almost dropped the filled bedpan in embarrassment. "Oh."

She avoided her patient's blistering glare, and wrapped up her work as quickly as humanly possible. Nurse Jensen was making a beeline for the door and freedom, when she stopped and fumbled for something in the pocket of her scrubs.

"Before he left, your friend asked me to give this to you when you woke up this morning. It seemed important."

Scuttling back over to Zuz in the center of the room, the nurse handed Zuz a folded scrap of paper before disappearing into the hall once more.

Zuz quickly unfolded the note. Torn from a piece of paper from a medical chart, Zuz read the clean half-cursive script Malcolm Weir had written on the back. It contained a phone number and the words:

"Call me anytime, my friend. -M."

David Zuzelo smiled, carefully refolded the paper and tucked it away. He knew everything would be OK.

EPILOGUE

Consciousness slammed back into Gordon Kiesling like a high-speed car crash. Consciousness and a pain so intense it took his breath away.

The pain bored its way into his skull through the bone just between his eyes and seemed to filter down along every nerve ending in his arms and legs.

What the hell is going on, thought Kiesling as he tried unsuccessfully to force his eyelids open. Why couldn't he seem to move? Where was he?

Muted voices from what felt like light years away touched his ears, along with the low frequency hum of large machines at work.

Straining against whatever was holding him down and keeping his body from rising, Kiesling tried to demand some answers from whoever was in earshot. To command them to set him free or face the consequences.

All the attempt produced was a series of garbled, unintelligible sounds from a jaw and tongue that refused to cooperate with Kiesling's desires.

The sound of the voices returned, this time in conversation with each other, in response to the prone man's outburst.

A series of slow, purposeful footsteps approached Kiesling's prone position. He could tell there were at least three people in the room with him: two pairs of flat soled shoes flapped roughly against the more familiar staccato rapid fire of a woman's high heels. The rich smell of lavender perfume filled the director's nostrils, causing his heart to speed up.

Melissa, he thought! He must be in one of the remote medical sites operated by Project: Hardwired. They'd rescued him from Weir's attack. He was saved!

Kiesling's voice grunted and grumbled once more and was answered by the sound of Ms. Roslan's own voice, "He's awake?"

"Yes," remarked a second, male voice, unfamiliar to Kiesling. "The speed of his recuperation is astounding."

The feel of cool, latex-wrapped hands moved across Kiesling's form, and up to his face, pushing it from side to side.

"Can he hear us," came a deep bass voice that caused Kiesling more than a bit of discomfort.

Fountain! What is he doing here, thought Kiesling as he tried to open his eyes once more, and failed. His arms seemed tied down and he was unable to reach up and find out what was keeping him blind.

"Oh, yes," responded the unknown voice. "The readouts are showing that the subject is fully conscious now. You may speak to him, but he won't be able to do much in the way of responding."

"Excellent. That's precisely how I've wished every conversation I've had with Former Director Kiesling would go," said Fountain, voice filled with gloating.

Kiesling struggled in place. "Former" Director Kiesling, his mind almost flatlined at the thought. He had to find out exactly what was going on. To set things straight.

"Can you do something about the tape on his eye?" asked the Congressman. "I want him to see me."

The former head of Project: Hardwired began flailing in a futile effort to sit up.

"Hold him down and I'll remove the tape from his eye," came the unknown voice.

Kiesling continued to squirm as two pairs of hands forced his body back down onto the cold metal table he had been resting upon. A third pair, the ones covered in latex, forced his head to one side. Shaking with rage, there was nothing Kiesling could do but lie back and give up the control he had fought his entire life to obtain.

One of the latex coated hands found whatever it had been

searching for and pulled back, sending a ripping, shredding pain along the skin of Kiesling's face as his right eye was freed.

The tearing pain was joined by a searing one as his eye fluttered open and allowed a cold, terrible light to shine directly into his optic nerves.

At first, blurry forms against a bright white backdrop was all Gordon Kiesling could make out. Slowly, after a handful of blinks and some squinting, the forms sharped into a trio of familiar shapes: Ms. Roslan, dressed in a sharp navy blue pants suit—Kiesling never let her wear the dreadful things, always preferring a more attractive skirt-jacket combination; the hated Representative Michael Fountain, in one of his famous off-the-rack jacket and trousers, looking as rumpled as ever; and the owner of the unknown voice, a small man wrapped in the trappings of a surgeon, with a shock of thinning red hair sprouting haphazardly out of the top of his wrinkle-covered head.

Kiesling immediately recognized the man as a member of a defunct bio-tech unit Dr. Ryan had been managing in the early days of Project: Hardwired. When the group had been unceremoniously fired due to the success of the Hardwired team, Kiesling had promptly forgotten the man's name and his existence.

Doctor Gostler? Gohrman? Grossman? Yes, that was it! Doctor Bruce Grossman filled the scope of Kiesling's vision, momentarily blotting out the harsh surgical lights hanging above the injured body of the man. The relief was short-lived as Grossman replaced the blocked light with one from his penlight.

After waving the transilluminator back and forth for a few seconds to judge Kiesling's reactions, Grossman stepped back and gestured to Fountain.

"He's ready for you, Congressman."

Vowing to have Grossman killed with his little flashlight once he was back to his old self, Kiesling wondered why the scientist had kept his left eye covered. Fountain's giant gray-haired head slid into view, replacing the little ginger doctor's visage, and chased the thought away.

"Hello, hello," Fountain wagged the fingers of his left hand as if to gain an infant's attention.

A grunt that tried vainly to be a rather vicious stream of obscenities directed at the middle-aged congressman tumbled out from between Kiesling's teeth and down his half-numb chin.

"Shhhh, it's ok, Gordon," smiled Congressman Fountain with all the warmth of a dead fish. "You're safe."

Kiesling calmed down, interested to hear what Fountain had to say before he had Ms. Roslan shoot him in the back for his insolence. Hopefully he'd learn what exactly happened after Designate Cestus blew up Abraxas-Prime.

"I can see you're wondering what happened to you. How you came to be in my...care," crooned Fountain. "One of the GMR teams..."

"GMR team Epsilon with Designate Ballista," finished Roslan in a manner all too familiar for Kiesling's taste.

From his spot on the operating table, Kiesling watched his assistant with haunted eyes as he listened to Fountain's story.

"Yes. Thank you, Melissa," the nervous tic burned in an unpleasant manner in Kiesling's forehead. Fountain continued, "GMR team Epsilon found you deep within the wreckage, clinging to life. Project: Hardwired, however was dead."

Moving to sit on the edge of the table Kiesling's inert form lay upon, Fountain loosened his tie and continued, "Needless to say, our overseers out in Washington were not pleased with the situation. Billions of dollars in collateral damage. Billions more in research and development lost. Hundreds injured or killed. It was a mess."

To Ms. Roslan, Fountain queried, "What's that military word they use when the shit hits the fan, Melissa my dear?"

The use of her first name ground into Kiesling's gut. He knew something was wrong.

"I believe the word you're looking for is 'fubar,' sir."

"Fubar! That's it," Fountain snapped his fingers happily at remembering the word. "The situation was Fubar." The politician gave an exaggerated sigh of exhaustion and continued, "While I was able to place most of the blame on our lovely Doctor Ryan, our bosses wanted someone's head for it. I'm afraid the bulk of that blame fell on you and I, my friend."

Fountain looked down, eyes dark. For a split second, Kiesling thought he caught a glimpse of regret. Of sorrow. It all vanished when a smile cracked Fountain's face from ear to ear.

"Fortunately for me, Former Director Kiesling, I wasn't as replaceable as you had thought," oozed Fountain, grinning with crooked teeth that had never known the touch of dental whiteners. "Unfortunately for you, Former Direct Kiesling, you were."

Fountain reached up to maneuver a steel framed surgical mirror down from the overhead lighting array for Kiesling to get a better look of what the clean-up crews from Project: Hardwired had found in the shattered remains of the US Bank Building.

The horror of what he saw nearly stopped Kiesling's heart.

Both legs were gone: the right taken just above the knee, and all that remained of the left was a bloody hodge-podge of gore soaking his hip socket.

The flesh of his left arm was gone nearly to his shoulder, with bones showing along his forearm.

More wires, tubes and hoses than Kiesling had ever seen in one place in his life ran in and out of the terrible puckered wound that now existed where his chest had been. Strange fluids flowed freely into his devastated body.

Worst of all was his face and the empty left eye socket that glared back at him.

The low, garbled rumbling of pure despair began to build deep within the remains of his chest as Kiesling snapped his eye closed to shut out what he had seen. The sound was strangled in his throat by a primal scream.

A geyser of nearly black blood and ooze caused Fountain to leap back, nearly stumbling over Doctor Grossman as he scrambled for a handkerchief from an inner breast pocket.

Once the outburst had subsided to a quiet sobbing, Fountain hunched back over, leaning close enough for the Kiesling to hear his whisper, "The government has invested way too much money in you to just let you go and die, I'm afraid. Lucky for you, we've got a position for you in Doctor Grossman's newly approved department."

Kiesling glared back at the politician as best he could with one bloodshot eye. He was greeted by another smile from Fountain and the sound of what seemed to be a virtual army of people entering the room.

Bobbing his head in faux-sympathy, Fountain added as he stood up, "Welcome to Project: Tiamat, Former...Director... Kiesling..."

As if on cue, what sounded like a virtual army of men entered the room behind Kiesling's trio of tormentors. Fountain looked around at the group of medical staff and scientists that had gathered around the table, then turned back to the battered Gordon Kiesling one final time and said, "As its first test subject."

Kiesling's eye snapped open with realization as Fountain stood and placed his arm around Ms. Roslan, pushing her towards the door the surgical team had entered through.

"Come, Melissa, it's time to get back to work."

All the blood drained from Kiesling's face, along with his hopes as he watched his two former colleagues navigate their way through the mass of men and women in lab coats and surgical scrubs, faces filled with hungry, anxious stares at the abomination spread out on the table before them.

"Doctor Grossman, he's all yours," grinned Fountain as he and Ms. Roslan moved for the exit. "And make sure Former Director Kiesling is awake for as long as possible."

Gordon Kiesling raged against his bonds, trying to get free, his remaining eye wide with fear. Again and again he called out to the woman who once answered his every beck and call, to no avail.

Stepping to the foot of the cool steel surgical table, Doctor Grossman adjusted his latex gloves with a snap and motioned to the waiting crowd.

"Ladies, gentlemen, let's begin."

The cadre of technicians, surgeons, chemists and biologists crowded around Kiesling, whose screams were silenced by the vile, wet sounds of progress.

ABOUT THE AUTHOR

Mat Nastos is a TV, Film, comic book, science fiction writer/director, known best for bad horror movies about giant scorpions, killer pigs & dinosaurs in the sewers. His work has been published by DC Comics, Boom Studios, IDW Publishing, Warp Graphics, Playboy and Highlights for Kids, and has been seen everywhere from the SyFy Channel to Cinema.. He is the author of the Amazon #1 best-selling science fiction action novel, The Cestus Concern.

Mat is a black belt in Aikido and American Form Karate. He is currently hard at work—splitting his time between writing and training minions to aid in his quest to take over San Dimas, California.

You can stay up to date with his latest work by going to his website at http://www.MatNastos.net

Curious about other Crossroad Press books?
Stop by our site:
http://store.crossroadpress.com
We offer quality writing
in digital, audio, and print formats.

Enter the code FIRSTBOOK
to get 20% off your first order from our store!
Stop by today!